Vaz

By

Laurence E Dahners

Prologue

Lisanne Frye pulled her blond hair back behind her ear and turned her eyes to glance at her teammate. He'd surprised her at every turn since Professor Albrecht had assigned them to be a team at the beginning of the semester. That assignment had been solely based on their positions in the alphabet. She'd had this Vaz Gettnor kid in some of her classes before but had never spoken to him because he seemed so weird. Stodgy clothes, weird tufty dark hair, never spoke unless spoken to and never looked you in the eye. She thought he must have some kind of psychiatric disorder.

When the Professor had listed them as a team, before even having a first meeting with Gettnor, she'd gone to Albrecht and asked to be reassigned. Albrecht had abruptly dismissed her, "Someday you vill have to work vis people you don' like," he'd said in his odd accent. "Just as vell start now." After cursing Albrecht for a suitable period she'd sent an email to Gettnor asking him to meet her in a study center.

His only reply had been, "OK."

At the meeting, Gettnor had been waiting uncomfortably at a table in the first floor study area as she'd specified. He'd been sitting staring at his slate which had been laid out on the table but not turned on. Lisanne had introduced herself and he'd shaken her hand. Even his hand shake had been creepy. It had been a "put your hand out, allow it to be grasped, twitch it, take it back." During the handshake his eyes had risen briefly, though not even to her face, then dropped immediately back to the table.

When she'd asked if he had any idea how they should go about the project they'd been assigned, he'd only shaken his head. Deciding *she'd* have to lead their team, she divided up the various tasks that would need to be accomplished to build the software controller module they'd been assigned. She turned her slate with its list of nine tasks to him and asked him which ones he would like to take on. He'd looked at it a minute and, to her astonishment, selected *seven* of them.

Bemused she'd picked four and left him with five. In view of his reticence to communicate she hadn't been surprised that "writing up the results" was one she'd been stuck with.

They'd met a week later to discuss their progress and determine if parts of the project were going to be problematic. She'd said "Hi Vaz," as she walked up to the table.

After a pause, without looking up from his blank slate, he'd said only, "Hello." Thinking like the programmer she intended to become, she decided he was running some poorly written software that required a lot of processor cycles to conclude that he needed to respond to the social debt created by her "Hi."

She sat beside him and flipped on her slate. "I've finished my first task and started on numbers two and three. Of course I haven't started on number four, the write-up of our results, since I don't know what they'll be." With some dread she said, "How are you coming with your parts?" She'd been developing ulcers over her fear that he wouldn't finish any of his tasks and she'd have to do the entire project herself to pull a decent grade.

He said only, "Done."

Lisanne blinked a moment or two, not sure what he meant. "Done with which part?"

"All of them. Well except the write-up... I suck at that."

Her eyebrows shot up, "You've finished all *five* of yours?"

"I did the first eight. Even though you're doing some of them I wanted the practice. We don't have to use mine though."

She drew back, "You've *finished* the first eight," she said dubiously.

He nodded.

Her eyes narrowed. "You haven't plagiarized some programming off the net have you?"

"No. I looked at a couple, but they weren't written very well."

Suspiciously Lisanne said, "Okaaay, send them to me and I'll look them over."

He mumbled to his AI (Artificial Intelligence) and a moment later a tone and a blink on her HUD (Heads Up Display) told her she'd received the files.

"Meet here again, same time next week?"

He nodded.

Back in her dorm room she pulled up the files he'd sent her and cursed. They were much too small to be able to achieve the complex goals the team had been set. Rather than start analyzing them line by line, she just tried them to see if they could possibly respond correctly based on Albrecht's specifications.

They did. *Every single one of them*.

She began looking through the code he'd written, feeling more and more awed as she went through it. Sparsely written, it didn't use any of the modules of code that were in such common use that programmers normally just plugged them in to accomplish certain tasks without trying to write something themselves. These common modules were in such wide use that no one knew who'd written them or thought that using them was plagiarism. In places Lisanne could find blocks of Vaz's code which did the same thing as the canned code blocks. She compared Vaz's code to three of the modules available out there in various libraries and his were

10-30% more economical of processor cycles. They also spread the load over the processors that were available very nicely,

With awe, she recognized that what he'd already finished on each of the eight tasks was head and shoulders above what she could do, even if she spent the entire semester on a single one of the tasks.

Lisanne shivered and set out to complete the write-up that would be her only contribution to their shared project.

Lisanne walked into the library the next week and found Gettnor waiting at their usual table. "Hey Vaz, I'm taking you for coffee, let's get out of this place."

"I don't drink coffee." He hadn't looked up from the table.

Lisanne grabbed his elbow and tugged. "OK, you can have a Coke or a juice or something."

Gettnor reluctantly got up from the table, "Where are we going?"

"Union coffee shop. Come on."

"I've never been there," he said, almost plaintively.

Lisanne didn't feel any surprise. "There's always a first time."

Once she had a coffee and he had a Diet Coke, they sat facing each other at a little table for two. As she sipped her coffee, she stared over the rim of her cup at him. "Vaz, you didn't use common code blocks in your programs."

"I know."

"You wrote everything new?"

"No, I've already rewritten most of the common code blocks. I do it for each one I come across. They're sloppy." He said this as if he were offended that someone had written code that was inefficient.

She realized that though he was staring down at the table, she thought he had a nice symmetrical face. He might not be model handsome but he wasn't bad looking either. "Vaz, look at me."

His eyes flashed up at her momentarily, then back to his blank slate. He sucked on the straw in his drink.

"No, really look at me. I don't think you've even seen my face."

"I *have*..." he said quietly, "You're very pretty."

"When?" she said in surprise.

"On line. There are many pictures of you available."

She giggled, trying to decide if she should be creeped out that this weird guy spent time looking at her pictures even though he couldn't bring himself to *actually* look at her. But he seemed so harmless. Just so exceedingly shy. Finally she said, "Well, I want you to look at me in person! Come on."

He slowly raised his head and eyes to look at her. His gaze danced around her face, but he never looked her in the eye, merely slid past her eyes on the way to examining other features. After about ten seconds his eyes dropped back to his slate.

"There that wasn't so bad was it?"

Even at the angle his downward gaze presented she could tell a grin appeared on his face. He shook his head.

"I want to look at you too. Look at me some more."

He looked up again and she studied him. He actually could be quite attractive she thought, if he could look you in the eye. She turned her head side to side, "What do you think?"

"You're very beautiful."

Surprised she said, "Aw, I'll bet you say that to all the girls."

He looked shocked, "No!" His head dropped back down and he almost whispered, "I've never said that to anyone!"

Realizing how painfully shy Vaz was, Lisanne resolved to stop teasing him. "I was only kidding. We should meet here again next week. You can tell me what you think of the summary I wrote. I sent it to your AI."

"I'm sure it's fine. Much better than anything I could write."

"So, you don't want to meet with me next week?"

Looking stricken, Vaz blurted, "Yes! Yes, I do."

Stifling a smile Lisanne said. "OK. This same table, next week."

Lisanne came to feel great joy that they'd been assigned to be a team. Vaz was weird; there was no doubt about that. But he was a genius at programming and would be going on to grad school in, of all things, physics. He may be weird, but weird in a sweet/brilliant sense and as time passed she'd found that she loved his bizarre, introspective sense of humor.

Chapter One

Twenty years have passed.

Vaz Gettnor stared in frustration at the graphic representation of the atomic spacing in his proposed hydrogen absorption alloys. He just couldn't seem to predict their properties like he'd expected to be able to. So tense he was nearly vibrating, he realized he'd reached under his shirt to begin twisting some chest hairs loose from their roots.

Disgusted, he stood so suddenly his chair fell over. He didn't pick it up. Instead he stormed down the hall to his office, closed the door behind him and dropped face first onto his couch. After a moment he pulled back an arm and slugged the cushions.

It felt good. After a bit he slugged the cushions again with the other arm. After a moment he began pounding the cushion mercilessly. His arms ached with exhaustion when he stopped but he felt... better.

More calm.

He slid off onto the floor, put his feet under the couch and started doing sit-ups. Remembering the days in high school when he could easily do 60-100, he was startled to realize that he'd begun struggling after only 30.

But, as he pounded out sit-ups anyway, a euphoric feeling flooded over him, a "second wind" phenomenon brought on by the release of endorphins. He realized the exhausting exercise had relaxed his tense state. While he sat, panting but feeling blissful, his thoughts wandered back to the hydrogen absorption problem, he... he had an idea about the alloy... a *good* one!

After making rapid notes about his new idea he turned to stare at the couch. It would be great if he could do this every time he got all worked up. Burning off the tension that seemed to cripple him would be so… helpful. He looked up at the ceiling… maybe he could get a pull-up bar and install it? And bring in some push-up grips. He noticed that he'd begun to split the seam on the couch cushion by pounding it. He'd need something else to hit he mused.

He wondered if Querx would object to his installing a pull up bar. After a moment's thought he decided that his boss Dr. Smint would be OK with it, and Smint seemed to be able to talk the company into whatever he wanted.

***

Stillman Davis walked into his new office with a tremendous sense of pride. He'd been working toward a department head position at Querx for three years now. He would rather have been put in charge of Marketing and Promotions, but R&D would do.

He stepped to his new desk and set down his case, looking around as the lights came up. A bit startled, he realized that someone was sitting in the visitor's chair in his new office.

Looking sharply at the man he recognized Jack Smint, the retiring head of R&D. Briefly he wondered what the old coot was doing here? Did he have some bizarre plan to try to keep running R&D by telling Stillman what to do even *after* he'd been put out to pasture? Stillman knew Smint had worked right up to the company's mandatory retirement age of 72. He straightened and raised his eyebrows, "Yes?"

Smint said, "I know you've worked hard to avoid having to take any advice from me Davis, but I feel it is terribly important to the company… and to some people I care about, that I try to keep you from stepping on that huge dick you think you have."

Davis narrowed his eyes and took a breath to retort.

Smint grimaced. "Sorry, sorry. My people skills are crap. My apologies. I'll leave but please, let me just give you one small piece of advice."

Davis applied a frosty smile, "Well? Let me have this amazing piece of wisdom."

Smint sighed, "Vaz Gettnor, one of your 'researchers' is an… odd fellow. My people skills are bad, but his are orders of magnitude worse. Nonetheless, he's a genius. So my advice… let him work how he wants to work. Don't give him a narrow project, or a deadline, or expect him to be here on a schedule, or to come to meetings. Make broad suggestions and wait patiently, he'll produce the unexpected, maybe not what you asked for… but the company will be the better for it."

Stillman felt his lip beginning to curl. "So if I mollycoddle this… Gettnor? Then good things will just mysteriously happen?"

Smint closed his eyes wearily for a moment. "R&D depends on people who see big things. Inspiration isn't something you can *demand* and direct. It is an event in the human consciousness that pops up at the most bizarre times and places. Gettnor has the potential to do… *amazing* things but if you pressure him, he responds like a turtle, closing up and becoming unreachable."

Stillman tilted his head curiously. "Why would we even *want* someone so bizarre? Why not just get rid of him and replace him with a better… engineer or whatever he is?"

"Physicist." Smint sighed, "Because, genius isn't something you can just order from Amazon."

Stillman rolled his eyes, "Oh, come on, there are plenty of smart people out there looking for jobs."

Smint sighed and stood. He knew his cause was lost. He said ominously, "Keep Gettnor happy… or you'll regret it." Smint took his leave, wondering if Vaz might be in so he could say goodbye.

***

Stillman Davis finished reviewing the files for the people in his new department. He still had a few minutes before holding his first department meeting so he called up Gettnor's file to see what Smint had been so excited about the other day. The picture was indeterminate; Gettnor had brownish skin but features that didn't seem African, Asian, Hispanic, Arabic or Caucasian. It was as if the man's facial features were a meld of all the races. He had straight looking dark hair, not clearly black, perhaps dark brown. It looked like there might be a patch of hair missing over his right temple with a clumsy attempt to comb other hair over it. The man's eyebrows were weird too, kinda short, reminding him of a "Hitler moustache" over each eye. He'd grown up in Virginia near D.C. and gone to Virginia Tech, obtaining combined electrical engineering-computer science undergrad degrees in three years. Then he'd completed a PhD in Physics in just three years too.

Davis sat back. Gettnor must have been an incredible grind to have taken enough hours of classes per semester to finish that quickly.

Gettnor had actually been on the faculty at VT for a couple of years then abruptly left, apparently in mid semester. He'd been hired here at Querx Tech six months after leaving Virginia Tech suggesting that leaving there hadn't been premeditated.

Stillman's eyebrows rose. Gettnor'd originally been hired at a pretty low salary for a PhD and had received only minimum cost of living raises since then. However, to Stillman's irritation, the company also deposited large amounts of money in a separate account for Gettnor. It wasn't clear why he was getting this extra money which was paid quarterly rather than monthly like a salary.

Davis' eyes narrowed. The extra money wasn't even the same from quarter to quarter. In any case, those deposits resulted in Gettnor taking home a lot more money than Davis, even after the raise he would get with his new job. He tried to ignore it, but it rankled him, especially because he wasn't sure why Gettnor was getting all that money. He wondered if it was a payoff of some kind?

***

"Hello everyone, and thank you for coming to meet with me today." Davis tried not to frown at the room filled with PhDs and techs. He had heard that the dress code was relaxed in R&D but was still shocked to see many of them wearing t-shirts. In fact his glance around showed him that only two of them were wearing ties. Nonetheless he forced a smile and began the speech he'd rehearsed.

"R&D is the bulwark on which Querx's business rests and this group has been doing very well for the company so I'm certainly not going to be making a lot of big changes. I do plan to tighten up reporting so that I can keep a little better track of what goes on," he frowned as he saw members of his audience glancing at one another, "but I assure you it won't be intrusive." For a moment he wondered if they were *all* misfits like Smint had described. After a moment he went on with his presentation, using graphs to emphasize the importance that R&D held for the company, but also to point out that they needed to continue to produce.

"Also I'm aware that Mr. Smint used to encourage you to spend up to one third of your time working on projects of your own interest. I don't want to stifle creativity, but I do believe that spending more than 10% of your time on unassigned projects is unwarranted." He tried another smile, "That said, if you have an interesting project of your own that you want to pursue, bring it to me and we'll see if we can't just make it into a project that Querx *is* interested in." Davis kept a pleasant expression despite the galling way they turned again to look unhappily at one another.

Sometime during his presentation he wondered which one was Gettnor. He became distracted trying to pick him out, then by the possibility that the man hadn't actually attended his presentation.

As he finished his presentation he had an idea. He stepped over to the door, asking each of them to introduce themselves to him on their way out.

No, that SOB Gettnor, had not *come to this introductory meeting!*

***

Vaz muzzily heard someone say, "Dr. Gettnor?" They sounded… not happy. He lifted his head off his desk, noting absently that he'd drooled on its surface. "Huh?" he responded.

Davis stared. The man had been asleep, head down on his desk! As Gettnor turned and rubbed the sleep out of his eyes Davis' eyes widened, he'd shaved his head! And his eyebrows! Bizarrely, his eyelashes constituted the only hair on his head. Davis wondered if the man had cancer and it just wasn't in his records. "Dr. Gettnor?" he repeated wonderingly, thinking this couldn't actually *be* Gettnor, could it? The man had on *sweats* for God's sake! Davis's eyes narrowed, taking in Virginia Tech's "VT" logo on the baggy sweatshirt.

Gettnor cleared his throat, "Yeah?"

"Do you know who I am?"

Gettnor rubbed his eyes and squinted at Davis's name tag. He read off, "Stillman Davis."

"Yes?"

Gettnor shrugged and lifted his nonexistent eyebrows.

"Your new department head?"

A furrow developed between Gettnor's eyebrows, "What happened to Dr. Smint?"

Davis blinked in astonishment. "He retired."

A distant look appeared in Gettnor's eyes. "Oh… yeah." He stood up woodenly and extended a stiff looking hand. "Welcome aboard."

Davis looked at his hand with distaste but then shook it. The hand was hard and calloused but the grip was weak. Somehow even the man's handshake offended him. Exasperatedly he asked, "*Why* are you asleep on company time?"

Vaz stared at Davis, then tilted his head. He examined Davis' face wondering whether the man was angry or not. Vaz knew he wasn't good at recognizing people's moods. Could Davis be joking around? Smint hadn't cared when Vaz worked, just about results. He sighed and said, "I didn't get much sleep last night, then suddenly just couldn't stay awake this morning." Vaz didn't realize that he hadn't made it clear that he hadn't gotten much sleep *because* he'd been here in the lab much of the night. He'd thought of a possible new hydrogen storage alloy while lying awake with one of his periodic bouts of insomnia last night. Excited about it and unable to sleep, he'd decided to come in to work and try casting a sample. His shoulders slumped as he realized that he'd slept through calling Lisanne this morning to tell her why he was gone. *She* would certainly be pissed.

Seeing the man's shoulders slump and thinking he felt guilty, Davis said, "You missed my introductory meeting with the research staff this morning."

Because he'd been told innumerable times that he should, Vaz expressionlessly said, "Sorry." Even though he wasn't at all.

"It's recorded on the Department server."

"Oh." Vaz said a puzzled furrow between his brows.

"So you can still watch it." Davis said impatiently.

"Did you say something important?" Vaz was genuinely curious. Department meetings seldom had anything relevant to his research, so he virtually never attended them. He didn't want to waste time watching something irrelevant and didn't consider the possibility that Davis might find the question offensive.

In silent fury, Davis' cheek twitched twice, but outwardly he only said, "Dr. Gettnor, *I* don't hold Departmental meetings to say things that are *un-*important."

Davis then turned abruptly and left, but the restrained calm of his words and Gettnor's inability to interpret the meaning of his stiff shoulders meant that Gettnor failed to recognize just how angry Davis was.

Gettnor stared at the screen containing his calculations for the new alloy for a moment, then with a sigh told his AI (Artificial Intelligence) to bring up Davis' talk from the Departmental meeting. He had the AI speed through the talk, gradually more and more irritated as he realized that *nothing* Davis had said seemed to be of any import or relevance to Gettnor's work. Vaz *hated* people who felt a need to talk and demanded that others listen even when they had nothing of significance to say.

Furious over the time he'd wasted, Gettnor closed his office door and leapt up to grab the bar he'd suspended from the ceiling. He slammed out 40 pull-ups, 80 pushups, and 80 sit-ups. He thought he might have to start over, but finally achieved an endorphin release at about the 70th sit-up. The endorphins relaxed him as they usually did. He didn't like wasting time on exercise like this, but since that day about six months ago that he first achieved an endorphin release pounding the couch and doing sit-ups he'd come to realize that exercising to such a release kept him from sitting and stewing. He would be feeling like his head was about to explode, and the relief of that sensation felt *wonderful*. He dropped panting into his chair and closed his eyes. He tried to stave off a grim sense of foreboding.

Vaz didn't think he was going to like working for this Davis. His mind tracked back to his time on the faculty at Virginia Tech. Small minded people on the faculty and students who were completely impossible to teach had wasted his time, frustrating him until he finally lashed out at one of the students. He'd nearly struck the young fool and been summarily dismissed from the faculty.

Davis seemed like the kind of imbecile he'd had to deal with back then. Controlling his temper could be extremely difficult around them.

Vaz sent Lisanne an apology for leaving in the middle of the night without telling her. He knew she'd still be pissed, but he also knew it would be worse if he didn't apologize.

When his breathing had slowed he went back out to check on the casting of his new alloy.

The casting's electrical properties weren't at all what he'd predicted! In fact they were so bizarre that he retested them five times thinking that he must have hooked up meters or leads incorrectly. Finally he removed the new casting and retested a disk he'd made a week ago. The old disk produced the same electrical results as it had a week before, confirming that there wasn't a problem with his test setup. He tested the new disk again.

It gave him the same bizarre outcome that it had minutes ago!

Vaz sat back, staring at the disk. He called up the calculations he'd made for this alloy and looked them over again. He got the same predictions... so at odds with reality. He tried to tamp down the irritation that he always felt when natural phenomena didn't obey his calculations. Closing his eyes he wearily reminded himself that understanding why something *didn't* follow expectations could be much more important than a result that came out as expected.

Vaz's mind raced through possible explanations for the unusual electrical performance, discarding one hypothesis after another. Suddenly, like a light blossoming in a darkened room he felt his consciousness expand to encompass the problem. He'd had this experience before, usually a short while after getting angry and subsequently exercising to exhaustion for a dose of endorphins. If he encountered a difficult problem during one of his endorphin induced euphorias, it could seem as if his intelligence had suddenly doubled. He felt omniscient as he pondered the electrical properties of the metal. *Aha!* In a moment of sudden clarity he saw *why* they were so bizarre and how a slightly different casting chemistry could make them even more astonishing!

A voice grated, "Jesus Christ! Are you asleep again?"

Vaz's stomach clenched as he felt his understanding begin to slip away. Squinching his eyes to keep out the world, he lifted his hands palm outward to fend this person off for just a moment until he could firm his understanding...

"Gettnor, open your goddamned eyes when I talk to you!"

Vaz felt it slipping away… Shoulders rigid, he opened his eyes and scrabbled for the pencil in his pocket, looking around desperately for a piece of paper to write down the few fragments of understanding he still retained. He still held up a deflecting hand. He saw no paper, so he began scribbling directly on the table.

A seething Davis ground out, "Gettnor! *Whatever* you think you're pretending to do so frantically can wait until you've spoken to your department head."

A despairing Vaz felt his vision of the problem slip completely away. Ashen he stared at the few notes he'd made on the table. They didn't make sense to him anymore. Slowly he looked up at Davis, head beginning to pound and shoulders tensing. Desperately he tamped down his rage, hoping that Davis wouldn't say something that made him explode. "Yes?" he said, trying to unclench his teeth.

"How is it that I visit you twice in my first day on this job and find you sleeping both times?"

Vaz's eyes narrowed. "I *wasn't* sleeping!"

Davis snorted. "*Excuse* me. Reclining your head on the headrest with your eyes closed." He raised an eyebrow, "I'll admit you weren't snoring. But…! I expect the people in *my* department to be working when I visit them"

Vaz grimaced, "I *was* working. I had just had a major insight that I was visualizing." Dispiritedly he said, "I've lost it now."

Davis scoffed. "Well, as soon as I've finished discussing my *requirements* of you, Dr. Gettnor, you can get back to your 'visualizing.'"

To Vaz's dismay, Davis had come to tell him that he would be expected to be *on time* to work. There would be no more of Smint's laxness regarding his working how and whenever he wanted and only being expected to produce results.

By the time Davis left, Vaz felt like he'd been punched in the gut.

**

Lisanne looked up as Vaz came in. "Vaz," she began, and then she saw he'd immediately turned and put his hand on the door to the basement.

He turned woodenly. Expressionlessly he said, "Sorry."

She wondered if he even knew what he was apologizing for. Wearily she said, "Go. Dinner will be in a half an hour. Will that be enough time?"

He nodded stiffly. She waved a dismissive hand and turned toward the kitchen. She wondered once again just what he did down there in his basement "man cave." She'd learned through bitter experience not to detain him from going down there when he seemed to want to. He didn't usually go down there immediately upon getting home from work, but if she stopped him from going down on the days when he did, he'd act like an asshole until she *did* let him. *Something* down there calmed him.

Glancing over at the basement door she wondered what would it be like to be able to cook dinner *with* him? He cooked—either slavishly following a recipe or creating the weirdest most wonderful meals completely from his own imagination. After finishing one of his impromptu meals he would be unable to write down a recipe for whatever he'd just made. And if she asked him to help her or, God forbid, she tried to help him, the meal they cooked together turned into an absolute disaster.

A tear trickled down Lisanne's cheek as she divided the hamburger into five parts and started squeezing out patties. She sometimes wondered how she could have fallen in love with someone so... odd. How could she not have recognized that what others

19

thought was weirdness and she thought was shyness, actually was an inability to relate normally to other human beings? And yet… somehow… she did fall in love with his brilliance… and shyness… and she still loved him, despite how intensely frustrating life with Vaz could be.

Vaz closed the door behind him, telling it to lock. Lisanne would be able to open it of course, but it would take a moment or two for the AI to accept her request. During that time he would be able to try to compose himself. He forced himself to go down the stairs calmly, one at a time, because pounding down the stairs like he wanted to would worry Lisanne. Once he reached the concrete floor of the basement he grabbed his gloves and slid his hands into them. He lunged out to punch the Everlast heavy bag hanging by the far wall.

Picturing Stillman Davis' face on the bag he pounded the bag steadily and as hard as he could for ten minutes. Then he pulled off his sweatshirt and switched to his speed bag, setting it thrumming for another ten minutes. Panting, but feeling relaxed and tranquil again, he stepped back from the bag and headed into the basement bathroom to towel off. The glance he saw in the mirror while reaching for the towel disturbed him. Over the six months since he'd found that exercising to exhaustion could exorcise his demons, he'd developed a bulging and to him bizarrely muscular appearance. His body seemed a caricature to him, at odds with his mental image of himself as a man who valued and depended on mental rather than physical capacities. He'd gone out and bought baggy oversized shirts and sweats to hide what had happened to him.

Vaz had his AI unlock the door to the basement so that Lisanne wouldn't find it locked if she opened the door to call down that dinner was ready.

Lisanne said a blessing as always. Vaz didn't believe, but he didn't object either. They all helped themselves to the hamburgers and buns and began choosing their condiments.

Lisanne turned to their son, "Dante, how was your day?"

"Fine." He took another bite of his first burger. Dark like his father, he was in the midst of a teenage growth spurt, eating more food than Lisanne could believe.

"Everything OK in your classes?"

Still chewing, Dante nodded his head without looking at his mother.

Lisanne closed her eyes; Vaz thought maybe she didn't like Dante's response? He didn't feel sure of it though. Lisanne picked up a slice of tomato and put it on her hamburger while turning to their daughter. "Tiona, how did you do on your English test?"

Tiona didn't meet her mother's eyes either. Well Vaz couldn't be sure, her wheat colored hair hung over her blue eyes. She took a bite of hamburger and for a moment Vaz thought she didn't intend to answer, but then, around a mouthful of food, she sullenly said, "Fine."

Vaz became aware that Lisanne's eyes were on him. He thought she was unhappy with the kids… and maybe with him? Did she want him to intervene or something? Surely not, whenever he did, it finished with *everyone* upset.

As soon as she finished her hamburger Tiona asked if she could be excused. Lisanne sighed and nodded. Both of the kids got up, took their dishes to the dishwasher and went upstairs to their rooms.

Still chewing his hamburger, Vaz felt Lisanne's eyes on him. Bringing his gaze up to her face, he swallowed and said, "What?"

21

"Did you think the kids' behavior was acceptable?"

Vaz felt his own eyes widen. He found a few hairs near his left elbow and began twisting them, uncomfortable because he wasn't at all sure what she wanted him to say. "Uh…" he began.

Lisanne waved a hand deprecatingly. "I know, you aren't even sure whether they were being rude." She shook her head despairingly, "So of course you didn't say anything, right?"

Vaz nodded, eyes still carefully on Lisanne's as she'd taught him. She sighed again making him even more uncomfortable. He said, "Did you want me to…?"

Lisanne tilted her head back and stared at the ceiling. Quietly she said, "No… no," she squared her shoulders, "I don't know why I even *think* you should get involved when the kids are a problem. You just make things worse."

Vaz narrowed his eyes. That sounded like a statement that should make him angry. He tilted his head considering. He didn't feel angry; it was a true enough statement after all. "OK," he said, and put the last bite of his hamburger in his mouth. He felt pretty sure that Lisanne was angry so he considered some of the strategies he'd been taught to deal with uncomfortable situations. After he swallowed that last bite he settled on, "The hamburgers were good, thanks."

Lisanne narrowed her eyes at him in turn, making Vaz wonder if he'd said the wrong thing *again*. But after a moment she shook her head, gave him a wry grin, and said, "You're welcome."

Long after Vaz had taken his dishes to the sink and retreated to his basement Lisanne sat at the table mulling over her little family. She knew teenagers were supposed to be difficult, everyone said so. Somehow, she'd thought that hers wouldn't be. They'd been so sweet back between the ages of three and twelve but...

She'd heard that the "teenage years" were grueling so you wouldn't be sad when your children moved out. But, the sullen and surly way Dante and Tiona had been acting this past year... she'd begun to think that they couldn't move out soon enough to suit her. Gathering the rest of the dishes, she resolved to get on the net and do some research on how to deal with these issues.

Lisanne spent a couple of hours looking around the net, trying to decide how to calm the issues she felt were tearing her family apart. She began to firm up a plan and sat wondering whether she should discuss it with her husband. Everything she'd read emphasized that the parents should agree on how to deal with such problems, then approach the problems together so that they didn't undermine one another in their strategies. But... Lisanne knew that Vaz would prefer that she simply resolve the issues if she could, without making him think about any interpersonal interactions if he didn't have to. Still, shouldn't she tell him about her plans?

No, she finally decided, her plans would just make him uncomfortable.

***

Stillman Davis had been out visiting the R&D staff. He didn't intend to be one of those managers who just sat in his office and interacted with his people through his AI. His mentors had emphasized the importance of personally knowing and relating to your staff if you wanted top performance from them. Even though he continued to be disturbed by the casual dress of the research scientists, he'd begun to appreciate that dress clothing might not be appropriate if you were working with chemical and physical processes.

He'd enjoyed speaking with Gerrold Rogers, a chemist whose assignment was to optimize fuel cells. Rogers had shown Davis some graphs demonstrating that a several percent increase in the power output of the company's cells might be achievable by doping the cathode catalyst with manganese. He'd even given Davis a sample of the new cathode to "put on his desk."

With a warm satisfied glow he opened the door to Gettnor's lab. This time, less frustrated than he'd been before, he noticed that the lab had a completely different look than any of the other labs. It looked compulsively organized, not a thing out of place. Pieces of equipment on lab benches, exactly squared in position with precisely the same spacing between them. It had the appearance of a lab someone had set up, then never used. Certainly none of the energetic looking clutter that Davis had seen in other labs.

Gettnor was slouched back in a chair staring at the big screen on the wall which displayed some kind of 3D multicolored graphic. The graphic changed slowly as Gettnor manipulated a touchscreen with his right hand. Gettnor hadn't noticed when Davis opened the door so he cleared his throat. Still no response so he said, "Dr. Gettnor?"

Gettnor still didn't respond! Was he really that focused? Or ignoring Davis on purpose? Davis leaned close behind him and heard the faint sounds of some kind of music coming from Gettnor's earphones. It sounded like some kind of new age or classical composition. Davis reached out to tap his shoulder, then paused. He stood undecided a moment, remembering Smint's admonitions and Gettnor's claim that his interruption the other day had ruined his understanding of something or another.

Personally, Davis thought that was just so much bullshit. He'd personally never had any trouble getting back to whatever he'd been doing prior to an interruption. On the other hand, he didn't really need to talk to Gettnor now. Maybe he should just come back later, when Gettnor didn't look so focused. After another moment with Gettnor still unmoving, Davis turned and went to talk to the folks in the next lab.

There were three PhDs and a couple of lab techs all working in the next lab. All bustled around, doing something in an atmosphere of purposeful disarray. One seemed to be assembling a mechanism. Three were measuring out solutions with pipettes. One cursed as she opened and closed drawers, apparently looking for something. All the activity made Davis feel better about his department. Something seemed to be getting done here as opposed to Gettnor looking like he might be playing some kind of game with his AI. They noticed him and one said, "Hello, Mr. Davis. Can we help you?"

With a warm feeling Davis said, "No, no. I'm just going around, trying to learn what my people are doing. If you aren't pressed for time, can you tell me what your objectives are in this lab?"

"Yes sir. We're trying to further optimize the nanoparticles for our old solid state lithium cobalt battery system. We hope to improve capacity another 15% without losing our safety margin. John is reassembling the lab's trial vacuum deposition system. Julius, Mary and Rick are making up our new trial solutions."

Davis nodded knowingly. Even though he didn't really have a clue what they were talking about, 15% sounded like a respectable improvement. He shook hands all around, and then asked if there was anything "administration" could do to help. They wanted more space and more lab techs to "get the job done more expeditiously."

Davis explained that they didn't have money in the budget to hire more help. He wasn't sure whether money was available or not, but wanted to work toward a positive, not a negative budget. Then he had an idea and grinned internally. "I see that there are five of you working in this lab. Isn't Dr. Gettnor all alone in the next lab?"

They nodded, though several of them glanced at one another, he thought with some apprehension.

"Would it help your overcrowding here if some of your equipment and experiments were moved into his area? I'm sure he's not using all that space all the time."

"Uh, I'm not sure that would be a good idea." Julius said.

Davis frowned at this rejection of what he'd thought of as a perfectly good idea. "Why not?"

"Uh, Dr. Gettnor doesn't do well if he's disturbed."

Davis snorted. "Well, maybe he needs to learn to adapt."

The group laughed nervously. Mary said, "I have a feeling *that* isn't going to happen. We'll be OK."

Davis frowned again but moved on to the next lab.

Pleased about his "morning with the troops," Davis headed back to his office. He only remembered his intent to check back on Gettnor after he'd passed Gettnor's lab. For a moment he thought about skipping it. After all, Gettnor set him on edge and might ruin the pleasant satisfaction he felt at present. But, he didn't like to think of himself as someone who skirted unwelcome tasks. Especially personnel issues where he prided himself on his skills. Resolutely he turned back and entered Gettnor's lab.

Gettnor didn't look like he'd moved since Davis had been in his lab earlier! Still slouched way back in his chair; same 3D graphics on his big screen, though they'd stopped changing. Davis narrowed his eyes, Gettnor's hand no longer moved on the touchpad.

Quietly, Davis moved up alongside Gettnor so that he could see the man's eyes. They were closed!

Indignantly Davis reached out and peremptorily tapped Gettnor's shoulder.

Gettnor didn't move except to slowly raise his hand as if halting someone.

Davis tapped again, a little harder.

Gettnor slowly waved the hand he'd lifted.

Davis pushed on Gettnor's chair, turning it toward him.

Gettnor exploded up out of the chair, ripping off his headset and boring into Davis with flashing eyes.

Davis stepped back uncertainly; suddenly feeling like Gettnor was looking down on him, even though they were much the same height.

Gettnor said, "I hope…" he closed his eyes and almost sighed, "Oh, I *so* hope this is *important* this time!"

Davis drew himself up. "Dr. Gettnor, you were asleep *again*! Do you ever do any work here?"

"I was not asleep," Gettnor grated out. "Just as before, I was attempting to visualize…" His voice faded out as he, for a moment, felt like he might get the picture back. He looked distantly up toward the corner of the room, and then slowly closed his eyes as he began to feel the pieces drop back into place again.

"Gettnor!"

Gettnor's eyes squinched shut a moment; then he wearily opened them with a discouraged look. "Go ahead. What's so important?"

"I'm going around learning what each group of scientists are doing. I dropped by your lab earlier and you were listening to music and staring at your display so I went around and talked to all the other teams. I came back here and found you, hours later, asleep in front of the same screen!"

With an aghast expression Gettnor said, "You destroyed a morning's work to *chat*?! Really?! You had *no* reason to interrupt me except that you wanted to talk?!"

For a moment Davis felt defensive; then remembered their relative positions in the company. "You weren't *doing* anything!"

"I was *thinking* man! *You* should *try* it sometime!"

Davis rolled his eyes, "And *what*, pray tell, were you thinking about?"

"I was *trying* to reconcile the actual electrical properties of a new boron-vanadium-palladium alloy with the predicted values, they're way off."

"What does that have to do with your mission?" Davis glanced up at his HUD, "I thought you were supposed to be working on hydrogen storage?"

Gettnor sighed, "The boron-vanadium-palladium alloy *is* a hydrogen storage alloy."

Davis narrowed his eyes, "Alloy? Are you saying that you're trying to create some kind of better tank to put hydrogen in?"

Gettnor's eyes widened. Then as if speaking to a particularly obtuse child, he said, "Some metals absorb hydrogen. Palladium can absorb 900 times its volume in hydrogen. We'd probably use palladium for hydrogen storage if it weren't so expensive."

Davis drew his head back, "Really?"

With a disgusted look Gettnor replied, "Really."

"OK, then. But *why* do we care about this alloy's *electrical* properties?"

"We should understand *all* the properties of anything we create here in the lab, there's no telling what we might miss if we don't completely characterize them."

"Oh, come *on* Gettnor. This *reeks* of a scientist who likes to piddle around. All Querx needs to know is how much hydrogen it absorbs right?"

"No! If its electrical properties are weird, other properties might be weird too! We need to understand them and have some idea *why* this is happening."

Davis sighed, "Wrong. *Querx* needs something that stores hydrogen. *That's* your job! Test that. If it's good, let's think about whether it's good enough to put into production. If not, *move on* to the next idea... for *storing hydrogen*."

Gettnor stared at Davis mulishly but said nothing. Eventually Davis stepped back and said, "Work on your assigned project." He frowned and as he turned to go said ominously, "You've been warned."

Vaz had to go to his office after the conversation with Davis and rip out his usual sets of pull-ups, pushups and sit-ups. Once the warm flush of an endorphin release rolled over him he sank gasping into his chair and relaxed until he fell asleep for a twenty minute nap. When he woke he saw the graphic representation of the electrical properties of the new alloy still displayed on his wall screen. Unmoving he found himself again in a state of expanded consciousness, able to grasp all sides of the problem. Desperate to avoid interruption this time he blindly groped out to close his office door. He told it to lock. His head felt fizzy with occasional events that he thought of as lightning bolts exploding in it. Goose bumps came and went.

An hour later Vaz had a good hypothesis and a plan for extensive testing. Mindful of Davis' demand, and because he needed to know, he set the disk he already had to evaluate its capacity for hydrogen absorption. Then he stoked up the automated casting system in the lab to make another hundred disks of the alloy. Ten of them were just more test disks of the same alloy, but the other ninety were distributed among slight variations in the concentration of the metals or the special crystallization conditions he'd been using.

He felt like he was back on edge again. His feeling of omniscience had faded and as he worked on the mundane tasks of setting up the lab for the absorption test and to cast the alloy he found his mind wandering repeatedly back to his confrontation with Davis.

Smint would *never* have told him to ignore bizarre findings like these. Smint would have asked what they were and puzzled over them with Vaz. He probably would have had some good perspectives and some suggestions of his own for further testing. Smint understood the value of *understanding*, not just applying a finding.

Everything was set up and in progress twenty minutes before his specified quitting time. Vaz stood uneasily shifting from foot to foot. There wasn't anything to do until sometime tomorrow morning, but Davis had told him that he was expected to be physically *at* work from eight in the morning to 4:30 in the afternoon.

Should he just sit in his office until 4:30? Just the idea of wasting time like that started to make his head pound.

Screw it, he thought and headed for the door.

A truck had broken down on Vaz's route home and his car's AI took him a little out of its normal way to avoid the resultant traffic jam. Normally completely oblivious to the sights on his way home Vaz found himself gazing around at the differences. "Stop," he said to the car's AI. Take me to," he had to turn in his seat to look back over his shoulder. "Mike's Mixed Martial."

Jen looked up as a man in his late 30's approached the desk. Completely bald, without even eyebrows, he wore a baggy muted Hawaiian print shirt over a loose long sleeved t-shirt and pants that looked like they didn't fit right. The pants were jeans that were... too big? They looked like they'd belonged to someone bigger than him and had been belted up into pleats to stay on him. She tilted her head as she examined him. Her first glance had made her think, *fat and out of shape.* Now she wasn't so sure. She could only see his head and hands but his face contained angular planes that made her think that he wasn't actually overweight. Yet, somehow he exuded a soft nerdiness. "May I help you?"

He glanced up at her face, then back down at the desk. "Do you have fights here?"

Jen's eyes widened, "We teach self-defense. We have sparring matches but not *fights.* If you want to watch fights you'll have to go to MMA events."

The man looked embarrassed, eyes darting here and there, "I'd... actually like to... get into a fight myself," he said, just above a whisper.

"What kind of training have you had?"

He looked down, "Haven't."

Jen snorted, "You do *not* want to get into a fight without any training."

"How many classes would I have to take?"

"Our minimum training program is a five session self-defense class."

"And then I could get in a fight?"

"No!" she snorted. "Then you *might* be able to defend yourself if someone attacked you."

The man stared up into the corner of the room considering a moment, then said, "When could I take a self-defense class?"

"The group classes start the first Mondays of each month. You can get 'one on one' training pretty much anytime."

"Like, right now?"

"Really?!"

He shrugged, "Yeah."

"But you don't have your stuff!"

He frowned. "What do I need?"

Jen looked him up and down, "Well, you could take it barefoot I guess. Usually you don't wear jeans, they bind."

"These are loose."

Jen rolled her eyes, "Mike," she bellowed, "you up for a one on one?"

Mike looked up from the strike pad set he'd been repairing and eyed the bald guy at the desk. He uncoiled and strode up to the front thinking that the guy was... odd. When he got close he said, "What happened to your eyebrows?"

The guy mumbled something.

"Huh?"

"Why do you care?"

"Because if you have some disease, I don't want you rubbing all over the equipment, or me either."

The guy dropped his eyes embarrassedly to the floor. "I have trichotillomania, a compulsion to pull out my own hair." He took a deep breath, "I shave it all off because my wife likes that look better than me having patches missing."

32

Mike lifted an eyebrow. "Humpf. OK, what kind of 'one on one' training do you have in mind, Mr....?"

"Gettnor. I don't know. I just like to hit stuff, work off anger and..." he trailed off.

"Why don't you just get a heavy bag and hit it?"

"Got one."

Mike chewed a lip, "You want to hit people?"

Gettnor shrugged. "When I'm hitting my bag, I imagine I'm in a fight. Helps me work out my anger. I wondered if a real fight might help me even more."

"Well we don't hold fights here, but we could help you get ready for one of the local MMA amateur fights if you want."

Gettnor shrugged again, "OK."

They discussed fees and Mike suggested that they do a one on one session, then decide what class Gettnor might fit into. After agreeing they walked into the back where Gettnor took off the Hawaiian shirt and his shoes. Mike handed him some 6 oz. gloves and said "Let's see what you do to the heavy bag since that's something you're familiar with." He stepped around and grabbed the other side of the big bag. Mike had glanced toward the front of the studio when Gettnor lunged out; hitting the other side of the bag so hard that it ripped out of Mike's hands and hit him in the crotch. Hard! It hurt! Gettnor didn't "box" it a few blows and bounce back. He *pounded* it with one heavy blow after another. Slower than fighters hit a speed bag but, holy crap, not much slower! He expected the guy to keep it up a few seconds and drop back exhausted but Gettnor just kept pounding. "Stop!"

Gettnor stopped immediately and stepped back, shifting his weight slowly from foot to foot. Not "dancing" from to foot, just shifting weight. He didn't look tired, he looked... elated? Mike wasn't sure what the expression on Gettnor's face meant. He looked more carefully at the man. It was hard to assess his fitness in that baggy long sleeved shirt. He narrowed his eyes. "Take off your shirt. Let me see what I'm working with."

Gettnor got an obstinate look on his face and just shook his head "no."

Mike shrugged. "OK. Can you kick the bag?"

Gettnor had terrible technique, telegraphing a huge roundhouse kick with his right foot. But, when it hit the bag, it knocked Mike off his stance even though he thought he was prepared for a heavy blow this time. Gettnor immediately kicked the bag with his left, then again with the right. Mike's eyebrows rose as Gettnor heavily battered the bag with his feet long past when anyone else would have quit in exhaustion. "OK, OK. Give it a rest." Mike shook his head and had Gettnor hit some target mitts. Accuracy wasn't great, but holy crap the guy hit hard! Even with Mike telling him to punch for speed instead of power the guy still hit the mitts *hard*. Pretty fast too, though by no means truly quick.

"You ever wrestled?" Mike asked handing him a disposable mouth guard and putting in his own.

"A little in high school."

"OK, we get down on our hands and knees and you can try to keep me from pinning you?"

Gettnor pursed his lips, "OK. No hitting?"

"No hitting. Just wrestling. I'll start behind you, arm around your waist."

"OK."

They got down in the "referee's position" with Gettnor on the bottom. Mike put his arm around Gettnor's waist and was startled to feel rock hard muscle instead of the soft belly he'd somehow still been expecting. Mike said, "One, two, three, go!"

Mike had expected Gettnor to be hard to pin after the power he'd displayed punching the bag. He hadn't anticipated Gettnor effortlessly ripping up out of his grip and turning to face him! "*Sheeit* you're strong!"

Gettnor tilted his head, "Really?"

"Really." Mike shook his head. "Let me teach you some stuff about 'how' to fight and we'll talk about how to spar safely. I don't want to actually spar with you until you know the rules; as strong as you are someone'll get hurt." Mike felt nonplussed to realize that he felt concerned that the person getting hurt might be himself. He'd been doing this for years after all, and he was a big guy, in good shape. Gettnor was smaller than he was; more average sized but somehow, just a lot... stronger. "What kind of workouts do you do to make yourself so strong? Weights?"

Gettnor shook his head, "No. Just pushups, pull-ups, sit-ups, hitting the bags, sometimes some other calisthenics."

"Cripes! That's all?"

Gettnor nodded. "They relax me... but I'll admit, they seem to have an excessive effect."

Mike laughed, "Relax you... right..." He snorted, "What do you mean 'excessive effect'?"

"They've made me excessively muscular. I think they have a lot more effect on me than they do on other people. It's kind of grotesque." He slid up a sleeve, showing layers of cut musculature in his forearm that Mike stared at enviously. "I mean, this just isn't right, is it?"

Mike shook his head and barked another laugh. "What you're calling grotesque is something that most of the guys that work out here would pay good money for."

Gettnor shrugged, looking embarrassed. "I really don't *want* to look like a muscle bound freak. I'm hoping that I can get the same relaxation out of sparring as I do out of my exercises without 'bulking up' so much."

Mike grinned at him in disbelief; then said, "OK, let's talk about how you can defend yourself from attack in the ring."

***

Lisanne got home late. She worked as a programmer at Radix, a local company that designed industrial process prototypes. She liked it because it was challenging work; collaborating with mechanical engineers to set up control systems for the machines they built. Some days were more challenging than others, like today, when the program for an industrial assembler had failed to place parts correctly. Because no one else could do anything until she figured out what was wrong, she'd stayed late to determine the cause.

Hopeful when she'd seen that Vaz's car was home she was delighted when she walked in and smelled something cooking. Vaz looked... relaxed and happy. Whatever he was cooking smelled great, though she wasn't sure just what it smelled like. "Hey Hubby, what'cha got cookin'?"

Vaz shrugged and twisted his lips, staring into the pan, "I'm not sure what you'd call it." He cast his eyes around the stove, "It's got fried flour tortilla strips, with mozzarella cheese, chopped tomatoes, garlic and the last of the pastrami, also chopped. I just shook in some spices at random."

"Sounds terrible," Lisanne laughed, "but from past experience it'll be somewhere between OK and amazing... Thanks for cooking."

"No problem. My day finished well and I felt like cooking. Hope it turns out OK."

Lisanne looked at him a moment, thinking about what a great husband he could sometimes be, good provider, great cook and just plain sweet. Recently he seemed to have even gotten over his tendency to occasionally fly into a fury. Those furies had been very frightening at first before she'd understood that he'd never actually hurt her. But he hadn't had one in months despite a few stressful situations. He would tighten up but wouldn't explode. Worst case he'd head down to his man cave in the basement and something down there cooled him off somehow. Whatever it was down there, she was glad it did whatever it did for him.

For a moment she thought back to how brilliant she'd found him when he'd been assigned as her partner in a college computer science class. Nerdy, quiet, shy, not a people person, but *wow* amazing when it came to writing code.

As she turned to go upstairs she glanced back and wondered briefly what had happened to his pants. They didn't seem to fit right. She'd recently begun noticing that his clothes fit funny. He'd gone out and bought a bunch of clothes himself recently. She had always tried to discourage him from shopping for clothes because he had awful taste in clothing. The new clothes seemed to bag on him... oddly... kind of oversized, but... not. She just wasn't quite sure what was wrong with them.

***

Stillman Davis arrived at work feeling unsettled. He'd laid awake a good part of the night, mulling over his confrontation with Gettnor. Thinking of what he *should* have said. Wondering if the manner in which he'd dealt with the situation demonstrated the leadership qualities that he wanted to become known for.

Gettnor was a goddamned loose cannon and Davis found himself resenting Smint for not dealing with such a personnel problem before he'd left. On the other hand, if he could prove that *he* could correct such antisocial tendencies and turn Gettnor into a team player, it would be something he'd be able to take pride in and list as an accomplishment.

Once he'd dealt with a few issues that had stacked up overnight he hopefully checked to see if Gettnor had come to work on time this morning. The building's security system logged all arrivals and departures. With some relief he saw that Gettnor had arrived at 7:50. A little early was *good* and Davis relaxed a little. However, just when he was about to close the security window he noticed that Gettnor had *left* work yesterday at 4:10!

Davis closed his eyes and sank back in his chair. *Christ!* Just a day after he'd warned the bastard, Gettnor'd flaunted his order to be at work for his scheduled hours. He rubbed the bridge of his nose, trying to stave off an incipient headache. They were going to have to have *another* talk! Davis really didn't want to talk to him but he forced himself to face up to his duty. If Gettnor couldn't or wouldn't toe the line then they didn't need him in this company. It would set a bad example for the way Davis planned to lead his section if he turned a blind eye to such a flagrant disregard for the rules.

Stillman looked at the schedule to see if he had time to confront Gettnor now. No he had an appointment. He felt a little relieved to avoid the impending conflict for a while, but told himself that it was good to have time to cool down.

Vaz stared wide eyed at the results of the boron-vanadium-palladium alloy's absorption test. Overnight it had sucked up 1,200 times its volume of hydrogen! Even though it was only 3% palladium the alloy was even more effective as a hydrogen sponge than the already astonishing but expensive metal. Well, that should make Davis happy. And if his new theory was right, it would absorb even more if he charged it electrically and more yet with an extremely high voltage, high frequency intermittent current that Vaz thought of as kind of "hammering" the hydrogen protons into the alloy.

He set up and applied the current, then turned to the freshly casted testing disks of his new alloys. If he was right, increasing the vanadium concentration and slowing the crystallization was going to further emphasize the bizarre electrical properties. He harvested and began carefully laser labeling the disks, placing them in a rack as he went.

Davis walked into Gettnor's lab. He found Gettnor hunched over an apparatus, pulling out small disk shaped semi-metallic appearing objects. He would put them momentarily in a small cylindrical device, close it, give it a command, then immediately open it and take the disk out. From there the objects went into a little rack. He cleared his throat, "Dr. Gettnor."

Gettnor glanced at him, said "Just a minute," and took another object out of the cylinder. He placed it in the rack, turned and said, "What now?" He didn't get up.

Davis' eyes narrowed. Gettnor sounded positively surly. Damn the man anyway! He didn't seem to have any conception of how the boss-employee relationship should work. Stillman had entered the room hoping for a reasonable explanation for why Gettnor'd left early yesterday, but now he found himself wanting to fire him just for his attitude. "You left the building yesterday at 4:10."

"Yeah."

"I *told* you that we expected you to be here for your entire shift!"

"I'm not a 'shift' worker." He'd held up his fingers and made little "quotes" signs at the word "shift."

"What the hell does that mean? You have assigned working hours, just like everyone else."

"I do projects. Sometimes I come in at night because something needs to be done, sometimes there's nothing to do. I'm not going to just sit here and twiddle my thumbs to keep you happy."

Davis drew back, face purpling and about to explode.

Gettnor's eyes widened as they jumped to stare at something behind and to Davis' left. Davis' eyes turned to see smoke begin to pour off of an apparatus on the bench there. The lower part of it turned red and it slumped over sort of sagging off onto the floor.

Davis danced away from splattering bits of melted material, his exposed skin feeling heat radiating from the mess. "What the Hell!?"

Gettnor had jumped up shouting an order, presumably to the lab's AI. The lab was plunged into darkness except for the red glow of the partially melted apparatus. Gettnor spoke again and the lights came back on. He slowly moved over to look at the mess on the floor. Davis noted with astonishment that Gettnor didn't look upset or horrified. *He looked excited and happy!* "What the hell just happened there?!"

Gettnor didn't turn, he simply shrugged and said, "I don't know, but we'll have to figure it out. *That was amazing!*"

"What in God's name have you got going on down here Gettnor?!"

Wide eyed, staring at the melted mess, Gettnor shook his head as if in amazement, "Where did all that energy come from?" he almost whispered.

"Do you mean to tell me that you don't even have any idea what just happened?! You sleep on the job, come in late, leave early and your experiments are *so* out of control that fires are starting in your lab!

40

Good God man, you're not just a terrible employee, you're a menace!"

Gettnor didn't even look up at Davis. He continued to stare at the smoldering mess on the floor as he scooted his chair closer to it and sat down. "What could *do* that?" he mumbled as if to himself. He stood again and disconnected some of the cables leading to the melted apparatus, then mumbled to his AI. The power came back on to the equipment that remained on the lab bench. Gettnor peered at the digital readouts on some of the equipment.

"Gettnor!" Davis practically shouted, "Forget that crap for now. We need to talk about your performance!"

Still mumbling, Gettnor picked up a meter and began hooking it up to fresh cables he jacked into the machines that had evidently been powering the melted apparatus. He didn't appear to have heard Davis.

Davis reached out and tapped Gettnor on the shoulder but Gettnor brushed at his hand like one might slap at an irritating fly that had landed.

Davis stared unbelievingly a moment longer then said, "Gettnor, I've had enough. You're fired! I'll send security to escort you from the building. I imagine we owe you some kind of severance pay and I'll make sure you get it, but for now, start packing up your stuff."

Davis stopped by his secretary's desk on his way back to his office. "Maddie, I've just fired Dr. Gettnor. Have Security escort him from the building. Put me in touch with HR. I'll need to talk to them about hiring a replacement and whatever severance package Gettnor's due."

Maddie stared wide eyed at him. "Are you sure?! Dr. Smint always said..." she trailed off at the incendiary look Davis gave her.

Davis ground out, "I know that Smint and Gettnor had some kind of *special* relationship. I, however, am not putting up with Gettnor's crap! He's *out* of here. I've already informed him. Though," he quirked an odd smile, "Gettnor's in his own little world, he might not have even heard me."

Davis slammed into his office and downloaded copies of all of his interactions with Gettnor into a file for the HR weenies to dither about. For a moment he wondered if he might have overreacted, but then decided no, there was absolutely no justification for the man's insolence, inattentiveness and just plain dangerous performance. Gettnor was *so* far from a model employee that no one in their right mind would tolerate him on their staff.

Allen checked the charge on his Taser; then put it back on his belt. He hitched the belt up and leaned in the door to Gettnor's lab. "Dr. Gettnor?" The broad backed man sitting in the lab didn't look up from studying the readouts on some of the equipment. With some surprise Allen noticed that the room had a burned smell as if there had been a fire. Allen stepped in through the door. His eyes widened as he saw what looked like a partly melted mass of material on the floor and noticed that part of the countertop on the lab bench had slumped down just above the melty stuff. His brows high, he cleared his throat, "Dr. Gettnor?" he said again, a little louder. The man held up his hand as if staving off the interruption while he continued studying the equipment on the bench behind the slumped area. Irritated, Allen waved his partner Jimmy into the room and put his hand on the Gettnor's shoulder, "Sir!" he began but Gettnor slapped his hand away and again put up a peremptory palm signaling him to wait."

Allen rubbed his wrist where Gettnor had struck it. It hurt! However he waited a moment, honoring Gettnor's signal to wait. The moment stretched to a minute, then two. Finally Allen cleared his throat again and when there was still no response, said "Dr. Gettnor!"

Gettnor simply put up his palm again, still focused on the equipment. This time when Allen put his hand on Gettnor's shoulder, he placed it low, where Gettnor wouldn't be able to slap at it. Gettnor shrugged the shoulder in irritation but still didn't turn. Allen began to pull, wondering what it would take to get the man to turn around.

Finally, Gettnor's head snapped around, focusing a penetrating gaze on Allen. Allen involuntarily took a step back, intimidated by the intense glare. Gettnor said, "What?!"

"Uh, we're here to escort you from the building." Allen waved in the general direction of Jimmy.

A crease appeared between Gettnor's eyes. "I don't need to leave the building! What are you talking about?"

"Uh, you've been fired. Mr. Davis, your department head, said he already told you."

"What!?"

Allen firmed up his stance and stuck his thumbs in his web belt. "You've been fired. We're here to escort you from the building."

A confused look passed over Gettnor's eyes. He spoke to his AI, asking it to connect him to Maddie in the Department head's office. "Maddie?"

After a pause in which she evidently responded, he said, "There are some of the rent-a-cops here saying that Davis fired me and they're 'escorting me from the premises.' Can he do that?"

Another pause, then Gettnor tilted his head and said, "Really?"

A moment more and Gettnor rolled his eyes and said, "OK. Thanks." He stood and picked up a rack full of small metal disks. He dumped the metal pieces out onto the lab bench; then swept them off the bench into his left hand.

Allen was already pissed at being called a "rent-a-cop" but he was flabbergasted when Gettnor pulled open the flap on the big thigh pocket of his cargo pants and dropped the discs into it. "Dr. Gettnor, you can't take Querx's material with you! That's what we're here *for*, to make sure you take only personal items."

Gettnor shrugged, "I *made* these."

"You made them while you were a Querx employee." Allen said, trying to project patience, "You used Querx equipment and Querx materials. They belong to Querx."

Gettnor shrugged; then said, "No one here knows what they are. No one here *cares* what they are or *needs* them for anything. They're *worthless* to Querx."

Allen frowned, "Nonetheless, they belong to Querx and they need to stay here." He reached for Gettnor's pocket.

Gettnor grabbed his wrist. Hard! Allen gasped and found his knees bending a little. Gettnor, eyes narrowed, ground out, "Do *not* touch me." Letting go he put his hand into the pocket and pulled out a handful of the metal disks, tossing them back onto the lab bench. He sighed, "Querx can keep them. Fat lot of good it will do them."

Allen suspected that some of the small pieces of metal were still in Gettnor's pocket, but he also suddenly decided not to make a big deal of it. "OK. Jimmy's brought a box. Do you have any *personal* items in here?"

Jimmy popped the flattened box open and folded it to hold things while Gettnor glanced around. "No." he said.

"OK, how about in your office?"

In Gettnor's office Allen was surprised to find that his "personal items" consisted of one picture, apparently of a wife, son and daughter, a chin up bar, which had to be detached from the ceiling, and a set of hand grips to do push-ups with. Allen shook his head. He had more personal stuff in his locker than this guy had in an entire office! He and Jimmy escorted the guy down and out the front door, then had the security system disable his access.

***

Back home Vaz wandered into the kitchen and made himself a sandwich. As he sat eating and staring sightlessly out the window he pondered the "meltdown" of the hydrogen saturation apparatus, still wondering what in the world could have happened. There wasn't nearly enough current being delivered to the apparatus to melt metal by itself. Though the small fragment of the alloy had absorbed over fifteen hundred times its own volume in hydrogen by the time the meltdown occurred, it was only a few cubic millimeters in size so that it really was only a liter or so of hydrogen. If the hydrogen had burned it would have made a pretty good flame for a few seconds but it wouldn't have had enough energy to melt the apparatus like it had. Besides it would have tended to melt the top of the apparatus, whereas the apparatus had been much more melted at the bottom than in the upper portions.

So not enough hydrogen, not enough electricity. What the Hell had melted the apparatus?!

When he'd finished his sandwich he went down to his basement and dug through his cargo pocket. Sure enough, there were seventeen of the alloy disks still in his pocket. He felt slightly guilty about taking them, but really did feel they belonged to him, not to Querx. No one at Querx would have any

45

idea what they were, nor care about them, or ever put them to use. He found a magnifying glass and inspected the laser cut numbers on them. Vaz breathed a sigh of relief when he saw that one of the disks was a copy of the original alloy that had just melted down. He put them carefully away and had his AI open his big screens so he could begin searching the net for possible mechanisms.

Lisanne came home, cooked dinner, called Vaz up and watched him eat mechanically without appearing to notice his food or Tiona's hostile attitude. He sat at the table staring into space long after his surly kids had excused themselves and gone upstairs. Lisanne put his dishes in the dishwasher and spoke to him several times without a response. She shook her head and went upstairs herself, wondering if he'd notice if she turned out the light.

Vaz got in bed with Lisanne in the middle of the night. She snuggled up to him but when she started to slide her hand under his pajama top he gently grasped her wrist and pulled it to the outside and around him.

In the morning when Lisanne left for work Vaz was still in bed. She knew Dr. Smint kind of let Vaz work whatever hours he wanted but it always worried her. This morning it irritated her because he usually made lunches for the kids and they had bitched about the sandwiches she made for them. "Make your own sandwiches tomorrow then!"

Dante said, "Why can't you just give us money to buy lunch like all the other kids?"

"We're not made of money like some of your friends' parents. And I seriously doubt that 'all of them' buy their lunches. But if you want to buy lunch, get a job. Spend your own money."

"Man, this sucks!" he said as he slammed out the door.

"Or make your own lunch." Lisanne shouted pointlessly at the closed door.

Tiona waited until Lisanne was looking her way to throw her lunch bag into the trash. Then she headed out the door too.

With a sigh Lisanne got Tiona's lunch out of the trash and put it in her own bag. She chewed her lip as she stared up the stairs to where Vaz was sleeping, thinking about waking him up. Finally she shook her head and went out to the garage to begin the drive to work.

When Vaz finally woke he started going over the numbers he'd come up with the night before. By his calculations there wasn't enough energy available in any conceivable reaction of the hydrogen with oxygen, or with any conceivable chemical reaction of the materials in the apparatus. An oxidation of the small quantities of vanadium or boron or palladium in the little disk wouldn't produce much energy. If the stainless steel of the apparatus around the disk could be oxidized, perhaps, but he'd looked carefully at the stainless steel. It had looked melted but not burned on the floor of the lab at the end. Even if he combined the entire power consumption of all the electrical equipment on the lab bench with some kind of chemical reaction he couldn't get enough power for the meltdown he'd witnessed.

Nuclear reactions would easily have enough power but there wasn't anything fissionable in the setup. Fusion shouldn't be able to happen because he was using ordinary hydrogen, not deuterium. Should it? He called up more websites…

A few hours later Vaz sat back feeling stunned. Though he'd never paid much attention to it,

47

he knew that people had claimed to have achieved "cold fusion" with tabletop devices operating at or near room temperature in the past. Paneth and Peters had claimed, but then retracted such a claim as far back as the 1920s. Fleischmann and Pons had made it famous in the 1980s. Though they'd never retracted their claims, their experiments had been soundly denounced by the scientific establishment and called "pathologic science" by respected investigators.

Others continued, even to this day, to investigate the possibility of cold fusion. However, most scientists accepted the tenet that it would be impossible to force large numbers of hydrogen nuclei close enough to one another for them to fuse using electrochemical forces alone. There actually were many ways to cause fusion of hydrogen nuclei on the table top and "neutron generator" devices built on these principles were in common use. However, such devices consumed more power than they generated. Those who investigated tabletop fusion nowadays usually said they were investigating LENR or Low Energy Nuclear Reactions because of the stigma associated with the term "cold fusion." Occasionally, one of them would claim that excess energy had been achieved but they always turned out to be crackpots or at least were unable to replicate their own experiments.

Even those who were crazy enough to flout established science with thoughts that they might be able to achieve LENR expected to achieve it with "heavy hydrogen." A light hydrogen nucleus contains only a proton. It is significantly easier to achieve fusion by forcing together "heavy" deuterium molecules which have hydrogen nuclei that contain a proton and a neutron. Even better with a mix containing deuterium and tritium, hydrogen nuclei that have a proton and two neutrons.

Vaz was using light hydrogen. He shouldn't be able to achieve fusion, but if he did it would emit a lot of radiation. He wished he'd thought to examine the lab meltdown with a Geiger counter, or some other method to detect radiation.

The other possibility because of the boron-vanadium-palladium alloy he'd used was that he had achieved hydrogen-boron fusion. When hydrogen and boron fused they would produce three helium nuclei and a *lot* of energy. But, such fusion *should* require temperatures over 6 billion degrees Celsius!

After another period of staring off into space Vaz started ordering equipment.

At the rate he spent on exotic materials and sophisticated equipment, after just a few orders, he'd emptied his personal debiting account. He considered a moment, then transferred money to his personal account from his "royalties" account, a separate account that he maintained just to contain the royalties from his inventions at Querx. He never touched that money and virtually never even checked the balance of the account. Lisanne didn't even know about the account. It had started as a small account after the first patent Querx took on one of his ideas. He'd shunted the money from each of the royalties into it as time went along. Just when he'd begun thinking that he really should tell Lisanne about it, she'd started talking about how she wanted to take a nice vacation in the Caribbean.

Vaz didn't like going to strange places, they made him uncomfortable. Lisanne had been working their budget trying to find money for the trip and he'd realized that if she knew about his royalty account she would immediately begin making reservations. So, he hadn't told her about the money and thankfully she'd eventually decided they couldn't afford the trip.

He only really thought about the money once a year when he had to put the income from the account on their taxes. Fortunately, because he was so good with numbers, Lisanne was happy to have him do the taxes and so he'd been able to continue hiding it. Each year at tax time he became stricken with guilt over the fact that he'd been hiding it. He worried that she'd be furious when she realized they could have gone on a vacation any time she wanted. He worried that she'd be angry that he'd hidden something so important from her, or that she'd think he didn't want her to know about the money because he wanted it all if they got a divorce. This despite the fact that he couldn't imagine life without her. Worst of all, hiding it felt… dishonest, and he hated dishonest people.

However, on this day, he felt better when he saw that the account had nearly three million dollars in it. Half a million dollars of new lab equipment wouldn't make a huge dent in that. And, why have the money squirrelled away at all, if not to be used for something important like this?

At four o'clock his AI reminded him that he had a self-defense session scheduled at Mike's Mixed Martial. At first he didn't want to go, feeling too excited about the meltdown to want to waste time at Mike's. But then he recognized that his jittery state could use some of the calming he got from an exercise session. He put on his sweats and headed out the door.

***

Mike watched his new pupil lumber in the door. Gettnor was in sweats this time but seemed on edge, shifting from foot to foot until he saw Mike and headed his way. He only said "Hi," when he arrived, then stood, still shifting his weight and waiting to be directed. Mike decided to have him burn away some of that restless energy hitting the bags, this time with Mike critiquing his technique.

As before Gettnor set about pounding the bags relentlessly and hard. Most of Mike's feedback had to do with decreasing the power of his punches and trying to improve his accuracy and speed.

After a session with the bags that most would find punishing and exhausting, Gettnor only looked like someone had calmed him. "What's next?" he asked.

Mike took him through a series of slow motion grappling moves, constantly having to caution him to slow down and be more gentle, "Jeez, Vaz, this is practice. Tone it down some more or one of us is going to get hurt."

"Sorry, sorry." Gettnor shook his head as if trying to clear it. "Sorry. I'm just wound tight."

Mike saw Rich Durson across the room. Bigger and younger than Gettnor, Durson really liked sparring. Mike uneasily worried that Durson might actually be kind of a bully when he was away from the gym. But, maybe he could give a Gettnor a little of what Gettnor seemed to want. If they both actually wanted to fight it seemed silly not to grant them their wishes. He turned to Gettnor, "Hey, there's a guy here that likes to spar. Would you like me to ask him if he'd spar with you?"

Gettnor nodded eagerly without saying anything. Mike eyed him a moment. He said so little, Mike realized that he had no idea how bright the guy might be. Could Gettnor be mentally retarded or something he wondered? He turned and pointed at Durson, "Before you say yes, that's the guy over there. He's bigger and more experienced than you. You sure you want to take him on?"

Gettnor nodded eagerly, staring at Durson like a dog might strain at a steak.

Mike shrugged and went over to talk to Durson. As he expected Durson glanced at Gettnor and agreed readily.

Mike got them fitted with gloves, headgear and mouth guards, then took them to the ring. He explained the rules for sparring to Gettnor who only asked one question, "I can hit him, right?"

"Yes, but he's a lot more experienced than you. I suggest you focus on defense this time. Remember keep your hands up. Try to take him down to the mat if you can."

Gettnor tipped his head dubiously. Then shrugged and walked through the gate in the netting that surrounded the ring. Mike entered the ring too, got between the two men and said, "Just one, two-minute bout. I'll call it if you look like you're getting hurt, or about to get hurt, or if you tap out." He'd addressed this last to Gettnor but also turned to Durson to make sure he understood.

Both fighters nodded and Mike dropped his hand between them saying, "Go."

Durson, who favored striking styles, got up on his toes and began dancing to his right while Gettnor stood flat footed, watching, hands not high enough.

To understand what happened next, Mike had to watch the video from his AI's cameras and from a couple of the security cameras in the studio a few times. Durson closed in and flicked out a testing punch with his left. When he did Gettnor blocked it aside with his left forearm while sending a right to the left side of Durson's head. Gettnor's punch had come from down low and was going up when it hit.

Durson's feet actually came up off the mat slightly as he sailed out to the horizontal, bonelessly crashing to the padding, out cold.

At the time, Mike's initial reaction was that Durson must have stumbled and would get up, then wide eyed he stepped over to look at Durson, palm outstretched to keep Gettnor away. Gettnor had already dropped his hands and stepped back, looking disappointed.

Not worried, disappointed.

Mike saw that Durson was out but still breathing. His headgear had twisted around. There was a glove abrasion on his cheekbone and a tear at the base of the upper part of his ear. He moaned and after a few minutes sat up and then staggered back to his feet. Mike recommended that Jen drive him to the ER but Durson refused. Mike called Durson's girlfriend and got her to agree to check on him in an hour or two. Mike followed as Durson unsteadily went out and got in his car and gave it directions to take him home.

Before he closed the car door Durson looked blearily up at Mike and said, "He got in some kind of lucky punch, huh?"

Mike shrugged and said, "Yeah," but a little shiver that ran over him said he didn't think so at all. When he got back in the gym, he couldn't help but eye Gettnor a little warily. Gettnor still stood just outside the ring, one hand on the netting. He'd taken off the headgear, but still had on his gloves and was chewing on the mouth guard. Expressionlessly, he said, "Sorry." He didn't really look sorry. He looked… relaxed. He said, "Anything else today?"

Mike shook his head, a little rattled. Real fights often ended with one good punch, but it didn't happen very often in arranged fights. Certainly, someone who'd only had two training sessions didn't knock out an experienced scrimmager.

Gettnor pulled off his gloves and put them away, then headed out the door.

***

Back home in his basement, Vaz was pleased to achieve another one of his periods of intellectual transcendence, apparently brought on by the heavy episode at the gym followed by the explosive release of tension from the fight. However, despite his omniscient grasp of the problem, he got no closer to determining whether something about the setup at Querx might somehow have been able to produce hydrogen-hydrogen or hydrogen-boron fusion without high temperatures that were thought to be needed.

He couldn't come up with any other explanations that would result in a sufficient energy release to produce the meltdown either.

He felt the rumble of the garage door opening that signaled Lisanne was home and checked the time with widening eyes. It was late! Now he realized that he felt hungry. He should have noticed that Lisanne was late and started cooking! He trotted up the stairs.

Lisanne stepped inside hoping that Vaz would be cooking. He was in the kitchen but seemed to be just starting to get things out of the fridge. Her shoulders slumped a bit but she resolved to make the best of it, at least he was trying. She walked into the kitchen, "What'cha makin'?"

"Something with fusilli pasta and hamburger I think."

"OK," she shrugged, "anything I can do?"

"Relax a minute; then make a salad?"

"Thanks," she said and headed upstairs to change out of her work clothes. She said, "Hi," to Dante and Tiona as she passed their rooms. Neither of them answered. She stopped just past Tiona's room and closed her eyes a moment in frustration. Deciding that it wasn't worth a fight at the moment, she went on into her own room.

By the time Lisanne came back down to make the salad the kitchen was filled with fragrant cooking odors. When she'd finished making a Caesar salad she stepped over to the stove to look at what Vaz was doing. He had a pan full of broken up hamburger that he was stirring. It looked like it had olives and tomatoes chopped into it. The fusilli was cooked and drained. While she watched he poured it into the pan with the hamburger and started stirring it around.

Lisanne put her head on his shoulder and arm around his waist. Her eyebrows rose, *his narrow, rock hard waist.* She realized suddenly that his clothes might be fitting poorly because his body had been changing. And if that had been happening, she recognized that he might have been hiding it from her. He'd stopped sleeping in his undershorts and started wearing heavy pajamas. He'd bought the ill-fitting clothes. He'd started taking his showers in the basement and had started turning the lights off before they made love. She'd been noticing that he felt firmer. If he'd been getting himself in shape, why wouldn't he want her to see his body? Her heart flip flopped, *could he be having an affair? Getting in shape for another woman?*

Unconsciously Lisanne's right hand had been rubbing Vaz's waist. His hand came down to capture hers, "That tickles."

Lisanne reached down with her left hand and suddenly lifted the front of his shirt. He let go of her right hand at his waist and grabbed the left one, pushing it and his shirt back down. But not before she'd seen the rippled muscles covering his abdomen. Her eyebrows rose, "Vaz?"

He blushed sheepishly but said, "What?" as if he had no idea what she was asking about.

She slid her right hand up to grab his arm. It relaxed immediately, but not before she felt that his biceps and triceps had become massive sometime in the recent past. Why hadn't she noticed these changes in her own husband? "Uh, you've been getting yourself in shape?"

"I, ah, uh… exercise relaxes me," he said with an embarrassed shrug.

"Are you trying to *hide* it from me?"

"Uhhh, it makes me look… kind of funny." He blushed, "I'm sorry."

She drew back to look at him, wondering if he were kidding. He really did look like he felt uncomfortable about it. "Oh, I don't think it's anything to be sorry for, my man." She grabbed the bottom of his shirt and started lifting it again, "Let me see."

He clamped his elbows to his side and hissed, "Not in the kitchen!"

Lisanne giggled. Vaz had always been surprisingly prudish for a man. She'd practically had to seduce him early in their relationship. When she asked him about it, he'd freely confessed to being a virgin, something she thought most guys in their twenties would have hidden. Inexperienced or not, he'd been pretty enthusiastic about sex once she'd introduced him to it. Of course, as shy as he was and as difficult as he found it to even talk to others, he'd never really had many male friends. So, no one to corrupt him with boorish male attitudes she guessed. And she'd been his first girlfriend. He'd really only been out on a few semi-dates before she'd… cut him out of the herd. Not many women would have found his combination of extreme shyness and mental brilliance all that sexy. She readily acknowledged that she'd been the aggressor in their relationship. "OK," she tapped him on the shoulder, "but when we get upstairs…" she waggled her eyebrows, "I'm gonna want to see what we're workin' with here." She patted his butt and looked into his eyes, not sure whether he was looking embarrassed or horrified by her behavior. "Shall I call the kids?"

He gulped and nodded.

Lisanne said the blessing, then started dishing up the food. "Dante, how did your big Chemistry test go?"

Dante sighed in a long suffering fashion, "Mom, please, please call me 'Don.' You *know* I hate my name."

"OK 'Don,'" Lisanne quietly sighed, "how did your Chemistry test go?"

"Fine."

Lisanne closed her eyes, "Don..."

"Ninety two."

"Thank you. Why do you make me pull it out of you?"

"Don't think it's any of your business." Dante mumbled.

Vaz tensed a little; then calmed himself. Lisanne would handle Dante much better than he would.

Lisanne calmly said, "If it isn't your parent's business, then you need to move out of your parents' house. I would be delighted to be rid of your surly attitude." She tilted her head questioningly and brightly asked, "Are you ready to take care of yourself?"

Taking a large bite of his pasta Vaz glanced back and forth at the members of his little family. He saw his daughter dart a surprised look at her mother. Lisanne didn't take a hard line very often. Vaz had been wondering if the backtalk their two teenagers had been giving Lisanne might be getting under her skin. It only bothered him a little, but he had long ago reconciled himself to the fact that many things that irritated other people didn't bother him. Conversely, some things that absolutely infuriated him didn't seem to bother others.

Speaking with his mouth full, Dante said, "Can't freakin' wait!"

Vaz looked at Dante in surprise; then shifted his gaze to Lisanne. Lisanne's eyes had focused intently on Dante who suddenly looked a little pale. Lisanne, still with a calm tone, said, "OK, find yourself a place to live and I'll help you move out. You can stay in your bedroom until then, but this is the last meal we'll make for you and if you eat food here in the future, you'll need to pay for it."

Dante stared wide eyed at his mother a moment then glanced at the expressionless Vaz. Turning back to his mother, he swallowed with some difficulty, "You can't *do* that!"

Lisanne put her elbow on the table and rested her chin on her hand, gazing steadily at Dante for a minute. At the end of that minute he was shifting in his seat. "Mmm," she mused, "I reviewed the law recently in view of your increasingly difficult attitude. As I read it, at age seventeen, if you refuse to obey reasonable rules set by your parents, you forfeit your claim to parental support..." She tilted her head questioningly, "Do you think that a judge would find our rules and expectations unreasonable? Because, if you do, you may want to take us to court."

Dante, though he hadn't put anything else in his mouth, swallowed again, still staring at his mother. He glanced again at his father, then looked back at her. "Mom...?" he began uncertainly.

Into his pause Lisanne quietly said, "Son, we *do* love you, we just don't *like* you very much at the moment. I actually *can't stand you* the way you've been acting lately. So you've got a choice... act like someone we can love, or go ahead and move out, get a job and get on with your life. But you *don't* have the right to stay here making *us* miserable. I hope that when you've matured we can be friends again."

Vaz swallowed the bite he'd taken a bit ago. He looked around the table at the tense faces of his family and wondered if he should say anything. *No, he decided, Lisanne's handling this much better than I would. I'd certainly make things worse.* He took another bite and tried to relax his shoulders.

Wide eyed Dante croaked, "I thought you wanted me to graduate and go to college?"

Lisanne closed her eyes a moment then whispered, "Of course we do… But, we don't want you destroying this family's peace and happiness. If you hate us, or hate living with us, so much that every word from your mouth must be contentious or derogatory or dripping vitriol, then we'll *all* be happier with you free and on your own, don't you think?" This last was uttered with an attempt to sound upbeat. "What'll it be?"

"But…" Dante glanced at his expressionless father again, then at his sister. Tiona looked appalled. Her normal pinched and offended expression had vanished and her face had paled. Dante closed his eyes… when he opened them he said, "Sorry Mom."

Lisanne nodded her head, "Thank you son. Might I suggest that you speak to your family members as you would to strangers? In other words, say 'please, thank you,' and 'sorry' as if you were trying to smooth a social situation with someone outside of your family."

Dante gulped and nodded.

Lisanne turned to his sister, "The same issues have cropped up with you as well Tiona. I'm going to ask you to follow the same suggestions."

Tiona's face had now reddened. Her lip twitched as if undecided about beginning a sneer, "Or what? Are you going to throw me out of the family too?" she hissed.

Lisanne's eyes narrowed and her gaze became intense but when she spoke she still sounded calm, "No. By law we must provide support to you for two more months, until you turn sixteen, or we may be charged with the crime of 'non-support.' However, we are not required to provide more than shelter, sustenance and health care."

Tiona's lip did curl, "*That's* all *I* need."

Vaz's eyes widened and he wondered how Lisanne would respond to this.

Lisanne looked sadly at her daughter, tilted her head querulously, then said, "OK," She spoke to her AI, saying, "Please disconnect Tiona's AI from the family's network plan, she will purchase her own connection if she wishes to be connected again."

Tiona's eyes widened, "You can't *do* that!"

"Hmm, I believe I can. Do you want to check and see if you're still connected?"

"But I can't do my schoolwork without a connection!"

"Shelter, sustenance and health care, Tiona. You *don't* have a right to be connected. But, we'll be happy to let you use the house AI to do your schoolwork."

"In the family room?!"

Lisanne nodded.

"How am I going to *talk* to people?!"

"In person. Or buy your own connection. But you'll need a job, even the cheap connections are kind of expensive and I don't think you've saved very much of your allowance, have you?"

"Where am I going to get a job?"

"Well, now, that's not really our problem, is it? But you could work right here in our home. Cook dinner, breakfast, make lunches, clean, do laundry."

"Mom!" Tiona looked as aghast as if she'd found her mother stomping kittens.

"Yes?" Lisanne asked, a gleam in her eye.

Tiona sank sullenly back in her chair, "OK."

"OK what?"

"OK," Tiona curled a lip, "you win."

"Oh, I don't want to win, I just want you to speak when spoken to, and speak pleasantly. And to help out around here instead of complaining all the time." Lisanne turned to Dante, "That goes for you too Don, instead of complaining about the lunches we make for you, you'll make your own in the future, OK?"

Dante nodded, Tiona got up without asking to be excused and took her plate to the sink. She went upstairs, but then called back down. "Mom!"

Lisanne glanced toward the stairs but said nothing.

Tiona shouted again, "My AI's *still* disconnected."

Lisanne grimaced and took another bite of her pasta.

Vaz stared at Lisanne with an awed look.

Tiona flounced back down the stairs. Demandingly, she said, "Mom, reconnect me…" then paused and sullenly said, "please."

Lisanne tensed a moment, then visibly relaxed herself before looking up at her daughter. She indicated Tiona's chair and said, "Please sit. Don't tower over me."

Tiona went around and dropped into her chair, crossing her arms and staring at the table.

Lisanne sighed, then gently said, "First, you apologize, then you speak to us, pleasantly, like we're strangers you're hoping to get something out of."

"Fine," Tiona pasted a patently fake smile on her face, "I'm sorry. Please reconnect me."

Vaz relaxed, not recognizing the false nature of Tiona's smile or the lilting spite in her request. Lisanne put her chin in her hand and stared at Tiona, saying nothing.

Tiona stared back a long moment, then her bravado crumpled. "I'm sorry," she whispered, a tear trickling down her cheek, "Please reconnect me." She smiled at her mother, though her lip trembled a little.

Lisanne spoke to her AI, "Please reconnect Tiona to the family plan... in two hours."

"Mooom!" Tiona exclaimed plaintively.

"Sorry Kiddo. I don't want you to think you can treat us badly, then apologize if you make us mad enough to cut you off and expect to get right back on. I plan to disconnect you for much longer in the future if your offense is egregious."

"Yes Mom," Tiona said throatily, "May I be excused?"

"Yes, thank you for asking."

Vaz was rearranging the basement to make room for the equipment he'd ordered when Lisanne came down the stairs. She felt great after her success dealing with the kids.

"What'cha doing?" she asked.

He shrugged, "I ordered some stuff. Trying to make room for it."

Lisanne tightened a little, but then relaxed and leaned up against him, "Not expensive stuff, I hope?" She slid her arms around him and under his shirt, marveling at the hard feel of his musculature.

Vaz shrugged noncommittally. He hated liars and refused to lie himself. He did, however, not speak sometimes—thus allowing Lisanne to believe what she wished. Usually he felt terribly uncomfortable about it and this was especially true just now as he thought about how much money he'd just spent ordering equipment.

Lisanne didn't push him because she really wanted to see what was under that shirt. She began to slowly lift the bottom of it, leaning back to look at what she revealed.

He tensed, and then visibly forced himself to relax.

Lisanne kept pulling the shirt up. *He's absolutely ripped!* It caught at his shoulders. "Bend over," she said and pulled it off over his head having to work it loose over his shoulders. Which, she realized, were massive. With the shirt off, he sat on his chair, crossing his arms in front of him as if to cover himself like a shy girl. "Oh Vaz," she breathed. His body was magnificent. How had this happened without her realizing it? How could he have hidden it from her for what? Months?

Lisanne straddled his lap and wrapped herself around him, marveling at how his body felt. After a minute she reached down for his belt.

He stiffened, "Uh, the kids…"

"I locked the door," Lisanne said breathlessly and pulled the band out of her hair, letting long waves of lustrous blond hair fall…

Upstairs, as he waited to fall asleep, Dante mused about his family. He hated that they were poorer than his friends' families. He hated that his Dad wasn't at all interested in sports and that his friends thought his dad was weird. Some of his friends hated the way their fathers focused on sports all the time and pushed them to compete. But Dante'd been on the wrestling team for two years and his dad had only made it to about half of their local matches, and of course none of the away matches. Many of his teammates complained about the way their dads acted at meets, but Vaz just sat there. Of course, Dante thought, he wouldn't *know* anything about wrestling, so it'd be hard for him to shout suggestions without sounding like an idiot.

His parents assumed that Dante'd go to college, but it didn't seem like they could afford it. Even though his dad had a PhD it seemed like he was more of a lab tech at the company where he worked. Dante'd seen one of Vaz's pay deposit notices he'd accidentally left up on the family room screen. It wasn't anything to brag about.

He wondered if he could get a wrestling scholarship. He'd been winning a lot of matches.

***

There wasn't much that Vaz could do the next couple of days. Until the equipment he'd ordered arrived he couldn't test any of his hypotheses.

So first he bent himself to the task of cleaning and reorganizing the basement. He went out and bought more lighting, cabinets and benches. He assembled and installed them. Then he carefully packed all the stuff that had been stored in the basement into a single large storage cabinet. Once the space was ready he began re-educating himself on nuclear physics. Once he was back up to speed with what he'd learned back in school he started pushing past it. During breaks he would try to ponder other mechanisms but he had become completely convinced that no electrochemical event could have provided sufficient power for what he'd seen that day in the lab. He worried that he might have blinders on, so every so often he'd recalculate the output of the various chemical reactions that might have occurred, versus the heat needed to melt the quantity of stainless steel that he estimated had been in the apparatus. It wasn't close, but the fusion explanation just seemed as ridiculously unlikely.

***

Vaz pulled into the garage from his session at Mike's and saw that Lisanne was already home. He still felt astonished that she liked the hard lumpy muscles his body had acquired, but he certainly appreciated the way she had been excited by it. He came in the door from the garage feeling some anticipation.

Then he saw Lisanne standing next to a large stack of boxes. Her hands were on her hips and she didn't look happy. "What's all this, Vaz? Scientific equipment? Why? Don't you get enough of that at work?"

His eyes shifted from place to place as his mind raced. "Uh, I had a really interesting finding at work. It doesn't really apply to the job but I want to follow it up." He carefully didn't say that he didn't work at Querx anymore and felt horribly guilty for the lie of omission. Lying and liars, something he despised, and yet he'd as much as lied by avoiding the question. Just like he'd been lying by omission about the money in his royalty account. Even though he was glad he didn't work at Querx anymore he also had some sense of embarrassment that he'd lost his job. He knew that most people would be horrified to have been "fired" though he wasn't really sure why it was such a big deal.

He knew she'd find out someday but he just couldn't face it now…

"How much did this stuff cost Vaz?"

He shrugged mulishly, not wanting to answer that question either.

"Vaz," she said dangerously.

He glanced at the boxes and recognized the labels of the companies for the five big ones. His facility with numbers let him add them up and he added a fudge factor for the unknown contents of the small boxes. He shrugged, "Thirty five thousand." He suppressed the fact that he'd ordered another $300,000 worth of equipment that just hadn't arrived yet.

"Vaz! We *need* that money for college for the kids!"

He shrugged and ventured, "I think this finding might be worth quite a bit of money."

"*Come on* Vaz. We can't risk the kids' education for a 'might be!'"

He stared at her a moment, wondering if he should tell her about the royalty account? But then he'd have to explain why she didn't already know about it. Why they'd never gone on a vacation like she'd wanted. He blinked, "I think we'll be able to get them through college anyway." He licked his lips nervously.

Lisanne tapped the biggest box peremptorily, "I want you to send this stuff back."

Vaz stared mulishly, "I need it."

"You do *not* 'need it.' Your *kids* need educations. *Send it back.*"

Vaz blinked again, then, without responding, turned and went down the stairs to his basement. He locked the door behind him and told the house AI not to unlock it for other family members besides himself. He'd felt calm on the way home from Mike's because of the exercise he'd had there, but now he was shaking again. As he ripped through another set of pull-ups he heard Lisanne knocking on the door at the top of the stairs. She stopped before he'd finished his sit-ups. After the sit-ups he still had to pound the heavy bag a while before the endorphins finally flooded over him.

Lisanne stared unbelievingly at the closed, locked door to Vaz's basement. What had gotten into him? More than ever, she felt like she had three teenagers in her house. Just last night she'd been madly in love again with the man she'd married eighteen years ago who suddenly had a sexy, muscular body with six-pack abs and ropy powerful arms. Today she finds he's done something this irresponsible! And when she insists he send the stuff back he just runs and hides?! What kind of husband and father would spend that kind of money on what would, after all, be a kind of hobby?

She sighed. She knew what kind of husband would do it. The kind she'd married all those years ago, equal parts brilliant, childish, and emotionally impaired. *Dammit!* She wanted to stamp her foot but restrained herself.

She closed her eyes. Well, he'd have to come up for dinner and she'd straighten him out then. Lisanne turned toward the kitchen, musing that she'd done pretty well with the kids the night before. She tried to think of a similar strategy to use on Vaz.

When Lisanne had finished making dinner she knocked again on the door to the basement. Vaz didn't say anything so she yelled through the door. "Vaz, dinner's ready!" Then she turned and called upstairs to Dante and Tiona too. She'd hoped that he'd come up when she knocked so she could confront him again without the kids there, but that was not to be it didn't seem. She tried not to cross her arms and tap her foot while she waited.

Dante and Tiona came down and sat but to Lisanne's astonishment, Vaz didn't budge out of the basement! Finally she sat down with the kids and said the blessing. Tiona frowned, "What's with Dad?"

Lisanne shrugged, not wanting the kids to know what was going on. "He's got some big project going in the basement. Doesn't want to take time for dinner I guess. You know how focused he can be."

"Is that what all those boxes are for?"

Lisanne nodded, wanting to say they were sending them back, but not wanting the kids to know they were fighting.

"It sounded like you and Dad were fighting about it. Is he going to send them back?"

Mentally, Lisanne rolled her eyes. Tiona did this to her all the time. Leading her on with questions, then turning out to already know more about what was going on than Lisanne had hoped. Trying to maintain a calm façade, she said, "Well, we *are* having a disagreement about it, and I do hope he'll decide to send that stuff back."

"Because it costs so much?"

Lisanne sighed, "Yes."

"You guys aren't going to have enough money to send us to college, are you?"

"We're *going* to send you guys to college," Lisanne gritted out, "Somehow, someway, it's going to get done. Rest assured on that."

A crease appeared between Tiona's elegant brows. She'd always thought of college as an "of course" proposition and had only recently realized how much money it cost. She was trying to come to grips with the issue, "Why do we need to go to college? It won't guarantee that we'll make good money."

Lisanne narrowed her eyes, "People with college degrees make more money than those who only finish high school."

"On average, yeah. But there are exceptions. Dad has a PhD and you make more money than he does."

"Programmers get paid pretty well."

"But why'd he go to school all that time if he wasn't even going to get paid as much as you?"

"You know, your dad got two BS degrees in three years and his PhD in just three more. He's unbelievably smart and incredibly hard working." Lisanne felt bemused to find herself defending Vaz… *Dammit, I'm starting to forget how pissed off the man's made me!*

Tiona flipped her hair dismissively, "Yeah, maybe, but what good is that PhD doing him? I'm not sure why I need to go to college, lots of people without degrees earn as much as he does."

Lisanne closed her eyes and tried not to grit her teeth. She knew that half of this discussion was just Tiona's attempt to irritate her *without* being rude and losing her net connection. "Tiona, *some* people without degrees earn more. *Most* do not. And college is an experience you shouldn't deny yourself, whether you earn more because of it or not, you will have a richer, fuller life for it."

"And," Tiona said, not to be dissuaded from her topic even though, deep inside she desperately wanted to go to college, "even with you making a good salary, and Dad bringing in some money, you still haven't been able to save enough for us to go to college."

"Because, Tiona, we've been spending a lot of money to send you to nice schools so far. Yes we'll have to spend even more when you're in college, but not that much more. We'll find a way to do it."

Tiona barked a laugh, "Not the way Dad's spending on his toys."

"Tiona, those aren't *toys*. They're scientific instruments. Your Dad hopes to do important work with them." Internally Lisanne felt almost cross eyed to be defending Vaz.

Tiona pointed her fork at Lisanne, "I thought *you* wanted him to send them back?"

"Well… I do. But that doesn't mean I think they're toys or that he doesn't hope to do something meaningful with them."

Tiona rolled her eyes eloquently to signal what she thought of them.

They ate in silence for a while then Dante said, "Steve and I are going to watch a wrestling match in Raleigh tonight. I've already finished my homework."

At first Lisanne's residual irritation with Tiona, and Vaz, threatened to spill over onto Dante. Despite her initial desire to say no, she took a deep breath and said, "OK, what time will you be back?"

"Before 11."

***

Steve picked Dante up at 7:30. "I thought you didn't think they'd let you go?"

"Well…" Dante grinned, "They think I'm going to a wrestling match."

Steve snorted, "Well, I guess there'll be some wrestling all right." He grinned, "And punching, and throwing, and other assorted mayhem."

Steve's family's car dropped them off at Eakin Auditorium, a local mixed use facility that served as a small venue for music and other events. Tonight it featured a roster of amateur MMA fights. It was crowded with boisterous people. It had a bar and some of the patrons were well on their way to being drunk. Dante and Steve found their seats in plenty of time for the first fight. Steve really liked this stuff and had started taking MMA training himself, intending to compete someday. Their wrestling coach was pissed off about it. Steve was their best wrestler and the Coach was afraid that he'd slip and throw a punch or something at a meet, resulting in a disqualification.

The first fight was boring. The combatants were grapplers who got tied up in the center of the ring and just struggled there providing little action for the crowd. Boos started quietly and built. The ref broke the fighters back to the standing position several times and started penalizing them for not progressing the match. Steve bitched about it, "Jeez, I hope they aren't all like this, I'll want my money back!"

Dante saw that the two fighters were actually struggling mightily and felt like they were just evenly matched. Even so, he thought one or the other should have tried shifting tactics. Their punches weren't convincing at all.

The second and third matches were much more exciting with a number of throws and in the third match a flurry of punches ended it with one of the fighters disoriented and confused in the second round.

In the fourth match the fighters were mismatched. Dante thought that the winner could have won in the first 30 seconds but held off just to give the crowd their money's worth.

In the car on the way home Steve was pumped. "We've got to go to some more of these. I'm sure I could compete. When I'm eighteen, I'm gonna make me some money."

Dante shook his head, "Those guys were only amateurs, and they were pretty tough. Going against the pros for money would be a *big* step up."

"There's supposed to be another card of amateur MMA fights in a few weeks, you up for seein' it?"

Dante shrugged, "Sure."

***

Lisanne woke in the morning and rolled over to have a serious conversation with Vaz. He wasn't there! His side of the bed looked undisturbed. Her heart flip-flopped, running away from this problem by leaving would be just the kind of thing that Vaz might do. She got up and padded downstairs to see if his car was gone.

At the bottom of the stairs she blinked. The huge stack of boxes was gone! With rising irritation she walked down the hall to the garage and peeked in. His car was still there. She went to the door to the basement. Locked! She commanded the house AI to unlock it but there was no response. She told it to override the locking command and gave it her owner's password. Still no response.

Lisanne wanted to kick the door or something. Speaking to her AI she said, "Connect me to Vaz."

A moment later it came back to say, "Sorry, a connection cannot be established."

Lisanne pulled back a hand to pound the door to the basement, but then slowly dropped it, realizing that it would wake the kids.

Frustrated, she went back upstairs to shower and dress.

***

At work, later that day Lisanne had her AI try to contact Vaz again. Still, "No connection."

Lisanne tapped her teeth a moment, then said, "Connect me to Querx."

A moment later an AI's voice said, "Hello, this is Querx. How may I help you?"

"Please connect me with Dr. Gettnor."

"One moment." After a moment the artificial voice said, "I'm sorry, Dr. Gettnor no longer works here."

"What!"

"He doesn't work here anymore."

"Are you sure?"

"Um, yes Ma'am, I'm sure. He's off our database of current employees."

***

72

Moving all that equipment downstairs had made Vaz grateful for his increased strength, though it had still been quite a struggle doing it quietly in the middle of the night. He'd gone out early in the morning to buy a hand cart to make it easier to move the rest of the stuff when it arrived. While he was out he'd gotten a small microwave and fridge. Then he'd bought some food he could cook in the basement so he wouldn't have to go upstairs and deal with Lisanne if she stayed mad.

After a lifetime of avoiding conflict, it just didn't occur to him that he should try to talk things out with his wife. Nor that he might be making things worse by putting it off.

Back home, he'd carefully listened for the delivery and when most of the rest of his equipment had arrived, had tipped the man to help him get the stuff down to the basement.

He felt pretty good about his control of the situation but then the Aerogas delivery truck came with his tank of liquid nitrogen. Just as he'd accepted delivery he heard the garage door rumbling. He quickly put the tank on his hand cart and started toward the basement. He'd just started it down the stairs to the basement when Lisanne came in the door from the garage.

"Vaz!" she said practically running down the hall toward him, "we need to talk! Don't you go hiding in your basement!"

Vaz quickly bumped the hand cart down a few more stairs and turned to close the door. Lisanne reached the door and started pushing on the other side. Even though he was still holding the hand cart with the heavy tank of liquid nitrogen with his left hand Vaz inexorably pushed the door shut with his right.

Frantically Lisanne said, "I called Querx today! They said you don't work there anymore! What happened? Vaz! Dammit, talk to me! If you aren't even working we certainly can't afford that equipment! You've *got* to send it back! I hope you haven't opened any of it!"

Throughout her tirade Vaz said nothing. He simply, slowly and relentlessly forced the door shut. Once it was shut he locked it using the AI override he'd set up to make sure she couldn't open it.

Then he bumped the hand cart the rest of the way down the stairs and over to the space he'd set aside for it. He took a few deep breaths and sat down trying to calm himself. He opened his screens and looked at the experiments he'd planned out, wondering if he could find one that he could start with the equipment he'd already set up. But he couldn't concentrate. He got up and opened some boxes getting out the equipment that had just arrived but he just couldn't focus.

Finally he put on his gloves and pounded the heavy bag, trying not to picture Lisanne's face on it. Mostly he managed to pretend it was Davis. He practiced his kicks on it for a while, then started in on his pull-ups.

Eventually an endorphin rush calmed him. He warmed himself a pre-prepared beef burrito from the little fridge. After he ate it he resumed his unpacking.

Lisanne went up to their bedroom so the kids wouldn't come in and find her crying. Once she'd calmed herself she asked her AI to check their accounts so she'd know just how bad their financial situation was.

Vaz had changed their passwords and locked her out.

Distraught, Lisanne wondered if she was going to have to divorce her husband. Just a couple of days ago it had seemed like things were great. She'd felt like she had control of her teenagers' behavior at last and she'd loved her husband's sexy new body. Now it all seemed like crap. With a sigh she searched the net trying to determine whether she would put herself and the kids at risk by not filing for divorce immediately. It seemed like the courts would divide their possessions evenly no matter when she filed. The only risk seemed to be that Vaz might continue to spend money that she didn't feel like they could afford. If the courts gave her the house, the contents of their accounts and he kept only the lab equipment she supposed that it wouldn't be too bad. Ultimately, she realized that they would have more money if he lived in the basement than if he went out and rented a place to live.

She wrote him an e-mail,

Vaz,

You've frightened me badly by locking yourself out of my life and me out of our bank accounts. I'm worried about our family. I'm worried about you. Are you OK?

With your expenditures on equipment, I've realized I don't know how much money we have, how much you might consider to be mine or how much you've spent. I have no way to buy food or pay bills.

I know you don't like conflict but if you leave me locked out of our accounts I'll have no choice but to file for divorce so that I can continue to provide for myself and our children. I've realized I don't even have any idea how much money we have available to pay our bills.

Please, at least communicate with me by email. I don't want to divorce you.

Lisanne

While Lisanne and the kids ate dinner she got a ping from her AI. When she looked up at her HUD she saw that she had an e-mail from Vaz. She waited until the kids had gone up to their rooms before she read it.

I've unlocked your accounts.

That's all it said. She shook her head. *Typical Vaz.*

She had her AI access their accounts again. They actually had separate "checking" accounts though they could both spend out of the other account. However they generally just debited money from their own. Her pay went to hers and his pay went to his. Their household bills and mortgage were paid out of his. Because she did the grocery shopping, food came out of hers. Still most of their family's expenses went on his account so it usually didn't have much money in it. When she saved some up in her account, she moved it to savings and if she accumulated quite a bit, they invested it.

She saw she was still locked out of his account. She opened her own and saw that there weren't any expenditures that she wasn't aware of. *Where did he get the money for that stuff?* With trepidation she opened their savings account. No expenditures there either. She sighed and opened their investment account, what she thought of as the "kids college and our retirement account." *He must have sold some stock,* she thought.

No withdrawals had been made from their investment account either. She sighed as she looked at it. It wouldn't pay for the kids to go to state colleges, much less have anything left over for retirement. Her job had a 401K retirement plan, she would have to raid it for shortfalls in the kids' college costs. *Maybe Vaz has some kind of 401K retirement from Querx?* She wondered if he'd thought to get it out when he left. Oh well, he could probably roll it over to a retirement account at his next job.

But, where did Vaz get the money for all that equipment? She sat staring aimlessly for a while, then realized that he might have received a severance package. She felt relieved, then realized, *we needed that money to pay bills until he finds another job!*

She sent him another e-mail,

> *I hope you're applying for jobs. Why aren't you working at Querx anymore?*

Vaz didn't answer that one.

***

Vaz had taken most of the past two weeks to set up each piece of equipment in his basement lab. Then, for the ones that were different models from the ones he'd been using at Querx, Vaz read the manual. Some of them required testing and calibration before they could be used. He'd had to run new cable to the breaker box for his new alloy furnace. Vaz knew that most people he'd worked with hated reading the manuals and would have, in fact, skipped most of them, assuming that the new equipment worked similarly enough to what they were used to. They may have skimped on the calibrations too. Vaz had always found such regimented busywork comforting, so he read the manuals thoroughly and complied diligently with their testing and calibration instructions.

He was finally ready. He had his rescued sample of the alloy mounted and it had absorbed hydrogen he'd electrolyzed from distilled water overnight. It was in a new chamber he'd had machined just for this testing, complete with thermistors, neutron and radiation detectors and a small window behind which he'd mounted a camera. Everyone was out of the house so he began applying the high voltage, high frequency intermittent current that he thought of as "hammering" or driving the hydrogen protons into the alloy while trying to keep an eye on the temperature and the video at the same time.

At first he sat forward on the edge of his seat as the temperature climbed.

But then the temperature leveled off at about the temperature—he had calculated many times now—that should be achieved by the electrochemical processes in this setup.

For a while he continued to sit attentively, thinking that there might have been a leveling off back at Querx. After all, he hadn't followed the temperature there. It could have leveled off, then started going up again after a pause.

Hours later, Vaz still slouched back in his chair, eyes on the screens but unseeing. The temperature remained the same.

When his AI reminded him that he had a training session at Mike's, he turned the experiment off, put on his sweats and headed out. He felt an ineffable sense of sadness at the failure of the experiment to reproduce its prior results.

Walking into Mike's he tried not to think about Pons and Fleischmann who had thought they had a wonderful finding, only to have it turn out to be irreproducible as well. He didn't even think about the fact that he had an alloy that absorbed over a thousand times its own volume in hydrogen. Such an alloy would be worth a lot of money but Vaz was oblivious to that possibility. Even though that was what he had set out to develop, it wasn't what he'd been thinking about for weeks now.

Vaz hoped that a good exhausting session with Mike would clear his mind.

Mike shook his head over the way Vaz attacked and punished the bags and training paddles. Mike had found a training partner for him and had Gettnor work in slow motion to throw his new partner. Then they simulated various submission holds.

When their time was up, Mike said, "Hey, you remember when you came in you were looking for a real fight?"

"Yeah."

"Are you still interested?"

Vaz got a distant look as he pondered his feelings. When he'd come in that first time he'd wanted to beat on someone as a surrogate for Davis. Now, he actually felt happy that Davis had fired him. He didn't want to work for Davis anyhow.

He realized that yesterday he would have said no. He had been happy yesterday. Doing his own research. No hassles from work.

Well except he'd been sleeping on a pad in the basement.

And he hadn't seen his family.

And he wondered how Lisanne was explaining his absence to Dante and Tiona.

He realized he wasn't happy after all. Now that the experiment had failed to reproduce, he was even less happy. He shrugged and answered, "Yes."

Mike said, "Remember Rich Durson, the guy you sparred with a while back? You laid him out with a punch?"

Vaz nodded.

"He'd signed up for an amateur MMA fight and paid the entrance fee. Their doctors won't let him fight because he's recently been knocked out. He's hoping that someone will take his place and reimburse him the entrance fee."

"How much is the fee?"

"Two hundred fifty."

"When's the fight?"

"Two weeks Thursday. You'd have to be there by 7. I'd be in your corner."

Vaz tilted his head a moment, then nodded once. "OK."

Mike said, "Remember that Durson was bigger than you? You'd be fighting up a weight class or two. You sure you're up for that?"

Vaz nodded.

Mike watched Gettnor leave after they'd agreed on some additional training sessions before the fight. This fight, Mike had a feeling, would be horribly lopsided. However, he wasn't sure which way. Gettnor sometimes seemed so clueless about fighting, but he was unbelievably powerful and frighteningly tireless. Sometimes it seemed that Gettnor moved so slowly and robotically that another fighter would be able to dance around him dishing it out, but then, unexpectedly, he would throw a lightning punch like the one that had knocked Durson out.

Back home Vaz ordered parts to make a testing apparatus *exactly* like the one that had melted down at Querx. He'd found the specs for it in his AI. His first searches hadn't used the correct keywords and he'd thought that its design was only on the Querx servers. Now, once the parts came in he could exactly repeat the bizarre experiment. It wouldn't have the built in thermistors, radiation detectors or the window for a camera that his new one had had. But the first order of business was to *reproduce* the experiment and he was pretty frustrated that he'd tried to do it with a completely different chamber. *Though perhaps I don't need to reproduce it all the way to meltdown,* he thought with a grin. As he sat looking at the plan for the apparatus he was replicating from the one at Querx, a chill went over him. The ceramic plate that supported the electrode at the top of the chamber, could it be...? He looked it up.

It *was* a piezoelectric ceramic! Which meant that the high frequency pulsed current he'd been running through the electrode would have generated ultrasonic mechanical deformations, creating waves which, because of the concave shape of the ceramic would have been focused… he had his AI calculate it… almost perfectly onto the thin boron-vanadium-palladium disk.

This meant that he had a boron-vanadium-palladium disk with huge numbers of hydrogen protons in it. Then more protons were being forced into the disk by his "hammering" current, some crashing into the disk. *And,* he had inadvertently been focusing high intensity ultrasonic sound waves onto it at the same time. And the current made it hot too, though not billions of degrees hot by any means. In any case, there were a lot of things going on at once. Absorption of the hydrogen into the alloy was forcing the hydrogen and boron molecules together. Then the "hammering current" was crashing more hydrogen protons into the matrix. Then, as the disk flexed up and down when the ultrasonic waves struck it, deformations in the matrix would squeeze molecules together as well. He ran another calculation, yes the ultrasonic wave frequency was very close to what he estimated would be the harmonic frequency of the disk which would produce large deformations. He tried to run some calculations to determine how much force would be impacting the nuclei of the molecules together, but there were too many unknowns for him to get a good approximation.

However, using the poor approximations he *had* made, it still wasn't nearly enough to cause nuclei to fuse in the numbers that might have caused his meltdown.

Vaz sat, arms crossed, staring in frustration at the numbers, then caught himself twisting hair follicles out of his upper arms.

He designed and ordered a concave piezoelectric electrode to go in his new chamber selecting an even more active piezo-ceramic for it.

***

Dante sat down at the dinner table and said, "Dad ever gonna eat with us again?"

Lisanne said, "Let's say the blessing."

Blessing done, Dante dug into his salad saying, "OK, what's the deal with Dad?"

Lisanne sighed, "I'm not really sure." She considered telling the kids that Vaz didn't work at Querx anymore, then decided there was no reason to get them even more upset. She'd tell them about that *after* Vaz had another job. "It seems that it's very important to him to carry out some experiments here in our basement." She'd almost said, "as well as at work," but stopped in time. "You should know, though, that I've checked our accounts and we'll be able to send you guys to college." *Even if we may not be able to retire,* she thought to herself.

Tiona said, "God, he's sooo weird. Why did you ever marry him?"

Lisanne drew back in disappointment, "Tiona! You wouldn't even be here!"

"So is that the only reason you can think of? Just because he stoked you with kids?"

Lisanne gritted her teeth. When she'd demonstrated that she was willing to cut off Tiona's connection to the net, Lisanne'd successfully stopped Tiona's rude refusal to answer questions and ended her sullen responses.

But, now Tiona asked questions, phrasing them as if she wanted to know the answers. However, the questions contained a subtext implying that Lisanne was an idiot. They weren't obviously rude or confrontational enough to push Lisanne to cut her off again, but they managed to dance right there at the edge. It made Lisanne want to explode.

Lisanne focused on Tiona, trying to remain calm, "No, Tiona. I married your dad because I loved him. Your dad, he's sweet, and smart, and a good friend. Admittedly he's not a 'people person.' None of us are perfect in every way. Your dad really has trouble with conflict. His mother told me that it's because he hurt another boy in a fight when he was young. So he doesn't want to argue with me about his equipment. He also really hates when he's not allowed to study whatever he wants to study in his research. I suspect that his job told him he couldn't follow up some finding he made at work, and he wants to study it so badly that he decided to buy the stuff to do it here at home. I don't agree with it, but I respect him for it."

For a moment Lisanne felt grateful to Tiona. Being forced to put those thoughts into words made her feel better about her husband's behavior.

Then Tiona said, "How much money has he wasted on this 'research project' of his anyway?"

"Come on Tiona! It might not *be* 'wasted.' He might discover something important. It could even be worth a lot of money."

"Really?" Tiona didn't say "really" like she wondered if it could be true. She said it like she couldn't believe that her mother was foolish enough to accept that such an event was even remotely possible.

Lisanne looked down at her plate, "I admit... it isn't likely." She put a forkful of meatloaf in her mouth.

***

The hallway of the school was crowded with the rumble of students leaving their classes. Dante found himself just behind Silvy France. Silvy was also a Senior, blond, beautiful and dating senior football fullback Jack Alexander. Dante and Silvy had been in school together since preschool, often near one another because their last names were close to one another in the alphabet. They were good "friends."

Friends no matter how desperately Dante wished they could be more.

Friends or not, he was admiring her lithe form as it threaded through the other students on her way to her locker near his.

He reached his locker and began to turn the combination, turning to say, "Hi Silvy."

Suddenly Dante found himself slammed up against his locker with Jack growling in his ear, "Stay away from *my* girl, wrestler *boy*. I've seen the way you stare at her—I don't like it!"

"Jack!" Silvy cried out. "Leave him alone, Don's my friend!"

Dante started to push back against Jack, thinking that with his wrestling skills he had nothing to fear. He was startled to find Jack nearly immovable. He realized suddenly that with the extra thirty pounds of muscle Jack had on him, wrestling skills or no wrestling skills, he would be in trouble fighting this guy. In his ear Jack hissed, "Yeah, struggle and squirm wrestler boy. You stay away from her or it's gonna go bad for you." Jack shoved back and stood, arms akimbo, brows lowered, staring at Dante.

Silvy smacked Jack on the arm, saying, "Don's my friend! Do *not* be mean to him." Dante noted distantly that she sounded a little excited. He stared balefully at Jack, but didn't move from his locker. After talking to him in heated whispers for a moment, Silvy steered Jack away and down the hall, speaking softly to him.

Filled with rage and thoughts of *I should have done this, or I could have done that...* Dante slowly pushed himself away from his locker, put on his jacket and walked out of the school.

    ***

Stillman Davis walked down the hallway in his R&D department, doing his weekly "walkabout" to talk to the "troops" who did the actual research at Querx. He almost always felt good after he made his rounds and talked to the scientists. They'd become used to his visits now and often had something set up to show him about what they'd been doing. As time passed, the presentations had become slightly formal, often with a few "slides" up on the screens in the labs and sometimes a demonstration. He felt like more and more he understood exactly what the people in his department were doing.

The battery people in the lab next to Gettnor's old lab had been startled when Gettnor had been let go but were happy to have been able to move some of their equipment into his space. They always had a nice presentation on their latest efforts when Davis visited. The presentations were so polished he sometimes had niggling doubts about the time they must have spent preparing them. He wondered if he shouldn't press them to invest that time in their research. However, he reassured himself that there was nothing to sharpen the understanding of a process in your own mind, quite like explaining what you were doing to someone else.

He stepped out of the battery lab and saw with surprise that that the CEO of Querx was standing in the hall, looking around in some puzzlement. "May I help you Mr. Vangester?" he asked.

Vangester turned, "Hello Stillman, good to see you out here where the work gets done."

"Yes sir," Davis said with pride, "I'm a big proponent of the old saw that managers should get out to see what's going on out at the sharp end of the business."

"Good man!" Vangester clapped Davis on the shoulder. "Actually, I'm doing a little of that myself. Every so often I like to come down here and see what Gettnor's doing. It looks like you moved him to a different lab; can you tell me where I can find him?"

An icy sensation crawled up into Davis' gut. The CEO was looking for Gettnor?! "Uh sir, he was a real problem employee."

Vangester grinned ruefully, "Yeah, I know what you mean. Like herding cats, working with him, eh."

"Yes sir. He wasn't on time to work, sometimes left early and I caught him sleeping on the job several times."

Vangester snorted, "That's our man Gettnor alright. Then here all night and all weekend the next time you check, eh? Did you tuck him away somewhere out of the main research flow?"

Davis felt muscles clenching in his buttocks, "Uh, sir, he had a major accident in the lab and I had to let him go."

Vangester looked horrified, "He was hurt?!"

"Uh, no sir. A piece of his equipment burst into flames"—Davis didn't feel like that was a lie, because even if there weren't any flames there had been a tremendous amount of heat—endangering personnel. "And it happened right after I'd caught him leaving early and then sleeping on the job. I, uh, I had to let him go…"

Vangester's eyes widened, then narrowed. He said, "What do you mean, 'let him go'?"

"Sir, he was a menace and a bad example to the rest of our employees. I fired him. I'm interviewing…"

"Fired him!?" Vangester exploded.

"Yes sir. I'll find a reliable replacement and the company will be better…"

"Good God man! Didn't you talk to Smint when you were taking over here?!"

"Uh," Davis's head throbbed over what Smint might say about how he'd avoided meeting with him until that morning on his first day, "Yes sir. He told me that Gettnor was a problem employee and that I'd need to cut him some slack. I took it as my mission to try to correct Gettnor's behavior, but I now believe the man has serious psychiatric issues. Nothing I did to bring him around had any effect."

Vangester had actually paled as Davis spoke. Now he said, "Surely Smint told you the man is a genius?"

"Well, yes sir. I think of him as a kind of 'idiot-savant,' but unfortunately, only the 'idiot' part seemed to be in evidence. We really don't need that kind of square peg in this department."

Vangester's hand had come up to rub his forehead and he'd begun to squint, as if he had a horrific headache. "Are you even aware that over 60% of Querx's revenues stream from products that depend on one of the twelve patents Gettnor filed in the nine years since he started here? I'm not even talking about the royalties Querx collects on the two patents for products that we licensed to other companies because they were out of our field!"

Davis felt his bowels clinch and had a sudden urge to visit the restroom, "I, I… I'm sure we can find a good replacement… someone who'll be more of a team player…" he trailed off at the livid expression on Vangester's face.

"No!" Vangester grated out. "You will do whatever it takes to get Gettnor back. *Whatever!* Understand! Apologize for being such a Goddamned idiot. Triple his salary. Quadruple it; we've been paying him a pittance. Give him a bigger cut of the royalties from his patents; we've been screwing him on those anyway. Give him a bigger lab, buy him more equipment. He loves equipment; *that* might actually work. Crawl on your belly, offer to fire yourself, *whatever* it takes."

In a small voice Davis said, "Fire myself...?"

Vangester exploded, "You've killed the goose that laid the Goddamned golden eggs! I *thought* your cocky attitude might cause some problems but I never dreamed you'd do something *this* stupid! If you can't get him to come back you'll *have* to be fired just to appease the board. Hell, *I'll* probably lose my job for putting an idiot like you in yours! If the only way you can get him to come back is by firing yourself, we'll Goddamned fire you." He muttered, "The best you can hope for is that we get him back and find something *else* for you to do. Hopefully something where you can't do any more harm." Vangester turned on his heel and stormed away. He stopped, calling back, "Let me know in two hours whether you've had any luck."

Davis turned and scurried to the bathroom.

***

While he waited for the replicated version of the original testing chamber and the new ceramic electrode for his new chamber, Vaz began testing the hydrogen absorption capabilities of the other test disks he'd had in his pocket when he'd arrived back from Querx that first day. His new chamber should work fine for that, so he carefully got one out from the drawer he'd stashed them in, unwrapped it and put it

88

in. He closed the chamber and turned on the hydrogen.

Vaz's AI said, "You have a call from Stillman Davis."

"Who?"

"Mr. Davis is the department head for R&D at Querx."

"Oh," Vaz initially felt surprise, then felt a rising tide of anger. He'd been much happier a moment ago, he thought. "I don't want to talk to him." Without anything active to do on his experiment he sat and stewed about Davis. Finally he got up and began pounding his heavy bag. Davis' face figured prominently on it in his imagination.

***

Stillman sat in his office trying to calm himself. His emotions cycled between rage at Gettnor, and panic that he was about to lose the job he'd worked so long and hard to get. *How could Vangester think that* Gettnor, *of all people, was indispensable! Now the SOB has the gall to refuse my calls!* Davis had sent an e-mail also but there'd been no response and he doubted there would be.

Eventually Davis settled his thoughts sufficiently and came to the crushing conclusion that if Gettnor was refusing his calls, there was only one way to get through. He would have to go to Gettnor's house. His AI had no difficulty determining the address. As he walked out he turned to Maddie and said, "I'm going out for a bit, not sure when I'll be back."

"OK." She said, an uncertain tone in her voice as she wondered where he was going. He left the office all the time without telling her where he was going, why this time? Why "out?"

Davis walked up to Gettnor's house and identified himself to the house AI, suddenly worried that Gettnor already had another job and he'd wasted his time. After a pause to speak to Gettnor, the AI said, "Mr. Gettnor does not wish to speak to you."

Relieved that Gettnor was home he said, "Please tell him I would like to offer him his job back."

There was a pause; then the AI said, "Mr. Gettnor said he does not wish to work for you."

Davis' stomach clenched at the specification that he didn't want to work for *him*. He desperately did not want to step down as department head; that would be his last offer. "Please tell him we can offer a larger salary if he will return."

The AI came back on, "He doesn't want a larger salary."

"We could double his salary."

"He doesn't want a larger salary."

There hadn't been a pause, suggesting to Davis that the AI had simply obeyed its earlier instruction, so he said, "Please tell him we could double his salary."

This time there was a pause, but then the AI simply said, "He said, 'No.'"

"Tell him we could triple his salary."

After a pause, "He said, 'No.'"

"Tell him we could give him a bigger lab."

After a pause, "He said, 'Don't need a bigger lab.'"

"Tell him we could get him more or better equipment."

After a pause, "He said, 'Go away.'"

"Tell him we could also quadruple his salary."

Davis waited quite a while and when the AI said nothing he finally asked, "What did he say?"

The AI responded, "He hasn't said anything yet."

Davis gritted his teeth, picturing Gettnor in one of his catatonic spells. He racked his mind for anything else but finally said, "Tell him I could step down as the department head of R&D if he doesn't want to work for me."

After a pause the AI said, "He asked if Dr. Smint would be department head again?"

"Dr. Smint is too old."

When the AI said nothing for a long time, Davis said, "Ask Dr. Gettnor if he would like to be department head."

After another very long pause Davis asked, "Did he respond?"

"He laughed. Then, though it wasn't very clear, I believe he said that you were an idiot."

Fury boiled through Davis. He grabbed the handle and struck the door itself with a fist. To his surprise, the door swung open. At first he expected Gettnor to be behind it, opening it to confront him. The entryway was empty however. Davis stepped inside, "Gettnor!" he shouted, wanting to confront the man who was destroying his career.

There was no response, so he stepped farther inside and shouted again, "Gettnor! I know you're here somewhere. Talk to me..." Davis trailed off before he said "you idiot!" fighting to remember, despite his trembling fury, that he must somehow convince Gettnor to listen to reason. He couldn't afford to anger Gettnor any more than he already had. He stepped into a large room, apparently a family room. Compulsively organized, all furniture perfectly aligned and stark, it looked like something arranged by a machine. "Gettnor?" he called out again.

From behind a door across the room he heard the tread of someone climbing stairs. Realizing he was in a home without permission he slowly backed toward the entry reassuring himself that, as a brown belt in karate he had nothing to fear from someone like Gettnor. The door opened and Gettnor stepped into the room, frowning at Davis. He carefully closed the basement door behind himself then started walking toward Davis.

Stillman said, "Look, Dr. Gettnor, you've got to listen to me! I… made a mistake letting you go. I have a temper and that fire frightened me! But I should never have let you go! What can I offer you to return to Querx?"

Gettnor grasped Davis by the arm just above the elbow.

"Hey, let me go!" Davis tried to jerk his arm out of Gettnor's grip, but it was unyielding. In response Gettnor lifted Davis by the arm until his feet were barely touching the floor and began to move him toward the door despite his protests. "You're hurting my arm!" he gasped with a sense of panic, it felt like his arm was in a vise. He struck at the hand holding him without noticeable effect. How could a weirdo nerd like Gettnor possibly be so strong? Gettnor strong-armed Davis through his front door and gave him a little shove. Davis stumbled back, "We could give you a bigger share of the royalties on your patents," he said, rubbing his arm. "Wait!" he gasped as the door inexorably closed before him. He stepped forward and called out, "Please! Listen to me. We can work *something* out." He thumped the door. Under his breath he said, "You idiot!" Louder he said, "Come *on*!"

After a while, shoulders slumping, Davis got in his car and headed back to Querx.

Vangester's secretary waved Davis into his office. "Mr. Vangester?"

Vangester looked around from his screen, "Any luck?"

"No sir, the man's completely unhinged! He assaulted me!"

"He came in to see you in person?"

"No sir. He wouldn't respond to calls, so I went to visit him. I'm trying to go the extra mile here."

Vangester frowned, "Let me see the audio-video of your interaction."

Davis' heart sank. For a moment he considered refusing. After all your own AI's audio-video records had been judged privileged and to require a warrant to examine without the owner's permission. Unless you gave them up voluntarily. But if he refused, it would seem he had something to hide. He decided his only hope was to show it to Vangester and hope that he didn't look as bad as he feared on the record. He told his AI to forward the record to Vangester's.

Vangester leaned back in his chair and looked up at his HUD, seeing the encounter from Davis' perspective. "Oh, Christ!" he said with a disgusted tone. Then he drew his head back and paused the recording to look wide eyed at Davis. "You entered his house without an invitation?!"

Davis said, "The door swung open when I touched it. I thought maybe the AI was inviting me."

Vangester rolled his eyes, "Touched it?"

"Well, knocked."

"Good God! If he'd *shot* you, the court would have found in his favor you know." Vangester sighed disconsolately, turning his eyes back to his HUD. When he finished watching the record, he said, "Could you have 'screwed the pooch' any worse? Of course," he shook his head sadly, "I guess I'm the *idiot* for thinking that someone so clueless he fired our most important employee was the right person to try to hire him back." He paused, then bowed his head, "Maybe there's some hope in the fact that he asked if Smint could be department head again."

"Smint's over the age limit."

"Don't be an idiot. We can work around that rule if it means getting Gettnor back."

"Sir, give me a chance. I'm sure we could find someone even more qualified to replace Gettnor. The man's unhinged!"

"'More qualified!'" Vangester snorted. "You just don't get it do you? There are a lot of people 'more qualified' in this world. Diplomas, degrees and grades—none of them measure whatever it is that Gettnor has. People who have *whatever* it is that he has frequently don't do all that well in those arenas. You can't hire them on purpose, you hire them by accident, then you do *whatever* you can to keep them. The one thing you *don't* do is *fire them* once you find one. Gods!" Vangester buried his head in his hands.

"Sir, let me work this problem. I'll figure out a way to fix it."

"Davis, the only reason you haven't been fired already is that I'm worried that I might need you for some reason, perhaps just so that I *can* fire you to make Gettnor happy! For right now, you continue to run your department, but do not contact Gettnor or otherwise interact with him in any way. I'm going to see if Dr. Smint can help us out." He shook his head morosely and waved dismissal at Davis, saying to his AI, "Get me Dr. Smint."

Back in his office Davis found himself wound so tight that he couldn't stop shaking. He paced as his mind darted frenetically from place to place. Maddie knocked to ask a question. He barked, "Get out!" Eventually, he couldn't take his own frantic edginess anymore and stormed out of the office a little before 4PM.

Downtown, Davis took off his AI and got out of his car, walking down and around a corner then another couple of blocks to Jerrod's Bar and Grill.

94

Stepping inside the door he waited a moment for his eyes to adjust to the dim light, then walked slowly over to the bar, surveying the patrons. Taking a stool he ordered a beer and asked the bartender if Jerrod was in. The bartender shrugged. "I'm a friend."

"Call him then."

Davis gave a little shake of his head.

The bartender frowned at him, then shrugged. Holding his hand back where it would be out of the view of his own AI's cameras and low enough that Stillman suspected it wouldn't show on the bar's AI either, the bartender pointed back toward Jerrod's office, all without moving his head. A moment later the man moved off to serve another customer. Davis picked up his beer and wandered off toward the small room at the back of the bar.

He knocked on the door and a gruff voice said, "Come on in Stilly."

Davis stepped in, concerned about how Jerrod had known it was him. He glanced around and saw a screen displaying the little hallway outside the office. He looked at Jerrod and meaningfully tapped his AI head gear.

Jerrod snorted, "Look at you, skulking around like the bad guy in a shoddy vid. Don't worry, my AI's not recording."

Davis pointed at the screen recording the hallway outside, "You're recording me coming and going."

"It records over the same memory chip every ten minutes. Unless you piss me off, then I dump it to real memory. What are *you* tryin' to do 'off the record' Stilly? It ain't like you to be acting like us 'unsavory' types. You ain't very good at it."

Davis studied his old friend. They'd known each other since high school when Davis had kept the books for a small time gambling operation Jerrod had run for students betting on local athletic events.

They'd drifted apart when Davis went to college and got a respectable job but still saw one another occasionally. Jerrod was still a big guy, but his muscles looked... soft. With modern medicine people rarely bulged with fat anymore, but Jerrod didn't look as powerful as he used to. Of course, he probably had younger, dumber people doing his "enforcing" nowadays. Finally he said, "I've got a problem."

"Don't we all."

Davis' shoulders slumped, "I just got promoted to department head."

"Don't sound like a problem to me."

"I fired this asshole that worked in my department."

Jerrod barked a laugh, "Good for you Stilly! Show some spine."

"Yeah... Turned out the big bosses think he's some kind of hot shit. He's patented some things that made the company some money."

Jerrod leaned back and grinned, digging in one ear with a finger, "So you got'cher shiny little dress shoe all down in da pooh, eh? Why'nt 'cha just hire him back?"

"I tried. He won't come back."

"So? Screw it. He's gone, the big bosses are just gonna have to deal."

"They're gonna fire me unless I get this guy back on the payroll."

Jerrod's eyebrows rose, "Really? They must *really* have the hots for this guy."

Davis shrugged despondently, "The CEO claims that the board will want someone's head to roll when they find out this guy's gone."

"Come on!" Jerrod leaned back and scraped a tooth with a fingernail. "How much are these inventions worth?"

"I tried to look into it since this shit came down. I think somewhere between five and ten billion dollars so far. Turns out his inventions are responsible for most of Querx's cash flow."

Jerrod sat up suddenly, "Really…" Jerrod looked much more interested. "I guess I'd want your head on a stick too. Don't they already have the rights to these inventions though?"

"Yeah, I think they're more interested in what he'll invent in the future."

"Huh, why's he been working for them anyway? He must be rich himself from inventions like that."

Davis shrugged, "I don't know. He's kind of… impaired. An idiot savant. Lord knows, they've been *shafting* him on the royalties, paying him about a tenth of a percent. His salary's crap too. But he's *so* weird, I doubt he could run a business himself."

Jerrod waggled his eyebrows, "Why don't we hire him ourselves?"

Davis snorted, "He'd never work for me!"

"Wouldn't have to know you're part of it."

"And if he never invented anything again? We'd be on the hook for his salary with nothing in the bag?"

Jerrod shrugged, "OK, we'll make sure he's actually inventing something before we hire him. Meantime, what are you wanting to do?"

"Make him go back to work for Querx to save my job."

Jerrod frowned, "How do you *make* a man go to work for someone else?"

Davis narrowed his eyes, "You've got people working for you… that don't really want to. Your accountant for instance."

"Yeah, but they owe me somehow. And they work for *me*. How do I make someone who doesn't owe me, work for someone else?"

"*I* don't know. You're the expert in these kinds of things."

Jerrod looked doubtful, "And you're going to pay for this?"

Davis tilted his head, "How much?"

"I'll have to look into it. At least ten grand."

"Jeez, for an old friend?"

Jerrod raised an eyebrow, "An old friend who might get me sent to prison."

Davis winced, "OK."

Jerrod leaned back, "So, this guy have any bad habits we can blackmail him over? Mistresses, drugs?"

"I doubt it, he's a real nerd. I'm pretty sure he'll crumble if someone threatens him though."

Jerrod stared doubtfully at him. Then he shrugged, "OK, we'll threaten him. You're new at this so I'll remind you, no electronic money. I'd suggest you buy some gold or platinum and pay me with that. Taking out large quantities of cash is looked on with a lot of suspicion nowadays."

Davis nodded.

"Buy a lot more of whatever you get than you need to pay me with. No matching transactions. Besides it might be more than 10G."

Davis nodded again.

"Do *not* contact me over the net. Check back in person in a few days."

Back home with his AI on again, Davis sent Vangester an e-message, "Working several angles to get Gettnor back for us. Please give me some time."

***

Dante and Steve walked around the corner to the wall they usually sat on to eat lunch. A large body leaned up away from the wall. Jack!

Jack said, "So, Gettnor." He sneered as he said Dante's name. "Silvy ain't here to protect you today."

Steve looked back and forth between them while Dante stared sullenly at Jack. "What do you want?" he said sourly.

"I want you to understand that if I see you sniffing after my girl again I'm gonna crush you like a bug."

Steve snorted, "I'd like to see you try Mr. Football hero. He's a wrestler you know?"

Dante didn't change his expression but after his experience the other day, really wished Steve had kept his mouth shut.

Jack grinned hungrily at Steve, "You just keep telling yourself that bein' a wrestler means jack shit." He turned back to Dante. "If you think it does, just keep sniffin' around my girl and we'll find out." He turned back to Steve, "And anytime you want to try your wrestling moves out on me, just come ahead pretty boy."

The three stood tensely staring each other down a moment, then Dante touched Steve's arm. "Leave it be. Get in a fight and we'll get thrown out of school."

***

Billy got out of the shower, dried himself and put on the latex gloves. He opened the bag and shook the clothes out onto the freshly washed counter. All synthetics. All new. Two layers. He put them on, carefully not allowing the outsides of the clothing to touch his skin.

Before he got in his car he put a plastic bag over the seat so none of the DNA he'd rubbed onto the seat over the years would get on his new clothes. He set the bag of other stuff on the passenger seat and gave the van an address near this Gettnor's address. The job seemed simple enough. Intimidate this science nerd into taking his old job back. Rough him up a little if needs be. Leave no trail that could be traced back to him or Jerrod if the guy went to the cops, but intimidate him on that score as well.

As the van took him to the address he'd given it, he thought through his plan again. He'd left his own AI at home, so no record would exist on it. Leave no DNA at the scene. Just before the van arrived, he got out the latex mask and put it on. It was just a cheap costume mask but it would make it impossible to identify him from the AI records at Gettnor's house. It didn't look so odd that people he encountered on the street would freak before he got there.

He'd left himself a long walk to Gettnor's and was irritable when he got there. *Oh well,* he thought, *it's got me in the right mood.*

When Gettnor's door AI asked him who he was, he held up the box and said "delivery" in his lowest pitched voice.

After a moment the AI said, "We're not expecting a delivery."

Billy tried the doorknob. The door opened. *Idiots,* he thought to himself as he put the heavy work gloves on over his latex gloves. He stepped inside, crossed the entryway and looked across the stark family room for the door to the basement he'd been told about. Seeing it, he started that way. The door opened and an average sized light brown dude with no hair stepped out. He was wearing funny gloves.

Billy was surprised when the man walked directly toward him. Most people hesitated when the confronted someone six foot six inches who weighed two ninety. Billy pitched his voice to a rumble again and had said, "Gettnor! I'm here to teach you a lesson. You need to go back to work for…"

The guy launched a full out punch into Billy's gut.

It felt like he'd been hit by a sledgehammer. With a gasp, Billy bent over.

Gettnor's fist rocketed up toward his face...

Lights were flashing on and off Billy's face. No, he fuzzily realized, people's heads were sometimes blocking the sun, other times not. "Can we get a hand here?" someone called, "This guy's huge!" A lot of faces gathered around, then he was lifted onto something, then lifted into the back of an ambulance. He wondered, *what the hell just happened?* He wanted to ask, but in his business you just didn't. A vague picture of that Gettnor guy throwing a punch at his gut rumbled through the back of his mind. His mouth tasted of blood and his teeth didn't fit together right. He felt incredibly weak.

Someone said, "Crap! Pressure's low, let's have some Trendelenburg. Turn on the sirens." Billy's feet went up, his head dropped and he heard the siren distantly as the world faded away.

Sitting in their police car, the cop and his partner shook their heads as they watched the video they'd downloaded from the house's AI. "Holy crap, run that back again!" The camera in the house's family room had a good angle to show the intruder step in from the hallway he'd nearly filled, putting on a pair of work gloves. You could see that he had on a costume mask of the President's face. He walked across the room and was near the edge of the screen when he spoke, saying, "Gettnor! I'm here to teach you a lesson. You need to go back to work for..." then out of the bottom of the picture Gettnor appeared, throwing the punch that crumpled the big guy. The big guy's head was descending out of the field of view when it suddenly shot back up from the crushing blow that busted up his face. Then the big guy lay out like a tree falling. Then this Gettnor could be heard saying, "Call 911," as he picked up the big guy's feet, pulled them around and towed him toward the front door.

They turned to one another, eyebrows lifted. One said, "Should we be charging him with anything?"

The other shrugged, "Seems pretty clear cut, he was defending his home from an unwelcomed intruder who was threatening him with harm. If he'd shot him with a gun, he'd be within his rights."

The first cop snorted, "If he'd shot him with a gun, he might not have done quite as much damage! How the hell did a guy like Gettnor take out a mountain of a man like Billy Ray Evarts with two punches?"

"I know, seems like such a nerd, right?"

"Not very talkative though."

"Yeah, let's go ask him some more questions."

Lisanne pulled into the driveway as the police were leaving. "What happened?"

The officers looked curiously at her. "Who are you?"

"Lisanne Gettnor. This is my house! What are you guys doing here?"

"Your husband didn't call you?"

"No." Lisanne considered telling them that she and Vaz hadn't been getting along but decided to wait to see if it had any bearing. "I hadn't heard anything. I'm just getting off work."

"Um, sorry Ma'am. You've been the victim of a home invasion. Your husband was home and stopped the intruder. Mr. Gettnor wasn't hurt. He's inside."

"My God! Was it a robber?"

"Um, no Ma'am. He apparently wanted to coerce your husband to go back to work... uh, we have no idea why. Do you have any ideas in that regard?"

"What? *I've* been hoping he would go back to work, why not?"

The cop snorted, "Apparently, Ma'am, he *really* doesn't want to go back to work. He said they offered him his job back, but he hates his new boss."

Lisanne closed her eyes and sighed in frustration. Then she opened them and frowned, "Someone wanted to *force* him to go back to work? Why would anyone want to do that?"

"We'd like to know that ourselves. Your husband says he doesn't know but we'll be questioning some folks over at Querx about it."

"Didn't you ask the guy?"

"We will. He isn't up to answering questions right now. Looks like your husband broke his jaw."

Lisanne drew back in startlement. Then realizing that if there'd been a fight Vaz had probably been hurt, she hurried inside.

Vaz was down on his hands and knees with a rag, washing blood off the floor when Lisanne came in behind him. She said, "Vaz! What happened?"

Vaz looked up at her warily. "A guy came in here and threatened me."

"And you fought him?! Why didn't you just call the police?"

"I did." Vaz felt that this was a true statement, even if he had called after he'd hit the guy. He desperately didn't want Lisanne to know how much he'd enjoyed hitting the guy. He'd been feeling really tense and having an intruder pop up—someone he could legally and in good conscience hit—had seemed like a godsend. The ecstasy of punching that huge guy had drained away all his tension and right now he felt great. He could hardly wait to get back down to the calculations he'd been working on.

Vaz hoped Lisanne wasn't going to feel like she had to talk about this for a long time. He didn't want to lose this uplifted feeling before he'd tried to apply it to the hydrogen-boron fusion question.

"Are you hurt?"

Vaz shook his head and turned back to his cleanup.

"He wanted you to go back to work at Querx?"

Vaz shrugged.

Lisanne narrowed her eyes, Vaz was hiding something. "Did Querx offer you your job back?"

Vaz nodded, getting up from the floor with the rag and heading to the sink to rinse it out.

Exasperated, Lisanne said, "Vaz! Talk to me! Are you going to go back to work?"

Vaz having wrung out the rag, started toward the laundry room to get rid of it. He wasn't sure how best to answer Lisanne to get her off his back. Finally he just said, "No." He turned toward the basement door.

Lisanne beat him to the door. He realized that she'd been keeping between him and the basement door the entire time. She said, "Vaz! Why not? We need the money!"

"No we don't. This new finding will be worth a lot of money."

"A bird in the hand Vaz! You can't jeopardize your children's future for something that *might* be worth money. Please!"

Vaz was wringing the rag that he'd never taken to the laundry room back and forth. His peaceful transcendent state was in tatters and tension was building. He wondered once again if he could explain that their financial situation was OK without making Lisanne angry that he'd been hiding it for a decade. He had a feeling that explaining it actually might resolve a lot of their issues, but he *hated* trying to explain things that he felt guilty about. Finally he stepped up to her and, gripping her by the arms, he gently but inexorably moved her away from in front of the door to the basement.

"Vaz! Dammit! Vaz, no! Talk to me!" She began to sob, "Come on Vaz…"

He shut the door in her face, feeling terrible, but unable to deal with the entire issue. "Don't cry," he said sadly through the door. "It's going to be OK." As he descended the stairs, he pulled the MMA gloves out of his back pocket where he'd put them after the fight. *That was a problem with* real *fights*, he mused, *they didn't last long enough to wear him out.* At the bottom of the stairs he lunged out to begin pounding his heavy bag.

Upstairs Lisanne sank to the floor and leaned her back against the basement door, gasping a little with her frustration. Vaz could be so stubborn, unyielding, and just plain difficult to communicate with! How could he just avoid talking about something so important in their lives?! Hiding in the basement like a child who'd done wrong!

She wiped angrily at her tears; then frowned a little. *Has he "done something wrong?" Besides the obvious of getting fired and refusing to take the job back when it was offered?*

***

Stillman Davis entered Jerrod's Bar and Grill and walked directly back to Jerrod's back office. He knocked and opened the door when bade to do so. With dismay he saw that Jerrod looked pissed.

Jerrod stood and leaned forward, "You didn't tell me the SOB was some kind of animal!"

"Animal? Gettnor? What do you mean?"

"I mean he took out the guy I sent over to lean on him!"

"'Took out?' You mean… he, he's, dead?"

105

"No! Ruptured spleen, broken jaw. Bunch of surgery. Worse, the police will be questioning him when he recovers enough to talk."

Stillman frowned, "He shot him?"

"No!" Jerrod barked. "Gettnor beat him with his fists!"

"But... but Gettnor's a science nerd. He couldn't beat up a cockroach!" Davis' eyes narrowed. "What kind of guy did you send over there?"

"Six foot six, three hunnert or so. I guess I should have sent an actual tank?"

"Wait, Gettnor? Took out a *big* guy? Are you sure you sent the dude to the right house?"

"Yeah, I'm sure... but I'll have to check, maybe somebody else was home?"

As he left, Davis uncomfortably remembered how strong Gettnor had seemed when he'd thrown Davis out of his house.

He shook his head, strong, maybe. A fighter though? That was just crazy.

***

Vaz studied the hydrogen absorption results for the other alloy disks. One of them had absorbed a little more than the original disk, but not by much. Most of them were much worse so his original estimates for the alloy had been surprisingly good. Several of them did have even more bizarre electrical properties but he'd kind of lost interest in that phenomenon.

The house AI interrupted his thoughts to tell him he had a delivery. Suspicious since that guy had come into his house last week, he checked the porch camera and saw a UPS man getting back in his truck and driving away. No one else was on the porch or in the house.

Excitedly he got the package which did indeed contain the replication of the apparatus he'd been using in the lab and his new piezo ceramic electrode. He went back down to his basement lab to try it out. His excitement made his hands tremble as he tried to assemble the devices. He finally had to break for a light workout to calm himself.

Having finally assembled the copy of the original apparatus, he started it absorbing hydrogen and turned to his new chamber. Gratifyingly the new electrode fit it like it was supposed to, so he installed a disk and turned on the hydrogen for that one too. He resisted the temptation to apply the hammering current immediately. Even though they should be saturated with hydrogen in just a few minutes, this time he wanted to wait to match the original conditions. That meant absorbing hydrogen overnight.

With a sigh, he thought that it was fortunate that he had that amateur MMA fight this evening. It would take his mind off of the experiment so he wouldn't sit around all night trying to resist the temptation to apply the current early.

***

Dante and Steve walked into Eakin Auditorium and headed for their seats. Steve was pumped again. "I talked to the Abe at my dojo. He thinks I'm good enough to fight in one of these as soon as I turn eighteen. If I win a few amateur bouts, he thinks I could get picked up for semi pro."

Dante shook his head, "Man, I don't know. Fighters get hit in the head a lot." Dante was becoming more and more disenchanted with Steve and his constant talk about fighting. Steve was neglecting his studies and Dante had begun to realize that very few fighters were successful enough to make a career out of it. Even those who were successful often found their careers cut short by injury.

"So?!"

"So, I've been reading. Fighters can have some pretty significant neuro problems later in life."

"Hah, who knows if I'll even live that long. I'm goin' for a short life, full of glory."

Under his breath Dante said, "I'll take a long life, and not as an idiot either."

"What?"

"Nothin'."

Some cheers rose from the crowd as the first fighters entered the ring and were introduced. The first one, Jack Alexander had 5 wins and no losses. The second, going only by a pseudonym "Dr. Demento" was in his first fight.

Dante hadn't been paying too much attention to the ring, having become more interested in the spectators. They were a varied group that seemed to have come from all walks of life but he thought most of them were there to watch someone get hurt. Drinking beer seemed to be an important part of the ritual for many. However, when he heard them announce "Jack Alexander" he turned to look at the ring with wide eyes. It *was* Silvy's Jack! He pulled off his robe and he looked enormously powerful. Dante suddenly realized it wasn't just his extra weight that had made him hard to shake off in the hallway that day.

Steve said, "Oh man, that new guy is smaller than the dude with the 5-0 record, he's gonna get killed." He elbowed Dante, "Check it out, he's shaved his head and his eyebrows like your dad does."

Dante looked curiously down at the ring, surprised that Steve hadn't recognized Jack. He saw that the other guy did look a lot like his dad. Dante snorted, the guy had on what looked like an ordinary bath robe instead of the flamboyant fighter's robes that most of the competitors wore.

Steve nudged Dante again, "Whoa! Look at the new guy. Holy crap, he's ripped! The big guy might have some trouble with him after all!"

For a moment Dante had narrowed his eyes. The "Demento" character looked *so* much like his dad that he'd begun to feel uneasy. But when the robe came off he relaxed. No way a narrow waisted, broad shouldered man with powerful thighs and massive arms like that could ever be confused with his dad, the nerdy lab guy.

The ref waved a hand to start the fight and the two fighters moved out into the middle. Steve said, "Oh man, the little guy better get up on his toes or he's gonna get creamed."

Dante stared. Jack Alexander was up on his toes, dancing toward the middle. Demento, hands up, simply plodded toward Jack, *walking* just like Dante's dad! What Dante thought of as his dad's "waddle," kind of wide based and robotic. Jack sent out some tentative left jabs that bounced harmlessly off Demento's upraised gloves. Then he launched a big hook to Demento's left ribcage below the elbow of the upraised left hand. Then Jack fell down... and didn't get up.

"What the Hell?" Steve shouted. "What the Hell!" He raised up on his tiptoes, "The little guy knocked him out?!" I didn't even see it happen! Jeez!"

Dante stepped out onto the stairs and began to walk slowly down to ringside. He had to *know*.

The big screens over the ring began showing a slo-mo replay. On the video from the side that Steve and Dante were on you could see Jack's testing left jabs, then the big hooking right to the ribs. From the camera on the opposite side you could also see the jabs, but then as Jack leaned down and in to throw the big hook to the ribs, Demento's right came around to wallop the side of Jack's head. The much bigger Jack simply went *down*.

Dante had reached the bottom steps and someone was getting up to block his progress. In the ring he could see Alexander still laid out with his trainer trying to bring him around. And Dante could see his own dad walking down the steps from the ring wearing a bathrobe Dante had occasionally seen him wearing at home.

One of the ringside bouncer types started shooing Dante back up the stairs to his seat. Dante made it up the stairs with only some minor stumbles, even though he kept almost all of his attention on his dad's characteristic walk heading out to the dressing rooms. He wondered if he could get into the dressing rooms himself. He felt torn between wanting to tell his dad he knew his secret, and worrying that his dad would be pissed that he was down here watching MMA on a school night. He might not. Dante hadn't even seen his dad for weeks. His mom and dad didn't seem to be getting along very well, so it seemed possible that his dad didn't even know that Dante'd told Mom he was going to watch a wrestling match.

When Dante got back to his seat, Steve said, "Where the Hell did you go? See a girl or something down there?"

"I went…" Dante suddenly didn't know if he should tell Steve. Probably his Dad didn't want everyone to know or he wouldn't be fighting under a pseudonym. But this was just too cool to keep bottled in. He desperately wanted to tell someone! "Down to see if that really was my dad."

"Hah! Funny! Check out this next guy…"

Dante never told Steve after all. Probably for the best. He didn't tell Steve that it had been Silvy's Jack either. He grinned a little. His dad had gotten even with that asshole for him, even if no one but Dante knew about it.

Dante kept his eye on the walkway to the dressing rooms thinking surely that his dad would come back out that way to watch the other fights. But his dad never came back in. If he was interested enough in MMA to participate, why wouldn't he watch the other fights?

The other fights had seemed a blur to Dante. When he got home his dad was down in the basement like he'd been for weeks. Dante thought about knocking on the door and going down to talk to him, but what would he say? "Dad, I watched you knock a guy out in that amateur MMA fight tonight. Thanks, that guy's a jerk. How did you get so ripped?"

Dante had enough trouble talking to his dad normally. This just seemed like a conversation he didn't want to start. He couldn't decide if this whole thing made his weird dad really cool, or just even weirder.

***

Vaz got up early in the morning, too excited to sleep. He made himself take time to nuke a breakfast burrito from his little fridge and eat it. Then he went to check the numbers for hydrogen absorption in his two chambers. Both were over 1,500 times the volume of the alloy disks. So far, so good. He made himself wait until his family had left the house before he switched on the hammering current and sat back to monitor.

He had installed temperature and radiation monitors on the outside of the old version. The new chamber of course, had the monitors built in. He worried more about the old chamber because the responsiveness of the measurements would be delayed by the time it took heat and radiation to make its way through the walls of the chamber.

111

Fortunately, this time he'd installed safety trips in the software that he had monitoring the system. He'd become so fascinated with what he saw on the broad spectrum video of the inside of the chamber that he didn't notice the sudden upswing in the readout of the x-ray detector. The software powered the experiment down, catching Vaz by surprise.

Seeing the x-ray graph in the red zone he noticed that several of the other detectors had suddenly jumped up and had approached their own safety limits. Large currents had developed in the frames of both test chambers and the heat levels were on their way up. Though the neutron detector had remained nearly silent it had definitely crept above zero too.

He sat back, stunned. Each hydrogen-boron fusion should produce three positively charged "alpha particles" (helium nuclei) which would induce large currents. Hydrogen-boron fusion should also produce x-radiation, but unlike deuterium fusion, it should produce only a few of the highly hazardous neutrons through "side-chain" reactions.

A few calculations confirmed that both devices had produced far more energy than he'd pumped into them, also suggesting that fusion had occurred.

Vaz thought for a while, then after carefully saving records of everything to do with this run, began designing his next experiment, aimed at seeing if he could harvest useful current from the phenomenon. The charged alpha particles would need to be directed into coils that would extract electrical current from them. Cooling to prevent meltdown had to be designed into the setup. Though in a working fusion reactor you could think of it as "harvesting" heat that could be used for other purposes, for this next run he would just cool it to prevent meltdown and waste the heat.

Most importantly, he needed to shield the device so that he could work around it while it was running. The shielding would have to include water and boron to absorb the low and high energy neutrons that would be emitted. Even though there wouldn't be high numbers of neutrons like there would with other fusion processes, they were still dangerous. Neutrons converted surrounding materials into radioactive ones so they had to be absorbed and water and boron were among the best materials for that. He also needed metal in the shielding to absorb the x-rays. Correctly done, the metal shielding should also be able to convert the x-rays into additional electrical current, but that would also be for future iterations.

Vaz had been working frantically for hours, planning the next experimental device. Trying to keep the costs down, he worked hard to find as many components as possible "off the shelf" from various vendors and then design his device around them. Trying to figure out how he would be able to cobble those together to make a workable testing apparatus with as few custom components as possible was mind bending but would save a lot of money. Several times he was tempted to just pay extra to get parts made from scratch, but he persevered.

His AI interrupted him, "You have a call from Dr. Smint."

He pondered refusing it. He really didn't want to think about anything else right now. But, Smint had been very good to him when he'd been the department head over at Querx and Vaz really liked him. Vaz sighed, "OK."

Vaz heard Smint's voice, "Vaz?"

"Yes?"

"This is Jack Smint. I heard from Vangester about your troubles with Stillman Davis."

"Who?"

Typical Gettnor, doesn't even know the name of the man that fired him, Smint thought to himself. "Davis, the man that replaced me as head of R&D at Querx."

"Oh, yeah. He's a jerk."

"Sorry to hear about it, I contended at the time that he was a jerk and the wrong man to head up R&D. I argued against letting him be my replacement but I was overruled."

"They should have done like you said," Vaz said sulkily, but distractedly as he kept staring at the unfinished design up on the big screen.

"Anyway, Mr. Vangester would really like you to come back to work at Querx."

"Huh?" Vaz said distractedly.

"Mr. Vangester would really like you to come back to work at Querx."

"Who's Vangester?"

Smint stifled a chuckle, "Mr. Vangester's the CEO of Querx. He'd like you to come back to work."

"Oh. I don't want to do that. I really hated working for... Davis, right?"

"Yeah. Vangester is firing Davis. He couldn't believe that Davis fired *you*. So, if you came back, you wouldn't have to work for Davis. They'd pay you more. They're willing to make a lot of concessions to get you back."

"That was a good idea," Vaz said, referring to the firing. His focus had returned to the design again, so he really hadn't paid much attention to the part about not working for Davis or the pay or the concessions.

Smint recognized a distracted Gettnor from talking to him in that state many times before. He tried to bring him back on topic, "So would you consider coming back to work for Querx if you didn't have to work for Davis?"

"Huh? Oh, I don't have to work for him *now*. In fact I'm not working for anyone and it's great. I can spend *all* my time on this amazing new phenomenon. No meetings, no interruptions. You're not going to believe this, but I'm getting fusion with excess energy!" Remembering how Smint had loved talking about his experiments with him, Vaz abruptly asked, "Do you want to come look at my setup?"

Stunned, Smint said, "Fusion?"

"Yeah! The day they fired me at Querx, my hydrogen absorption apparatus overheated and partially melted. It looks like what happened was that the hydrogen in it was fusing with the boron in a new alloy I'd been testing."

Staggered by what Vaz had just said, Smint said nothing for a bit. It was *so* absolutely typical for Gettnor. Anyone else would have kept any possible fusion a secret for fear of someone trying to steal the method and patent it themselves. They would never have considered inviting anyone to look at their apparatus. Certainly anyone with knowledge of how intellectual property law operated would *never* have admitted that some of the work on it had been done at Querx, possibly giving Querx some claim to the idea. Smint had been urging Vaz to return to Querx so one would think he had Querx's interests at heart.

Smint had been aware that Querx paid Gettnor less than he was worth and suspected that they might be screwing him out of part of his share of his previous inventions' royalties. He'd always felt that it was a somewhat reasonable arrangement because Gettnor was just as clueless as he'd demonstrated a second ago and would never be able to negotiate a better deal for himself at another company, or bring his own ideas to market. Maybe Querx hadn't treated him right, but he'd been better off than he would have been out in the world.

But… fusion?! From everything Smint knew about fusion, it was absolutely ridiculous to imagine that anyone could have achieved it with any kind of small device like Gettnor might have in his home. On the other hand, no matter how clueless Gettnor might be about how the rest of the world worked, he was virtually *never* wrong about anything to do with physics. "Vaz?" he finally said.

"Huh? Oh sorry Dr. Smint, I got distracted. Did you want to come look at my setup?"

"Yeah, Vaz… I'd like that very much. Thanks. At your house?"

"Huh?"

"At your house?"

"Uh huh."

"Tomorrow morning, say 8 AM?"

"Yep, that'd be fine."

"See you then." Jack waited a bit for Vaz to say something else, but he didn't. Smint eventually just signed off.

***

That night Smint lay awake searching his soul. Querx had hired him temporarily as a "consultant," *just* to have him try to hire Gettnor back. They were paying him on a "consulting fee" schedule that was much more than he'd been paid when he worked there full time. As an employee-consultant he felt he owed Querx something toward the goal they'd set him. On the other hand, he'd always liked Vaz. Smint found Gettnor's incredible social clumsiness somewhat endearing and he *loved* talking to him about science. He thought of Vaz as a friend and sometimes wondered if he might be the only friend Vaz had. It just seemed so unlikely that Vaz would have made other friends. So many people were simply… "put off" by Gettnor's… odd behavior. Few hated or actively disliked him, like Davis apparently did, but it was hard to think of anyone who'd ever expressed interest in spending any time with him.

On the other hand, Smint had met Lisanne, Gettnor's pretty blond wife. She seemed very intelligent and as normal as they came. And she truly seemed to care about Vaz. She'd borne his children so she *must* get along with him. Perhaps Vaz had friends and Jack just didn't know about them?

But, didn't he owe Vaz something as his friend? Perhaps he owed Vaz more as his friend than he owed Querx as a consultant? Niggling underneath all these thoughts was a guilty feeling that perhaps he was considering helping Vaz stay out of Querx's clutches with some hope of getting a "piece of the action" if the fusion claim panned out? That wouldn't be ethical either.

It was probably all moot anyway. There was no way that Vaz had really achieved fusion, no matter how much he hoped he had.

***

Smint was surprised when his car announced that he had arrived at Gettnor's house. Considering how many of his inventions Querx had patented—and made a killing from—Smint had been expecting something much more... ostentatious. This was simply one more ordinary house in a row of houses. Gettnor's share of the royalties on his inventions should have been worth tens of millions... shouldn't it?

Smint identified himself to the Gettnor's house AI. After a couple of minutes the door opened and Vaz said, "Dr. Smint! Come in. I'm sorry, coming up the stairs I realized I shouldn't show you the device while it's working because it emits a lot of x-rays and I haven't set up any shielding yet. Right now I'm only

117

designing the next iteration. But we could look at the data from the last run together if you'd like?"

Smint uneasily suspected that the *real* reason he didn't want to repeat the experiment was that it wasn't repeatable. Or that it only worked in Gettnor's imagination. Smint had spent some time last night looking into the science of fusion and according to everything he'd learned, the kind of fusion Vaz claimed was patently impossible without massive equipment. Nonetheless he smiled and said, "Please, Vaz, call me Jack. I'd love to see whatever you've got to show me."

He followed Vaz across the room and over to a door that proved to lead down into a basement. There was another door at the bottom of the stairs, Vaz opened it and they stepped into a large, well lit basement. Smint looked around in amazement. Typical Vaz, everything was impeccably arranged like for a catalog display. The basement appeared to be significantly better equipped than the lab Gettnor had worked in at Querx. Of course, at Querx, Gettnor had had access to other equipment in other labs so it probably wasn't really better equipped than Querx as a whole, but, still, there was an *amazing* amount of very expensive equipment here. As he turned he saw in one corner a cot, a mini-fridge, a microwave, a set of drawers and some clothes hanging from a pipe running under the ceiling. "You sleep down here?"

Gettnor looked embarrassed and shrugged, "Yeah, sometimes."

Jack also noticed a heavy punching bag and a speed bag like boxers practiced with, as well as a pull-up bar and some weights. They looked worn. "Looks like your son works out down here too."

Gettnor looked embarrassed about that too, "Uh sometimes," he mumbled, then perked up, "Here, sit, let me show you the data from the run."

Smint sat in one of the two rolling chairs and looked up at the large wall screen. It lit with a strangely colored image. Gettnor pointed at it, "That's a compressed spectrum video of the inside of the chamber. Over on the right you see graphic representations of the output from the chamber detectors for heat, alpha particles, x-rays, and neutrons. On the video image what you're looking at is a disk," he highlighted it, "of a new boron-vanadium-palladium disk which has already absorbed 1,500 times its volume of hydrogen overnight."

Smint's head pulled back in surprise at the huge amounts of hydrogen absorbed.

Vaz continued, "Which means that the boron atoms just have hydrogen protons absolutely *packed* in among them. The video starts when I turned on the pulsatile current that I had calculated would 'hammer,'" here Vaz put up his fingers and made little quotes marks in the air, "more protons into the alloy." Vaz turned excitedly to Smint, "And this is really freaky, it didn't work when I tried the same experiment without an odd electrode I used in the original device. I'd used it just because I had that electrode lying around the lab. That electrode was mounted on a ceramic base that had a concave shape and that ceramic turned out to be piezoelectric. So, with the pulsatile current it generates ultrasonic waves in the compressed hydrogen. I mean, that's just such a freak accident! Because of the concave shape, the ultrasound waves happen to focus on the disk. And, by my calculations they just happen to be about the right frequency to create a harmonic that should cause huge physical distortions in the molecular structure of the alloy. It would have been incredibly difficult to calculate how to achieve all these things at once if you were doing them on purpose, yet they all happened at the same time *by accident*!"

"All these things?" Smint said bemusedly.

119

"Yeah," Vaz said, "I mean, I had calculated that, by my new alloy theory, this particular alloy should absorb huge quantities of hydrogen. I'd also calculated that this particular frequency in the current should harmonically force the protons into the alloy. But it was just freaky luck that the current would generate ultrasonic waves and that they would be the right frequency to harmonically vibrate that particular thickness of disk so violently!" He waved at the screen, "Look, you can see that the alpha detector is starting to rise, now the x-ray detector is starting to rise, heat had been going up for a while because of the electrical and acoustic energy being pumped into the system… wait… wait… There, that's when the safety triggers shut it down because the x-rays had reached the safety limits I'd set. There already had been tremendous energy output in the form of alphas at that point."

Vaz turned excitedly to Smint, "Now I know exactly how much energy went into the system, just a little more than a quarter of a megajoule. My best estimate is that it put out about two megajoules, almost all of it in the few seconds after the x-rays appeared! There's no oxygen in the system to oxidize the hydrogen and really no evidence of substantial chemical reaction of any type to power that output. Even though I really can't believe it's from fusion, nothing else makes sense."

Smint had to grin at the rapidity of Gettnor's pressured speech.

Vaz said, "I'm thinking something about the highly compacted structure of the protons in the alloy, along with surging motion imparted by the current and harmonic motion from the acoustic impulses is forcing the protons to fuse with the boron nuclei at a significant rate…" He'd finally run down, "Though… I still find it… hard to believe… really, it's impossible." He grinned, "But you know what they say about 'when

120

theory and calculation comes into conflict with data'… 'you've got to go with the data.'"

Smint sat back in the chair, wondering if *he* could believe the data. Data could be faked, or made up, or be coming from sources an investigator didn't recognize. Fleishman and Pons weren't the only ones that had thought they had data demonstrating positive energy out of "cold fusion," then later been unable to replicate the data, or to have someone else point out where the extra energy they thought they had, had actually come from. "Ha… have you replicated the experiment yet?"

Vaz tilted his head, "Well there was the meltdown over at Querx. I don't have much data from that one except that there must have been a *lot* of energy released to melt a mostly stainless steel apparatus. Then I tried to replicate it without the piezo electrode and it didn't work. After that I simultaneously replicated it with a copy of the original Querx device and my new device with a new piezo electrode.

"So, I guess you could say three successful replications, except that two of those I don't have much data from. The one at Querx and the replication with the copy of the Querx device didn't have any internal detectors for the heat, alpha particles etc. because I tried to copy the original device exactly. I've been wanting to do another replication, but have been making myself wait until I have the new properly shielded reactor with coils to harvest the energy from the alpha particles. Then I'll have an even better measurement of the energy output." He turned almost eagerly to Smint, "Do you think I should do another replication with the device I've got? I could buy some lead sheeting to shield the x-rays."

Bemused, Smint said, "No, no, I think you should wait and do it right."

Vaz sighed, "Yeah, that's what I think too." He grinned and rubbed his hands together, "And this time

I'll be able to publish my results! I hated that Querx always wanted to keep the results secret."

Feeling like a traitor to a friend, Smint said, "Speaking of Querx. Is there any chance that you'd go back to work for them? They're ready to offer a lot."

Gettnor looked uncomfortable, "Lisanne wants me to. But… you know they sent a guy over here to threaten me, telling me to go back to work. Like I'd work for someone because I'd been threatened!"

Smint drew back, wide eyed with startlement, "They what?!"

"Well," Vaz tilted his head considering, "a big guy showed up here saying, 'you need to go back to work for…' He didn't actually say Querx, but the police figured it had to be Querx. It's the only company I've worked for in years."

"Christ!" Smint breathed. "I doubt that Querx authorized that. It sounds like something that idiot Davis would have done on his own once Vangester put pressure on him."

Vaz shrugged, "Besides, I like being able to do whatever projects I want. I hated always being told to work on this or that. And it'll be cool to be able to publish my results again."

Smint nodded and sighed, "Why does Lisanne want you to go back to work??"

"She's worried about having enough money to send the kids to college."

Surprised, Smint said, "But you must have a *lot* of money from your royalties."

Vaz nodded, "Almost three million, but Lisanne doesn't know about *that* money."

Smint was startled on many levels. First, that Vaz would share his net worth so freely. Second, that it was so much smaller than he'd expected, and third that his wife wouldn't know about it. He addressed the last one first, "Lisanne doesn't know?"

"Uh, yeah. When the money first started coming in she'd been pushing me to go on a vacation to the Caribbean or somewhere." He looked sheepish, "I don't like strange places." He shrugged, "So I put it in a separate account, didn't tell her about the money and she finally decided we couldn't afford the trip. I haven't figured out how to tell her about the money without making her really mad about that vacation. And… and…" throatily he finished, "I hate hiding it from her. It's almost the same as lying I think."

Smint resisted the temptation to ask why Vaz was afraid to travel. Then he decided not to point out that Lisanne would almost certainly be more relieved to have money to send her children to college than she'd be mad about missing a vacation. Instead he said, "Still, I would think you'd have saved up a lot more than that from your inventions. Have you been spending the money on something else?"

"No. The inventions don't pay all that much. You'd be surprised."

Smint sat back, astonished, "Don't pay that much? Querx has made *billions* on them. Last I saw, it was over nine billion. One percent of a billion is ten million. Aren't they paying you…" he frowned, "I thought the company hiring agreement said they were supposed to pay somewhere around two percent of gross to the inventor? And I think 30% of net royalties collected when they license to others?"

"Yeah, they were paying that much initially. Then they said that after the first five hundred thousand it dropped to a percent and after the first million, to a tenth of a percent. Three percent of licensing."

Smint's eyes widened in dismay. He'd thought that they might not be paying him quite what they should but, if this was true, they had been absolutely *screwing* Gettnor for years. And *he'd* had no idea. "Holy crap!" he breathed.

"What?"

Smint held up a finger, asking for a moment to think. He was there at Gettnor's house to negotiate for Querx. He'd taken that assignment in good faith and he liked to think of himself as an honorable man. But it didn't sound like there was any way that he could talk Vaz into going back to work for them anyway. *And*, he'd developed a sudden loathing and distrust for the company that he was negotiating for. Finally he turned to Vaz, "They shouldn't have done that."

Vaz frowned, "No, they said that's how things were done."

"Vaz, you're too trusting about things like this."

"Really?"

"Yes!" Jack said patiently, "They should be paying you two percent on the entire thing. And thirty percent of what Querx gets if they license it to someone else. I'll bet they show the change to a tenth in their records as a 'renegotiation.'"

"Why would they do that?"

"Because, they legally can't change it without a renegotiation, but I'll bet they just told you that was how it was and when you didn't object called it a 'renegotiation.'"

"No, I mean why would they change it?"

"It probably wasn't so much for the money." He frowned, "Though it *was* a lot of money. But they're getting plenty after all. I'll bet that they were worried that if you had too much money, that you'd quit working for them and they wouldn't have you inventing more stuff."

"Really? Why did they fire me then, if they wanted me to work for them so badly?"

"Case of the right hand not knowing what the left one was doing. They put that idiot Davis in charge of R&D without telling him how important you were. I tried to tell him, but he didn't want to listen to me."

"So, if I went back to work for them, that's what they mean by paying me more of the royalty?"

"Yeah, they're paying you a pittance, so they'd be happy to pay you more to get you to go back to work for them."

"So, do you think I should go back to work for them? So that I could 'renegotiate' that royalty?"

"Well... you could. You could also have a lawyer look into the legality of their paying you less than their original agreement. But, you know, if you went back to work for them they'd feel like they owned your new stuff on fusion, assuming it works."

Gettnor frowned, "I hate that kind of legal stuff... Do you know anyone who would do it for me?"

"Do what?"

"Figure out the legal stuff."

"A lawyer you mean?"

"Well, hire a lawyer, and figure out what's the best thing to do. Go back or stay on my own."

Smint tilted his head, thinking. If this fusion thing actually did work, he'd like to be a part of it, he thought, though he wasn't sure why. He had already retired. He had enough money to live on. Everything he knew about fusion said it wasn't going to work. But, the things he'd seen Gettnor do so far were... amazing. Betting against him on something scientific seemed crazy. And it would be nice to have plenty of money, and to leave something of substance for his kids and grandkids. He said, "I... could do it... kind of be your 'business manager.' First I'd have to resign the contract work I'm doing for Querx, because it'd be in conflict."

"What are you doing for them?"

"They hired me on a contract, just to try to get you to come back to work."

"Really?" Vaz said, a puzzled look on his face.

"Really."

"And... instead, you'd actually work for me?"

125

Smint nodded.

"How much would you charge?"

"A percentage? Say five percent?"

Vaz frowned, "Percent of what?"

Smint wasn't sure whether Gettnor was kidding or could actually be that obtuse. "Uh, if I negotiate you another one percent on your royalties, I get a tenth of a percent. I could help you with patenting your fusion tech, if it works, too. Also for five percent of whatever you get."

"Really? But what if you work hard on it and don't negotiate anything, or we can't get a patent, or something?"

Smint tilted his head again, "Then that'd be my loss. An impetus to work hard to negotiate something for you, eh?"

"OK, if you really want to… sure, I'd appreciate it. I'm really not any good at any of that kind of stuff."

Smint left Gettnor's house with a plan to come back in a few days with a legal agreement for them to sign. First he had to get out of his contract with Querx, then figure out what legal firm to work with. Gettnor estimated it would be several weeks before the parts arrived and the next version of the fusion device was finished. This apparently depended on how many parts he could buy and how many he'd have to have machined or constructed. They'd get together then to see how it worked.

While Smint was there, Vaz hadn't been very upset, but after he left Vaz sat and thought over the things he'd learned about Querx. Eventually he was shaking with tension and anger. He couldn't concentrate on the design of the new fusion test device until he pounded the bag a while and flogged himself doing sit-ups, pull-ups and push-ups. Near the end though, he achieved a giant endorphin release and afterward experienced one of his omniscient periods that allowed him to rapidly see the way through to finishing his design.

***

Lisanne sent Vaz a message,

"You haven't seen or talked to your children for weeks now. If I promise not to try to talk to you about your job, would you eat dinner with us tonight?"

Vaz had just finished ordering the last parts for his fusion device and had begun to wonder what to do next, so he messaged back, "Sure." He climbed the stairs and started looking through the kitchen to see what there was to cook for dinner.

Lisanne stepped in from the garage and her heart leapt to see Vaz in front of the stove. She took a deep whiff of the delightful smells wafting out of the kitchen and she crossed the room. "Thanks for cooking Vaz." She put her arms around his narrow waist and marveled once again at how firm it was.
"Hey, no problem."
"What'cha makin'?"
He shrugged, "I guess you'd say it was Mexican."
Lisanne desperately wanted to talk to Vaz about a thousand different things including whether he had applied for any jobs, however, she bit her tongue in favor of having her family together for a dinner. "Can I do anything?"
"Call down the kids. It's about ready."

Dante came down the stairs and his eyes widened to see his dad dishing up the food. He'd been thinking that his parents were getting a divorce.

127

He hadn't seen his mom and dad in the same room for weeks now and wasn't completely sure his dad still lived in their house. As he pulled out his chair he said, "Hey Dad, welcome back."

Lisanne's eyes widened at a cordial greeting from one of their surly kids. Though, upon reflection, the "welcome back" comment might have been a dig.

Vaz looked a little surprised, "I haven't been gone."

"You haven't been eating with us."

Vaz looked embarrassed, "Uh, yeah, I've been... working on a project."

"And not eating?"

"Uh, yeah, I just heat something quick in the basement."

"Whatever..." he studied his dad, "I've got a wrestling match tomorrow night. Can you come to it?"

Vaz looked even more surprised. Though Lisanne had badgered Vaz to go to meets and he did go sometimes, Dante had never actually invited him to one himself. He glanced up at his HUD to be sure he didn't have anything scheduled and said, "Sure. Is it at your school?"

"Yeah. Five o'clock. Maybe you could give me some pointers?"

"Uh, I haven't wrestled since I was in high school."

Dante hadn't known his dad had ever wrestled. But of course, he hadn't known he fought MMA until recently either. He grinned, "Yeah, but... you know." Dante shrugged and lifted an eyebrow enigmatically.

Looking puzzled, Vaz shrugged and said, "Sure, if I see anything."

Sounding irritated, Lisanne called up the stairs again. "Tiona!"

A moment later Tiona bounced down the stairs, still talking to someone over her AI. Her eyes widened when she saw her dad sitting at the table. "Dad?"

Vaz looked blandly up at her. "Uh huh?"

"You're eating with us?"

Vaz only nodded.

Tiona looked back and forth between her mother and father. "What's going on between you two?"

"Nothing," they answered simultaneously.

Tiona rolled her eyes. "So, do you have enough money to send us to college or not?"

Lisanne said, "Somehow," while Vaz only nodded.

Tiona lifted an eyebrow doubtfully, "Okaay. If you say so."

With some frustration Lisanne said, "Tiona! Don't *worry* about it. We'll get you through school somehow. Your education is our first priority." She turned to Vaz, "Right?"

To Lisanne's immense irritation, Vaz frowned as if considering, then said, "Uh huh."

Dante pointed his fork at his plate, "This is really good. What's it called?"

Vaz, looking a little embarrassed, said, "Mexican food."

"Well, yeah, I can tell that, but what... what's its name?

Vaz shrugged again, "Mexican lasagna?"

"Oh, with tortillas instead of noodles?"

"Kinda."

Abruptly, Tiona announced, "'Vita's parents just declared bankruptcy."

Lisanne put her hand over her mouth, "Oh! That's terrible."

Dante exclaimed, "But... they're rich! They have that big house and... and... her dad drives a Mercedes..."

Vaz said calmly, "Just because you *spend* a lot of money doesn't mean you *have* a lot of money." He put a forkful of the lasagna in his mouth.

Indignantly, Tiona said, "But you guys don't even spend any money! You aren't actually going to be able to send us to college, are you?!"

Vaz looked at her, a furrow between his brows. "Yes we will."

Tiona snorted, "I think I'll be taking out loans *if* I decide to go."

***

Vangester looked up as Smint entered his office. "Any luck?"

"No. Not a chance in Hell. Davis completely burned any chances of your ever getting him back. Do you know a big guy showed up at Gettnor's house and threatened him if he didn't go back to work for you? Who does that sound like?"

Vangester grimaced, "Davis!" He said it like it was an expletive. "Goddammit!"

***

Vaz climbed the stairs from the basement to go to Dante's meet. When he opened the door, Lisanne got up off the couch and picked up her purse. He looked at her warily.

She smiled, "I thought I'd go to the meet with you."

"I thought you didn't like wrestling."

"I don't. But I love my family. This way I get to go *with* one of them, to *watch* another and get ulcers about whether or not he's going to get hurt."

"Are you going to badger me...?"

Lisanne quirked the corner of her mouth. "No. I'd like to, but I promise I'll leave you alone."

"OK."

At the meet, Vaz found himself comparing the wrestling moves he saw to the things he'd been learning at Mike's. Though he thought that some of the things he'd learned would certainly help win matches, he wasn't sure how many of the things he'd recently learned would be legal moves in wrestling. It felt odd to him to be watching a sport that only had grappling, no striking allowed.

He thought to himself that wrestling wouldn't be nearly as satisfying to him. When *he* fought, the opportunity to actually hit someone provided a huge release.

If only he could find an opponent that he could hit more than once or twice.

Then Dante came out into the ring. Vaz leaned forward in excitement; Lisanne gripped Vaz's hand and gave a little shudder. Dante aggressively shot a takedown but his opponent successfully sprawled and despite valiant efforts Dante couldn't take him down. The first period looked like a draw to Vaz. In the second period Dante started in the down position. He exploded out of the defensive position, scoring points for that, and then surprised his opponent with a sudden takedown. Vaz rose to his feet in excitement. Lisanne said, "Is he winning?"

Dante shrugged and said excitedly, "I think so." Then Dante's opponent tried an escape that Dante appeared to have anticipated. He caught him mid move and suddenly pinned him.

The ref stood them up and raised a grinning Dante's hand. With a tone of wonderment, Lisanne said, "He won?"

Vaz nodded cheerfully, "He won."

Lisanne clapped her hands and stamped her foot enthusiastically. She hugged Vaz. "I'm glad I came. I thought I'd hate it, but it's really pretty exciting… Well, I guess it is, as long as he wins… and doesn't get hurt."

When the meet was over, Lisanne surprised Vaz by wanting to go down and congratulate Dante. Vaz had always just gone home once the meet was finished. Sometimes as soon as Dante had wrestled. Dante's team had won the meet and so everyone was pretty excited and bouncing around. The hyper crowd made Vaz a little uncomfortable but he managed to stay calm. Dante saw them and came over grinning, "Mom! You came too? How'd you like it?"

"It was fun, though I don't think I would have liked it if you'd lost."

"Bite your tongue! *That's* not gonna happen."

The coach turned, "Mr. and Mrs. Gettnor?"

Dante turned to him, "Yeah, Coach Avery. This is my mom and dad. Mom's never come to a meet before. Afraid I'll get hurt."

"Oh, no Ma'am. Don't worry about that. It's the other guys that have to worry. I'm pretty sure Don's going to win State if he can just stay in the 74 kilo weight class."

Vaz and Lisanne glanced at one another. Dante had implied he was winning some matches but not that he might be doing that well.

Dante had turned back to his parents, "I might get a scholarship to help pay for college."

Lisanne said, "That's wonderful!" at the same time that Vaz said, "You shouldn't worry about that."

They glanced at one another but then Dante asked, "Got any pointers for me Dad?"

Coach Avery said, "Did you wrestle, Mr. Gettnor?"

Vaz shrugged, embarrassed. "Back when I was in school. I certainly don't have anything to offer that your coach wouldn't be able to tell you better than

I, Dante," at a grimace from Dante, Vaz quickly corrected himself to, "Don."

As they broke up Lisanne started talking to Steve's mother, leaving Vaz and Dante next to one another. Dante raised an eyebrow, "Suggestions, Dad?"

Vaz tilted his head. "Really, Vaz, it's been forever. You're a much better wrestler than I ever was. I couldn't offer you any suggestions."

Dante said, "Come on Dad! I *know* you know more about it than you're letting on."

Vaz drew his head back in surprise. "Why would you think that?"

Dante waved a hand in dismissal, "OK. You can't help, I get it. I'm goin' out to dinner with Steve, OK?"

"Sure...?" Vaz watched Dante walk away in bemusement. *What gave him the idea that I'd be the right person to ask for wrestling tips?*

***

Gettnor's house AI unlocked the door for Smint and said, "Go on down to the basement Dr. Smint. Dr. Gettnor is waiting for you."

Jack opened the door, went inside and headed down the stairs. For a moment he wondered if he should knock on the door at the bottom of the stairs, but decided he'd already been invited. Opening it he said, "Vaz?"

"Hey Jack. Almost ready."

Gettnor was sitting on his rolling chair, screwing bolts down the side of a long stainless steel pipe about a foot in diameter. Cables appeared to be entering the pipe in several locations and it was suspended from the ceiling above with sets of ropes. Since Smint had last been there, a huge steel tank had been installed in the basement. "Wow, that's quite a setup!"

"Yeah," Gettnor said, standing up and patting the pipe. "The apparatus is inside this big tube. Now we've got to get it into the tank. Can you man the ropes over there?"

Smint took hold of the ropes at the right end of the pipe, saying "Tank?"

"Yeah, we need neutron and x-ray shielding so I welded up this big stainless steel tank and lined it with boron. With the device in the center of it we'll have a meter of water, surrounded by boron to absorb neutrons and two layers of steel to absorb x-rays." Vaz directed Smint and they used the ropes to lift the pipe up over the edge and slowly out to the middle of the tank where it floated on the surface. Then they changed to a different set of ropes and pulled it down into a cradle inside the tank, watching their progress with a tiny video camera inside the tank. Other cameras inside the pipe confirmed that the contents of the pipe were staying dry. Finally they pulled covering plates over the top of the tank.

Vaz pushed his chair back over to his control station saying, "Still dry inside, good." He washed his hands together excitedly, "OK, the disk is already loaded with hydrogen. You ready to fire it up Jack?"

Smiling at Gettnor's enthusiasm Smint said, "Sure."

"OK, here goes the hammering current."

They sat watching for a while without much happening. Then some of the graphic indicators started to rise on one of the screens. Vaz excitedly said, "OK, x-rays and heat climbing. Oh, and look at the current! Wow, we're really generating some power!"

"Do you have detectors out here in the room to be sure we aren't getting any x-ray leakage?"

"Yeah, the two flat lines at the bottom are the x-ray and neutron detectors out here in the room with us. Wow! It's really starting to heat up." He gave a command to his AI and turned back to Jack, "I'm running some liquid nitrogen through the frame of the device to keep it cool. We're not going to have any meltdowns today!"

Later that afternoon Smint and Gettnor leaned back and looked at one another in giddy near disbelief. There could be no doubt; the device had generated enormous numbers of alpha particles which had induced *huge* currents in the coils. Fusion was the only possible explanation for that and for the much greater energy produced as compared to what the device consumed. The fact that there were relatively few neutrons released confirmed that it was aneutronic fusion which pretty much had to be due to the hydrogen-boron reaction. Smint put up his hand for a "high five."

Vaz stared at his hand.

"You're supposed to slap your palm against mine."

"Why?"

"Celebration, congratulations, high five! Haven't you ever done it?"

"Oh, no. But I've heard of it." He smacked Jack's palm so hard it stung, leaving Jack shaking his hand out.

"Damn! You don't have to break my hand! It's more like a clap."

"Oh, sorry." Vaz looked embarrassed.

Jack looked surreptitiously at Gettnor. The baggy sweats he wore gave the impression of someone hiding a big gut… but might just be baggy. To look at his face, he wasn't carrying much extra fat. "I'll start talking to someone about a patent. I'm thinking that I'd like to work with Jim Milton. He's done most of the patent work for Querx so I've gotten to know and trust him over the years. I don't feel like his relationship with Querx will affect his ability to work with us. Would that be a problem for you?"

Vaz shrugged, "I don't know much about these kinds of things Dr. Smint, that's why I'm so grateful that you're willing to deal with them. Whoever you think we should go with is fine with me. I'll be happily working on the apparatus, trying to improve it 'cause it's pretty inefficient right now."

"Call me Jack."

"Uh, OK, please call me Vaz."

***

James Milton leaned back in his chair. "Cold fusion! Come on! You don't *really* believe it works do you?"

Smint shrugged, "Yes, I know, it *shouldn't* be possible. That's what everyone says, but I've watched him run a cycle on his apparatus, it actually *does* work."

"Well, we can't just submit a patent for that like you can for other things. Just like perpetual motion machines, you have to have a working model to submit a patent on cold fusion."

Smint said, "We have that, how are we going to show it to them though?"

Milton laughed, "*I* don't know. Never had to do it. I'll have to call them and ask. Probably whoever I talk to won't know how it's done either, 'cause it probably just doesn't get done."

"Can they fly down here to look at it? It might be pretty hard to take it up there and set it up?"

"I'll ask, but that'll cost more money. Querx probably won't mind that though. Not if they think they'll get a patent for fusion anyway."

Smint's eyes had widened, "We don't work for Querx anymore! I hope you haven't said anything to anyone over there about this?"

It was Milton's turn to look startled, "Uh, I was at a local dinner meeting for patent attorneys last night and saw Phil Dennis. You know, the in house counsel for Querx. Because I knew we were meeting today I said something to him about Gettnor 'doing it again.' Of course, I didn't know anything about what the IP (intellectual property) was and certainly not that you thought you had cold fusion, so I couldn't have given much away. Come to think of it, he did look a little surprised when I said it."

Smint sighed. "Crap! I really didn't want them knowing about it until much later in the process."

"Why not, if neither of you work for them anymore, it doesn't have anything to do with them does it?"

"No. But they may try to claim it does," Smint said ominously. "On another issue, they modified Gettnor's contract with them to reduce his cut of the royalties from all of his other inventions, reducing it from an original two percent of gross or thirty percent of licensing, down to a tenth of a percent of gross and three percent of licensing."

"Why did he agree to that?"

"Come on, you've talked to him haven't you? He's absolutely clueless about this kind of stuff."

"But they must have gotten him to sign a modification of his original employment contract. Wouldn't even *he* have gotten suspicious over that?"

"I don't think they did. He says he's sure he didn't sign any documents to that effect. I think they just told him they were changing it, implying that that was what was supposed to happen after he'd gotten a million dollars from it. Then I'm betting that when he didn't object they put the audio-video record of his lack of complaint on file as 'agreement' to the change."

"Damn!" Milton breathed, "I suppose it would depend on exactly how it was done but I don't think that would hold up in court. The courts have been accepting a lot of audio-video recorded agreements as binding but generally there needs to be evidence that the parties both understand they are entering a negotiated agreement."

"Would you be able to help us take them to court?"

"Oh my goodness no. That's not my field, and besides, I'm hardly an uninterested party. Querx is my largest client. You'd never be sure I was doing my best for you. I can refer you to someone who has a lot of experience with the ramifications of 'contracts' bound by audio-video records."

***

Phil Dennis knocked on the door of Gettnor's lab and stuck his head around the corner. Gettnor was supposed to tell Dennis about patentable IP before he talked to any attorneys and obviously he needed a reminder. "Dr. Gettnor?" His eyes widened as he saw a couple of the lab techs from the battery lab in there. Gettnor was famous for being a loner and Phil had never seen anyone but Gettnor himself in his lab.

The people in the lab looked curiously at him, "Uh, Dr. Gettnor doesn't work at Querx anymore," one of them ventured.

"What? That can't be, he's talking to our patent attorney about a new patent of some kind."

"Not a Querx patent then, he got fired weeks ago."

"Who in the world would have done a dumb ass thing like that?"

138

"Uh, it was Mr. Davis, the department head. Uh, Davis has been fired too and the rumor is, that it was, like you say, because he did something truly 'dumb ass,'" he grinned, "like firing Gettnor."

After an hour or so spent trying to track down what happened to Gettnor, Phil wound up in Vangester's office. Wide eyed he began his conversation with "Davis fired Gettnor?!"

Looking grim, Vangester nodded. "*Goddamn* him anyway."

"Nobody told him how important Gettnor was?"

Vangester sighed. "I assumed Smint would brief him before he left. Apparently, hard as it may be to believe, he avoided talking to his predecessor." Vangester closed his eyes and shook his head, "Smint even went to his office unannounced to try to 'give him a clue,' but it didn't sink in. Ultimately, I'm the idiot who put Davis in position to screw things up so royally. The board is probably going to have my ass if I can't find a solution for this debacle."

"Jim Milton let slip that Smint and Gettnor are applying for a patent on something. I don't think he knew that they weren't working for us any more or he would have kept it confidential."

Vangester's eyes had widened, "Smint!?"

Phil nodded.

"You've got to be shittin' me! We hired Smint as a consultant to try to get Gettnor back on our payroll. He said it couldn't be done! I'll bet the SOB found out that Gettnor had some cool new IP and decided to do an end run on us, trying to get a piece of it for himself."

Phil shrugged, "Maybe. But Gettnor only left a few months ago right?"

Vangester's eyes widened, "Yeah. Are you thinking that whatever they're patenting is something he figured out while he worked here, so we own it anyway?"

Phil frowned and pulled on his ear, "Maybe."

"That'd be great! You start checking through the records of what Gettnor was working on here before he left. Materials requisitions, lab records, video records from the security cameras in his labs, conversations he might have had with other researchers. Whatever you can find. I'll start working on finding out what those bastards are actually patenting. Then we'll determine if the two are related."

Phil scratched his head uncertainly, "I'm not sure I'd know what Gettnor was doing from watching vids."

"Then have one of the scientists analyze whatever you find."

***

Ben Carter looked up as a student stepped into his office. He glanced at his HUD. "Ms. Gettnor?"

She nodded and took the seat he indicated.

"How can I help you?"

"I'm trying to figure out what kind of college scholarships I might be eligible for?"

"Your parents can't afford to send you?" He was a little surprised. Most families that sent their kids to Allenton Prep could afford college for those selfsame kids. There were a few kids here on scholarship of course but, he glanced up at his HUD again, Tiona Gettnor wasn't one of them. Generally if you couldn't afford college, you couldn't afford Allenton.

"I don't think so." Tiona shrugged, looking uncomfortable.

He frowned, "What do they say?"

"They say they can, but they seem broke. I think I'd better come up with… something on my own."

Carter studied her. She looked like she might break down and cry. "Are there other problems in your home?"

Eyes glistening, she nodded.

Carter felt himself tense at the thought that this pretty young girl was being abused. "Who's doing it?"

She looked puzzled, "Doing what?"

"Whatever… they're doing that has you upset."

"My Mom and Dad."

Feeling like he was pulling teeth, he asked, "And what are they doing?"

In a small voice she said, "I think they're getting a divorce." She hadn't grasped until that moment just how worried she felt about the possibility of a divorce or how much she didn't want it to happen. She realized that if someone had asked her a couple of months ago if she cared if her parents got a divorce, she would have said "no." But now that her family actually seemed to be falling apart, she realized suddenly that their little unit of four held tremendous importance for her.

Relief exploded over Carter that it wasn't abuse, though he carefully didn't show it, "So they aren't actually doing anything *to* you?"

She looked puzzled a moment then exclaimed, "Oh! No!"

Relaxing back into his chair he said, "But if they aren't getting along, it must make you feel pretty awful, huh?"

She sniffed and nodded, a tear beginning to track down her cheek.

Carter picked up the box of tissues he kept for these occasions and offered her one. "It's important

141

that you understand that your parent's relationship with one another is not your responsibility or your fault. Are you comfortable with that?"

Tiona shrugged uncertainly.

"In any case I'm very sorry to hear about this. Have they already started proceedings?"

She shrugged and whispered, "I don't think so."

"So, is your biggest concern that your family will break up, or that you won't be able to go to college?"

She sniffed, "Both."

He thought for a moment. "Let's talk about college first. What do you want to study?"

Gettnor wiped her nose and said, "Physics."

His eyes widened. He just hadn't expected that. "Physics! That's great! Not all that many girls want to go into the field. What do you like about it?"

"I'm good at math," she said quietly. "And I like all science classes, but especially the parts that I think have to do physics, even though I haven't had an actual physics class yet." She frowned, "Though I'm not sure that I should study it."

"Why not?"

"My Dad's a physicist, but he doesn't make very much money. That's a big part of why I don't think they'll be able to send me to school."

"I think most physicists make decent money. Who does he work for?"

"Querx."

"I've heard of them, they're doing pretty well. I'm surprised that they don't pay well."

Tiona shrugged.

Carter had his AI call up data on the average physicists salary and throw it up on the screen on his wall. "Here, check this; it looks like most physicists get paid pretty well."

She looked up at it a moment, then sniffed disconsolately, "My brother's seen one of his pay statements. He doesn't get paid nearly that well." She drooped, "But he's pretty weird… so I guess he might not be very good at it."

"Weird?"

"Yeah, he shaves his head… and eyebrows… and," she dropped to a whisper, "he kinda lives in the basement. We don't see him very much."

Carter didn't say anything for a bit. He'd seen Tiona in the hallways of the school many times and would never have guessed that anything was wrong. He was often caught by surprise to find that the same young people he saw laughing and apparently full of confidence around their friends, frequently turned out to feel quite insecure when he talked to them in his office. Tiona had seemed so ebullient and self-assured whenever he'd seen her around the school. Finally, he said, "Let me look at your grades." He glanced up at his HUD and his eyebrows rose. She took a lot of advanced placement classes and so far had perfect grades leading to a GPA far above 4.0 by their current grading system. In fact he hadn't seen a GPA that high for years. She might be displaying a lack of confidence here in his office, but she was on the track team and had won a lot of middle distance events last year. She had just been elected was vice president of her class. He looked back at her, "You've got great grades and activities. We should be able to get you an academic scholarship of some kind. Have you taken the SAT yet?"

She didn't look up as she said in a low voice, "Next week."

"All right then, do well on that and we'll get you a scholarship!" He tried to sound upbeat.

She nodded, eyes still on the floor. "What about my parents?"

He felt helpless, wondering how she thought that he could do anything about her parents' marital problems. "Do you know why they're having problems?"

"Money."

Carter sighed, *it's always money*, he thought. "Are they in debt?"

"I don't think so. I think they're just worried that they don't have enough to send us to college."

Carter glanced up at his HUD. Dante Gettnor was her brother. He must be the other part of "us." He leaned back, "So you feel like if you got a scholarship it might take some stress off of them?"

Her eyes widened. It didn't look like she'd thought of that before. "Maybe."

"Sometimes kids bring their own problems home with them and are in a bad mood around their family. They might not even realize it, but that can put a lot of stress on their parents. Do you think that might be happening?"

Tiona looked a little bit embarrassed, "Uh, maybe."

"So, can I offer a summary of suggestions?"

"Uh huh."

"Do well on the SAT, we'll get you a scholarship. De-stress your parent's money concerns by telling them that you're *planning* to get a scholarship and that I think you've got a good chance. *Talk* to them about your worries and ask what you might be able to do to help them. Especially, try to be upbeat around them so your own funk doesn't contribute to theirs."

She stared at him for a moment. Her voice broke, "You make it sound easy, but it's not."

He shrugged, "All you can do… is all you can do."

She sighed and stood, "Yeah."

After she'd left he stared after her a moment, wondering if he'd made any dent in her problems.

***

Jack Smint opened the door of James Milton's patent office and went inside without noticing that the car behind him had gone on to park a little farther down the street.

The PI inside the car focused his laser acoustic transducer on the window of the small office building. He expected to have to turn it from window to window until he heard Jack Smint's voice but it picked him up on the first window it hit. He heard Smint say, "It worked again! Without a doubt! We can demonstrate it to whoever you want. Even though it would be good if they could come here, we can work out a way to take the equipment up there too."

In his office Milton stared at Smint. "You're absolutely sure? 'Cause I've done some reading and a lot of very smart people say it just isn't possible."

Jack said, "Yeah, I've read the same stuff. Because of that I've checked every instrument and reading Vaz has done and unless he's gone to extreme lengths just to fool me, it's real."

Milton leaned back, "OK, I've drafted a preliminary application. Give me the diagrams of the final setup. I'll finish the app, have you guys look it over and we can send it in. Then we'll wait for them to tell us how and where they want to look at it."

***

Vangester looked up as the PI stepped into his office. "What have you found out?"

"Smint just left Gettnor's place and drove over to James Milton's patent office. They're pretty excited about something. Don't know what it is yet, but they're applying for a patent and it sounds like they have buyers interested. They're already talking about 'demonstrating' it to someone. I assume as soon as they have 'patent applied for' status."

"Sons of bitches! They're gonna regret crossing me like this." As he walked the PI out, he turned to his secretary and said, "Have Phil Dennis come up and talk to me."

Phil stepped into Vangester's office. "You called?"

"Yeah, it looks like you were right. Smint and Vangester are patenting *something*. What can we do about it?"

Phil shrugged, "Maybe nothing if there isn't any evidence that it was actually invented here."

"Well? What have you found out? Was Gettnor working on something before he left?"

Phil tilted his head, "Of course he was working on *something*. He was assigned to work on hydrogen storage and was doing just that. Right before he was fired he'd been casting little disks of a variety of compositions, all containing palladium."

Vangester interrupted, "Casting disks? What would that have to do with hydrogen storage?"

Phil shrugged, "I had the same question. The geeks downstairs tell me that palladium absorbs large quantities of hydrogen. We're assuming that Gettnor was trying to find an alloy that absorbed more, or maybe that absorbed nearly as much but didn't cost so much."

"So, did he succeed?"

"We don't know. The day Davis fired him he had one of the disks in a device he'd made in the lab. We think the device was to measure hydrogen absorption but we aren't sure."

Vangester frowned, "Can't you just test it or take it apart and figure out what it does?"

146

"The device melted down quite spectacularly in front of Davis. The meltdown was a big part of Gettnor getting fired. Davis called him a menace and yelled at him about sleeping on the job, then told him that security would be down to escort him out. Of note, Gettnor didn't seem upset about it melting down; he looked excited."

"What?! Why wouldn't he be upset?"

Dennis shrugged, "Damned if I know. One thing we're pretty sure of, and that might give you some leverage, is that he took some of the disks when he left."

"Really…" Vangester breathed, "*how* do we know?"

"When the security guy was trying to get him to leave, Gettnor scooped up a bunch of the disks and put them in his pocket. The security guy insisted that he put them back, but we're pretty sure that there were still quite a few left in his pocket when he left."

Vangester drew his head back, "Can we prove it?"

"Maybe not conclusively, but I think 'any reasonable observer' of the record would conclude that he took a lot fewer disks back out of that pocket than he dumped in."

"'Any reasonable observer' being some kind of legal term right?"

Dennis nodded.

"All right! Good pickup. Now, just what can we do with this ammunition?"

Dennis shrugged, "Who knows? Depends on what his new invention is. If it's a new kitchen slicer and dicer, we probably can't do anything. If it has one of those disks in it, then we can probably claim a share."

Vangester enthusiastically rubbed his hands together, "Now we're getting somewhere. We just need to know what they're patenting."

"We won't know that until the patent application is published in eighteen months."

"You might be surprised."

Dennis raised an eyebrow, "I hope you're not going to tell me how you plan to do that."

"My little secret. You *have* made sure that nobody's going to throw away the rest of those disks haven't you?"

"Yeah, oh and that's another indication that he kept some. The machine he used to cast samples made a run of 100 disks of different compositions the night before he got fired. There are only 83 of them left in the stuff we boxed up from his lab."

"Even better, right?"

Dennis shrugged, "Sure. My advice?"

Vangester raised his eyebrows questioningly.

"*Don't* do anything illegal. In these days, with audio-video records of everything, it's too easy to get caught."

Vangester's face smoothed, "Of course not," he said.

Dennis thought, *he protesteth too much.*

***

Mike shook his head. Gettnor had come in and asked to be taught wrestling techniques. Mike had tried to point out that striking had worked pretty damn well for him in his sparring with Durson and in his amateur MMA bout. Gettnor had insisted however.

That had been during last week's lesson. Mike had confessed he didn't really know what grappling holds were legal in wrestling but had promised to look it up by this week's lesson. Today he'd spent the lesson teaching legal wrestling techniques to Gettnor and Durson who'd recently become his regular training partner.

Then he'd suggested that Gettnor and Durson try the moves out full on. Normally Mike trained all moves slow motion and practiced with great care to be sure no one got hurt. But, since wrestling skills seemed much less likely than striking techniques to really hurt someone, he'd thought it would be OK for them to actually take each other on, as long as they followed the wrestling rules.

Since Durson was quite a bit bigger than Gettnor, and seemed to be nearly as muscular, Mike had thought that Durson would have the definite advantage.

Hah! Gettnor had scored takedown after takedown, quickly wrapping Durson up and pinning him in 30-60 seconds each time. The expression on Durson's face was priceless. Durson had always thought his knockout was pure luck and apparently believed, like Mike had thought, that when and if they sparred again, he would win like he should have the first time.

The power in Gettnor's limbs seemed all out of proportion to his size. Sure he looked really muscular when the baggy sweats he always wore got pulled aside, but Mike had known a lot of guys who *looked* ripped, yet didn't seem to be all that strong. The appearance of being ripped was as much a lack of fat covering the muscle as it was actual muscle. But Gettnor was *strong*. If Durson got a good hold on him he just broke it. Gettnor didn't have to have a decent hold on Durson to pin him with it. Durson's eyes were wide with surprise each time he got pinned but he seemed as helpless as a beginner in the hands of a powerful and experienced fighter as his limbs were forced inexorably into whatever position Gettnor wanted.

While Durson was putting away his stuff, Gettnor turned to Mike and said quietly, "Durson is big, but doesn't really seem to be all that strong."

Mike raised an eyebrow, "Oh, Durson's strong all right. You're just unbelievable. Would you like me to arrange some more amateur MMA bouts for you?"

Gettnor shook his head. "No. I'm not mad at anyone anymore so I don't really need a fight. In fact this is the final lesson of the last set I bought, so I'm going to stop the lessons for a while. Thanks for what you've taught me." He turned and walked out the door.

Mike shook his head as he watched Gettnor leave. *Completely typical*, he thought. *No "goodbye," no handshake*. Mike had the feeling that to remember to say the "thanks" or other polite niceties Gettnor had had to consciously give it thought. Not that he was opposed to uttering niceties, just that he had to give it significant conscious effort. Mike wondered if he'd ever see him again. He shrugged and went back to talk to Jen at the desk.

***

Milton looked up as his secretary ushered Querx's CEO Richard Vangester into his office. The CEO had never been down to his office so he felt a little perplexed as to what it could be. "Mr. Vangester, please sit. How may I help you?"

Vangester took the seat and waited until James took his own. "You can tell me just what Smint and Gettnor are patenting down here."

Milton's smile froze on his face. "How would you know about that?"

Vangester gave a predatory smile, "You don't have the 'need to know' on that. You just need to tell me what they're doing."

"Mr. Vangester... that would be... a betrayal of a client's confidence."

Vangester snorted, "Come on, Milton. We both know that Querx is your biggest client by far.

Which client do you value most? I don't think you'd like it if we cut you off, would you?"

Milton leaned back and folded his hands in his lap. He fixed Vangester with an enigmatic gaze for a minute. He cleared his throat, "Querx is my biggest client. Yes. But, not my only client. And they've been my biggest client, *only* because Querx has had a steady stream of Vaz Gettnor's intellectual property for me to patent. Querx hasn't submitted anything to patent since you fired him. With a choice between a corporation and a genius, I'll take the genius every time… *especially* over a corporation that comes down here to lean on me."

Vangester obviously hadn't considered this aspect of the equation. He began to turn red. Before he said anything though, Milton added, "Of course, I'd love not to make a choice, but if there is a choice to be made, my legal obligation is clear as well."

Vangester stood, "You're going to regret this!"

Milton stayed in his chair but raised an eyebrow, "And you're going to regret firing Vaz. But I suspect you already know that."

     ***

Anbala Singh motioned Smint to a seat in her little conference room. Once they were seated she said, "Dr. Smint, I've reviewed the electronic copy of Dr. Gettnor's contract you sent me. It seems straightforward. Can you tell me what you would like to know about it?"

"Jack please. Here's the issue, Querx has only been paying Dr. Gettnor a tenth of a percent on the gross for products they make themselves and three percent of their net on his IP that they licensed elsewhere."

"Really?! Anbala looked up at her screen and had her AI bring up the relevant part of the employment contract. After skimming up and down a few moments she said, "Well there's no provision for that in this contract. There must be a codicil or superseding agreement?"

"Vaz doesn't remember agreeing to one and we've had his AI search through its AV memory for the time he's been employed there. Of course, we might have used the wrong keywords for our search. It's a lot of data."

"You just searched the time between this contract and the change in income from the patents?"

"Yes, we did find a conversation about it. Shall I play it for you?"

"Sure." She waved at her screen, "put it up."

Smint spoke to his AI and a moment later an unstable video popped up on the screen, obviously recorded from someone's AI headgear. It was focused on some lab equipment. A nervous sounding voice spoke from the speakers, "Dr. Gettnor?" There was a pause, then she said "Dr. Gettnor?!" again and a little more emphatically. The video picture rotated and swung up to show an anxious appearing redheaded woman on the screen.

"What?" a male voice grunted impatiently from close to the microphone, almost certainly the wearer of the headgear. Anbala assumed it was Gettnor.

The woman washed her hands together, "I, uh," she glanced up at her HUD, "about your royalties. I, uh, wanted to tell you that now that you've collected a half million dollars… that your percentage," she glanced up at her HUD again, "drops to one percent of gross, with fifteen percent of licensing." She said the last in a rush as if rehearsed and distasteful.

After a long pause the image tilted and Gettnor's voice said, "Is that what's *supposed* to happen?"

The woman looked almost panicked but she nodded spastically. Gettnor turned back to his lab equipment without saying anything. They could tell, because the video image didn't bob, that he hadn't nodded his head either. On the audio track the woman said, "OK, see you later."

Anbala, eyes wide, turned to Smint. "Gettnor didn't think she was acting weird?"

Smint lifted his shoulders a tiny bit, "You'd have to know Vaz Gettnor. He isn't really very good at interpersonal interactions and really has a hard time reading other people's emotions.

"This is all you've found?"

Smint said, "Well, there's another one later, much the same. It mentions reducing the royalties to a tenth of a percent with three percent of licensing."

"And that's what Dr. Gettnor's receiving currently?"

Smint nodded again.

"And you're thinking that they may try to claim that his failure to object constitutes acceptance of a new contract?!"

Smint shrugged. "I don't know. These are the only things we've been able to find that relate to changing his cut of the royalty."

"Let me see the second one."

They watched it too. It was much the same except that a different minion from the financial office talked to Gettnor.

Anbala sat forward and drummed her fingers on her desk, "I certainly hope they aren't really claiming that constitutes a contract. That would be laughable in court."

"I have a feeling that someone decided that Gettnor would never think to object. So far they've been right. If I hadn't mentioned that I thought he should have tens of millions of dollars from his inventions he wouldn't have thought there was a problem."

"So, what do we do?"

153

"Is it a lot of money?"

Smint nodded, "As I said, tens of millions, probably close to thirty million."

She grinned, "Have Dr. Gettnor *ask* them for copies of his employment contract and any modifications, supplements or addendums. If *that's* all they've got, they are just going to crap their pants."

"What if they refuse?"

"They can't legally do that. If they do, we'll take them to court."

***

Dante lowered himself to the "down position" for the second round of his match. As he lifted his eyes he noticed his father sitting in the stands. He felt frustrated because he'd expected to pin this guy in the first round but the guy had successfully sprawled out of Dante's takedown attempts. Dante thought he had won the round on points but he wanted to feel dominant. *Dominant* wins were what he thought he needed to get a scholarship.

The ref started the match and Dante "sat out," explosively scoring an escape. He turned to his opponent and decided to let the guy attempt a takedown instead of shooting his own. They circled a bit and finally the guy shot an attempt at a double leg takedown. Dante successfully sprawled on him, and then pivoted to a dominant position.

When the match was over Dante had won but was disappointed that he hadn't managed to pin the guy. When he was declared the winner he saw his dad turn and leave without showing any emotion. He sighed, thinking, *what did I expect, that* my *Dad would suddenly get all weepy and run over to high five me?*

When Dante opened the door and stepped into his home he was surprised to see his dad sitting in the family room. His dad looked up at him and Dante worried that he'd done something wrong. "Hi Dad," he said giving a little wave.

Vaz said, "Hi," then as an afterthought waved. As if he had suddenly remembered that he should return a wave. So typical of his dad.

Dante looked up at the wall screen his dad had been looking at. It had esoteric diagrams all over it. "What 'cha workin' on?"

"Trying to design a better iteration of my new project."

"Wow, you're sure doing a lot of work at home. Do they pay you overtime when you do this stuff here instead of at Querx?"

Vaz stared unblinking at Dante without saying anything for a while, then abruptly said, "I don't work at Querx anymore."

Dante's eyebrows climbed, "Where *do* you work?"

"At home."

"Damn," Dante breathed, seeing his college chances shrinking. "Will you be able to get another job?"

"I'd rather work for myself."

"Yeah, but…" Dante felt his throat work a little. He felt surprised to find this hitting him so hard. Suddenly, he found himself angry, "You're just going to let Mom support the family by herself?"

Vaz blinked, "No."

Dante rolled his eyes, "You're going to make money in the basement?"

Vaz stared at him another moment, then without addressing Dante's question said, "I have a wrestling 'pointer' for you."

Dante felt torn between wanting to tell him to shove his pointer because Dante was pissed that his dad had quit his job, and feeling that after a lifetime without fatherly advice, he desperately wanted some.

This, despite realizing that most of his friends hated the advice they got from their parents. Finally he said, "What?" with a little surliness.

Vaz didn't appear to notice his tone, "You never seem to use a 'switch' when you're below. Since you almost always seem to be stronger, it should work pretty well."

"I've tried it, works in practice, not in competition, at least for me."

Vaz blinked a couple of times, "Can I show you how I think you should do it?"

Startled, Dante shrugged and dropped to his knees on the carpet. "So, I'll be on your left...?"

Vaz rose from the couch and stepped to Dante's right, kneeling in front of him in the down position. "Slow speed, OK?"

"Uh huh," Dante grinned as he reached around his dad's waist with his right arm and grabbed Vaz's left wrist with his left hand. *This could be fun,* he thought, *showing the old man what a real wrestler could do.* For a moment his eyebrows rose as he gripped his dad's stone hard waist. He'd forgotten how ripped his dad had looked at the MMA fight. Still, the guy was old, "OK, go."

Dante felt his dad's left hand reaching up for Dante's right wrist where it gripped Vaz's waist. Dante tried to hold it back, which should be easy to do at low speed since his dad couldn't jerk it loose or otherwise violently twist it out of his grip. Instead his dad's wrist relentlessly towed his hand with it as it moved deliberately up to grip his own right wrist where it wrapped his dad's waist. Once he had captured Dante's wrist, Vaz rolled slowly to the right pulling Dante over his body despite Dante's strongest attempts to resist. Eventually Dante flopped wide eyed over onto his back. Vaz straightened, "Now I know you could have stopped me at any point there

156

since we were working at low speed, but it's a lot harder to resist when it's done quickly."

Dante stared wide eyed at his dad. The irresistible power his father had just demonstrated flabbergasted him. Dante'd become used to being the stronger wrestler in virtually all of his matches. Despite knowing that his father appeared muscular and had won his MMA bout with one punch, Dante had thought of it as a fluke, a lucky punch, an overrated opponent. He'd been thinking that Jack Alexander wasn't as tough as he thought he was. Now his dad had just easily overpowered Dante's best efforts and apparently didn't even realize he'd been trying as hard as he could! Vaz seemed to be assuming that Dante had only given 50% effort to allow the demonstration to flow to its natural conclusion.

Someone cleared their throat and they turned to see Lisanne standing on the stairs in her robe. She raised an eyebrow, "What are you guys doing?"

Vaz just stared unblinkingly at her so Dante said, "Uh, Dad was just showing me a wrestling move."

She snorted, "Well, at least you didn't break any furniture."

Vaz said, "We were going half speed, half power, in full control the whole time."

Lisanne snorted again and turned to go back up the stairs. "Men!"

    ***

Vangester stepped into Phil Dennis' office. Without waiting for a greeting he said, "Fire that son of a bitch Milton."

Phil rocked back a little theatrically, "Why?"

Vangester quirked the corner of his mouth, then pointedly reached up to switch off his AI headgear. He waited until Phil switched his off too. "'Cause I said so should be good enough. But, in any case, because he pissed me off. I asked him for help with Smint and Gettnor and he refused."

Phil's forehead furrowed, "What kind of help?"

"We need to know what those bastards are patenting and we're his biggest customer, he owes us."

Phil stared, "He'd be… he couldn't violate their confidence like that!"

"Oh, come Phil. Grow up and play with the big boys."

"Jesus, boss," Phil breathed, "I hope you didn't say anything like that to him where it could be recorded, that kind of stuff is 'discoverable' in court."

Vangester looked a little uncomfortable, "I'd turned mine off but I couldn't very well ask him to turn off his AI."

Phil closed his eyes, "So you asked him to do something unethical and illegal 'on the record'?" He opened them again and reached up to rub his temples.

Vangester shrugged. "Fire him anyway. He needs to be taught a lesson."

***

James Milton stood up from inspecting the fusion device in Gettnor's basement. He looked at Smint and Gettnor, "So the actual device is this little thing, the reason it would be hard to take up to the patent office is all the shielding?"

"Yeah," Smint shrugged, "we could break down the tank and reconstruct it near the patent office, and then fill it with water there, but it would be cheaper to pay for a couple of plane tickets to fly them down here."

"OK, on to another issue. The CEO of Querx showed up at my office to ask me what you're patenting."

Smint frowned, "You didn't tell him did you?"

"No, of course not! But they obviously know you're patenting something and are thinking that it might be something you were working on when you were there at Querx. Do we have any exposure there?"

Smint turned to look at Gettnor who stared stone faced at Milton.

"Come on guys, I'm on your side. Tell me about any problems there might be and let me be the judge of how significant they might be. You *do not* want me to be blindsided by them later."

Gettnor still said nothing so Smint turned back to him and said, "The first fusion reaction occurred at Querx."

"What!?"

"Yeah, you know that this finding was mostly a freakish accident?"

Milton nodded.

"So Vaz was only trying to push more hydrogen into a new alloy he'd casted and the device melted down because it accidentally induced the fusion reaction we're patenting. Combination of heat from the reaction and extreme currents in the apparatus generated by the alpha particles. It melted down in front of Stillman Davis, the guy who fired Vaz. It pissed Davis off because he thought Vaz had let an experiment get out of control. Probably a big factor in Vaz getting fired."

Milton narrowed his eyes, "But there had been no intent to induce fusion, nor any recognition that it had happened at that time?"

Gettnor said, "*Something* bizarre had happened."

"But you didn't know what?"

Gettnor shook his head.

"So you came here after you were fired and figured out what happened and improved it without any help or equipment from Querx. You never worked on it there because, after that meltdown, you were immediately fired?"

Vaz nodded. Smint turned uncertainly to look at him.

Milton sighed, "What else? You've got to tell me."

Smint said, "Vaz…"

"Yes?"

"Vaz took some of the disks he'd made up there at Querx."

"Oh Christ! Are those the same kind of disks that are in the fusion device?"

Smint said, "*The* same ones in fact."

"Shit! And I suppose there were security cameras there that might have seen him taking them?"

Smint slumped and said, "Yeah, and a security guard. How bad a problem is this?"

"Not the end of the world, but Querx will have a strong argument that they own at least part of it. In fact, rather than getting into an expensive court battle, you'd be better off negotiating the size of the piece they'll get with them."

"How big a piece should they get?!"

Milton held up his fingers with a small space between them, "A little piece."

    ***

Tiona walked up to the front of the room and the man handed her back her AI. It had been weird to spend hours without it. As she put it on he said, "Very impressive, Mizz…" he glanced up at his HUD, "Gettnor. Very impressive indeed."

"What did I get?" she asked, looking up at her HUD. Electricity seemed to sparkle over her scalp as she saw that she'd gotten a perfect 800 on the math section and made the 86th percentile on the language section. "Oh!" she exclaimed in a small voice."

The man waggled his eyebrows, "*You* won't have any difficulty getting accepted wherever you want to go." He put out his hand and Tiona shook it.

As she walked out of the testing center she skipped a step. She'd been worried about the SAT, even though she'd done well on some practice tests. She knew that Dante hadn't gotten a great score and that had spooked her. He'd never told her exactly how he'd done, but she knew it wasn't what he'd hoped for and that he worried that if he didn't get a wrestling scholarship to help him in the door he might not get into the school he wanted.

She took a deep breath, maybe now she'd be able to get a decent academic scholarship.

***

Phil Dennis leaned into Vangester's office, "Mr. Vangester, got a minute?"

Vangester sighed. The board was putting enough pressure on him from above without his being constantly nagged by underlings that couldn't decide what color tie to wear. "What now?"

"I got a call from Reid Hapler in the HR office. It seems Dr. Gettnor has contacted them, asking for copies of his employment contract, specifically seeking any modifications or amendments. He seemed worried about it and said I should talk to you about it."

Vangester squeezed his eyes shut, "Shit!" he hissed.

"I assume then, that you aren't going to tell me that there's nothing to worry about?"

161

Vangester sighed, "Well there shouldn't be. But..."

Dennis sat down uninvited and pressed fingers to his temples. "Tell me."

"Well he'd only been here a year or two when some of those patents of his started bringing in a *lot* of money."

"That's a good thing right?"

Indignantly, Vangester said, "Yeah, but the way the employment contract is written in reference to royalties he was going to be taking home more money than anyone in the company!"

Dennis took his fingers off his temples, "So?"

"So, it was irritating to a lot of people that we've got this weird guy who can barely tie his own shoes and he's making more money than they were. Plus, someone suggested that if he got too much money he might retire."

"So?"

"So, we modified the contract. Now, after the first half million there is a reduction in the percentage the inventor gets and after a million it is reduced further."

Dennis narrowed his eyes, "You retroactively modified his contract?"

"We changed it for new employees. Then we told him..."

"Yesss?"

"We told him we were going to pay him on that scale."

"He signed off on it?"

"He didn't object."

"You're not going to claim that because you *told* him and he didn't actually object that that constituted a contract?!"

Vangester shrugged uncomfortably, "Doesn't it?"

"Crap! Let me track down the relevant record. I certainly hope it looks better than what you're describing!" He turned to walk out of the office, then stopped. Without turning he said, "How much money are we talking about here? Maybe it's not worth arguing about."

Vangester said, "Probably somewhere between twenty and thirty million. We don't want to take a hit like that."

"Good God!" Dennis sighed as he left the office.

An hour later Dennis was back. "I don't think you can say that Gettnor 'accepted' a modification of his contract either time. He might not have objected but he did ask, 'Is that what's *supposed* to happen?' as if he was casting doubt. Then he never said, 'Yes, OK, or even nodded.'"

"Yeah." Vangester said disgustedly, "That's just the way the SOB is, but I suppose that wouldn't hold up in court?"

With raised eyebrows Dennis shook his head.

Vangester grunted, "Those women were supposed to say, 'OK?' or something at the end of their little speeches to him in order to have him confirm that he agreed, but *both* of them flubbed it. We even wrote them out scripts and put them up on their HUDs," he shook his head with dismay, "and they still couldn't get it right."

"Well, whatever's the right or wrong of how you tried to get him to accept a modification of his contract I don't think it will hold up in court. You'd better start figuring out how you're going to pay the man the money he didn't get."

"Dennis! We didn't hire you to tell me I have to pay the man. We're *paying* you to figure out how we can get out of it!"

Dennis stared at him for a while, then said, "I'll search for precedents, but," he said darkly, "*I* don't think you can." He turned on his heel and left.

***

Tiona saw her brother walking out of the school ahead of her. "Don," she called, feeling weird. She'd spoken to her brother at the school less than ten times during the three years she'd been in high school. Mostly they pretended that they didn't see one another. He turned and waited for her, "Did they offer you a scholarship?"

He nodded, "ECU did. I still haven't heard from NCSU."

"Oh," she knew he wanted to stay in Raleigh. "Good luck with State. When will you hear?"

He shrugged, "Next couple of weeks. Did you know Dad quit working at Querx?"

Horrified, Tiona found her hand over her mouth stifling a little squeak. "No! When?"

"I don't know. He told me last night."

"Oh no," Tiona moaned, eyes glistening, "after he spent all that money on equipment too. Do you think he'll be able to get another job?"

"'T'... he's not even applying," Dante said in a hushed tone.

"Oh my God!" Tiona said feeling her world crumbling. "With just Mom's salary they'll be broke! There's no way they'll be able to help us in college; Mom's already worried about money." She wiped an eye and sniffed, "What's *wrong* with him?"

Dante snorted, "This the first time you've ever noticed your dad's a little weird?"

She shook her head and dabbed at her eyes.

Suddenly, Meri, Tiona's best friend appeared and put an arm around her, "What's the matter girl?!"

164

Meri shot a glare a Dante, evidently thinking he must be at fault.

In a choked voice Tiona said, "My dad quit his job."

"Oh," Meri said in a freighted tone. Quietly, she asked, "Are you going to have to go to public school?"

Tiona's eyes widened, she hadn't considered that. She shrugged, choked and unable to speak.

Meri said, "Well at least you'll get a scholarship to college. Think on the bright side."

Dante's eyes widened, "She will?"

Meri looked at Tiona with surprise, "You haven't told him?"

Tiona shook her head, still having trouble speaking.

Meri turned to Dante, "She maxed the SATs."

Tiona shook her head as Dante stared at her and said, "What?!"

"Just the math," she choked out.

"Just the math," Meri snorted. "That's maxing to me. She made a great score on the language section too."

Dante stared at his sister with a mixture of admiration and jealousy. Finally he said, "Hey, way to go Sis." He reached out and clumsily patted her shoulder. "Don't cry, 'T,' *you're* gonna get through college. It's gonna happen, even if you have to take out loans. Those scores are gonna help a lot."

Head still bowed, Tiona dabbed at her eyes and nodded minutely.

***

Stillman Davis walked to the back of Jerrod's place again. When Jerrod told him to come in he asked, "How's your man doing?"

165

"He's gonna live. And he's kept his contract with me a secret, if that's what you're worrying about."

"Did he say what happened... you know; how Gettnor put him in the hospital?"

Jerrod quirked his mouth, "Says Gettnor sucker punched him in the gut, then when he bent over with the wind knocked out of him, the SOB hit him in the face too." He grinned, "Billy's pretty offended by the unsportsmanlike behavior of your man. Kinda wants to get even some night."

Davis leaned forward, "Maybe we should give him a chance."

Jerrod, "I'm not trying any more of that kinda crap for you. Payin' Billy's upkeep while he's 'inactive' has eaten up all the money you paid me. It's windin' up that I did that little service for you out of the kindness of my heart for an old friend."

Davis snarled, "*But,* you *accomplished* exactly *zip* for my money buddy." He took a deep breath, remembering who he was talking to. "Sorry, Jerrod, we both took a loss on this. But there's something that's potentially a lot more lucrative here."

Jerrod frowned, "Lucrative?"

"You know, money making."

Jerrod lifted his chin indicating Davis should continue.

"I still have contacts at Querx and they tell me there's a shit-storm there over Gettnor patenting something else."

"So?"

"It may be something that's worth a *lot* of money?"

Jerrod snorted, "So you want to go steal his *idea* from him?!"

Stillman shrugged, "Maybe we could make him give us the plans or design or whatever for the thing. I could find a buyer and we could turn over a pretty profit."

Jerrod frowned, "What good is a design for something if Gettnor has the patent. No one else could build it?"

Davis grinned in a predatory fashion, "That's where *my* contacts come in. I know some folks in China who don't care all that much about patents. They just need to know how to build it and then they make the product anyway, patent or no."

"And you think you could sell it to them for… how much?"

"I don't know, we don't even know what it is yet. But when I find out, if it looks good I'd like to be ready to move on it."

Jerrod looked dubious, "Do you really think we'd be able to force him to draw us up some plans?!"

"No, they're probably too complex to put on a napkin. But he'll have them stored away. All we have to do is make him export us a copy."

"And how much is this Chinaman going to pay?"

Davis shrugged, "Again, depends on what it is. Potentially millions."

Jerrod rolled his eyes, "Talk to me when you have *some* idea what you're talking about, OK?"

Jerrod felt like he'd dismissed Davis for being clueless but Davis felt he'd agreed to go along once Davis had the info. He left with a jaunty step.

***

Vaz heard someone stumping down the stairs to the basement. He'd stopped locking the door now that Lisanne wasn't riding his case. He hoped that she wasn't coming down to yell at him.

The door opened and Tiona stepped in, blinking a little in the bright lighting. He straightened from where he'd been bent over "Mark 3" as he thought of the latest version of the fusion device and watched her expectantly.

Startled at the transformation in the basement Tiona looked around in amazement. Lab type equipment seemed to be everywhere. All highly organized as she would expect from her Dad. Towards the back stood a huge, featureless metal... structure. For a moment she wondered what kind of physics experiments her dad was doing down here and if it would be interesting to talk to him about. Then she remembered her purpose in coming down here, "Dad! You quit your job?!"

Vaz stared blankly at her. After a moment he said, "Fired."

"What?" Tiona said not registering the meaning of what he'd said.

"I didn't quit. I was fired."

"Oh!" she gasped. "What did you do?"

After another unblinking moment Vaz said, "I left work early and one of my experiments melted down."

Tiona's gaze swept again over all the expensive looking equipment in the basement. Her hand had risen to her mouth. "Dante says you aren't even looking for another job..." in a small voice she asked, "that isn't true is it?"

Vaz nodded.

Appalled, she said, "So you're just going to let Mom support the family?"

He slowly shook his head.

Relief flooded through her, "You are going to apply for a job?"

He shook his head again.

Incredulous she said, "What *are* you going to do?"

He pointed to the device he'd been working on when she entered, "This should be worth quite a bit of money."

Uncertainly she said, "What's it do?"

"Fuses hydrogen and boron."

Tiona had finished Chemistry and didn't know of a particular reason you'd want to make hydrogen-boron compounds, "Why would you want... boron hydrides?" a lift in her tone indicating she wasn't sure that a hydrogen-boron compound would be a "hydride."

"Not a chemical reaction. Nuclear fusion."

She wasn't quite sure what he meant by "nuclear fusion." She stared at him a moment, then let her eyes wander around the lab again, "Why would you want to do that?"

"It produces energy."

"Oh, OK." Tiona felt confused and uncertain. She turned and opened the door at the bottom of the stairs.

"Tiona?"

She stopped, "Yes?"

"We have enough money to send you to college."

Without looking back she rolled her eyes and shrugged her shoulders. She closed the door and started up the stairs.

Vaz stared after her. Once again he pondered how he could explain the money in his royalty account to his family without making them angry that he'd hid it for so long. There would be a lot of distressful emotions. For a moment he considered that the happiness of having the money might outweigh the anger that he'd been hiding it. But then he considered that Lisanne might want to use the money to travel and his stomach clenched. He'd never left the "Triangle" area near Raleigh and as he aged he seemed to be developing more and more apprehension about being in unfamiliar places. He felt so comfortable in his basement and loved the fact that now he didn't even have to leave the house to go to work. He wasn't even going to Mike's Martial anymore.

Occasionally, he worried that if he kept this up, he might eventually reach the point that he would be unable to leave the house.

His mind ping ponged back and forth around these uncomfortable thoughts but then his eye caught on the coil for the Mark 3 version of the fusion device. He bent back over it. Working on it brought a comfortable feeling gently back over him without his even having to hit the bag.

Tiona went back to her room and started searching the web for information about hydrogen-boron fusion. It was fascinating! The amount of energy available from fusion astounded her. She also came to realize that hydrogen-boron fusion in particular had very desirable characteristics because it didn't release neutrons except through accidental side reactions. The fact that the majority of the energy was released as electrically charged alpha particles meant that this type of fusion didn't have to heat water to create steam like standard atomic energy plants. The high energy particles could generate electricity simply by passing through coils!

Then she started reading about the prerequisites for fusion. Enormous heat had to be generated in order to cause atomic nuclei to crash into one another hard enough to fuse. The repulsive forces between nuclei were enormous. They hadn't successfully produced more energy than it required to achieve fusion of heavy hydrogen yet, and they had been trying different methods since the 1950s! Hydrogen-boron fusion required ten times as much heat as heavy hydrogen fusion!

Tiona sagged back in her chair, wondering how she could have believed, even for a moment, that her bizarre father could have achieved fusion. No one else had been able to, despite decades and decades of trying. In fact, if his own family thought he was weird, was it any wonder he got fired? No matter how smart Mom said he was, they'd have to be able to talk to him down at the job, wouldn't they? Hell, his own daughter could barely make sense of a conversation with him.

She got up and walked slowly into her parents' room. Her mother lay propped up on the bed working on something on the big screen in their room. She closed it when she saw Tiona.

"What 'cha workin' on Mom?" Tiona said in a quiet voice.

"Tryin' to work out how to send you kids to college." Seeing the look on Tiona's face, she quickly said, "Hey kid, it won't be impossible, we just need to figure out how to shift money around."

Tiona grimaced, "I talked to my counselor. I should be able to get a scholarship. He said he'd put me up for some." As she said this she climbed up on the bed and leaned her head against her mother's shoulder.

Lisanne clapped her hands together delightedly, "Hey! That's great! What kind of scholarship? Academic?"

Lisanne could feel Tiona nod against her shoulder. She put her arm around her and hugged her, ecstatic to have Tiona leaning against her like she used to when she was younger. But Tiona seemed so sad. "Is something wrong 'T'?"

"I'm worried about Dad."

Lisanne tensed but tried not to let Tiona feel it. Had Tiona learned that Vaz wasn't working? Or had he done something else. "What's worrying you?"

"I think he might be delusional."

Lisanne blinked over the top of Tiona's head. *Not* what she'd expected. Her brow furrowed, "Why would you think that?"

"I went down to confront him about... about his not working and leaving it all on you."

Lisanne wanted to ask how she'd found out Vaz wasn't working but Tiona continued, "He gave me this story about how he'd built a fusion machine and that it was going to make money. Then he told me not to worry about money for college... Mom, I looked up fusion and *that* just isn't possible. Then I looked up delusions and... claiming you can do impossible things is a pretty typical thing if someone's manic. If you're religious you might claim you're Jesus. Since he's into physics... I think that's why he's claiming he can achieve fusion."

Lisanne's heart climbed into her throat. She wanted to dismiss Tiona's concerns, but... she'd sometimes worried that Vaz might have a breakdown someday. Not having a job could have put a huge amount of stress on him. After he'd lost his job at Virginia Tech he'd spent a long time in a deep funk and it had been incredibly difficult to get him to go out and apply for jobs. He hated changes in his routine after all. How could she not have seen that something similar or worse might be happening now? Just the thought of going out to talk to new people in the process of making applications would have driven him right into his shell. And Lisanne hadn't helped; she'd just ridden him about how he *needed* to get another job.

So, he'd climbed into his basement cave and, she thought, started doing research. But maybe just *deluded* himself into thinking that he was doing something important. After all if he'd been successful at Querx they'd have paid him more than they did. What was she going to say to Tiona?

At that moment, worried about her mother's lack of response, Tiona said, "Mom?"

"Uh, yeah girl. Just been thinking. I didn't know your dad was working on fusion and I don't know much about it. I guess I'll have to look into it before I know what to make of your worries. Delusions… seem… like something that *couldn't* be true, but I've got to look into it. He can be pretty… odd."

"Mom? Why did Dad get fired?"

Icy fingers slid down Lisanne's back, "Fired?"

Tiona drew back, "You didn't know?"

Eyes glistening Lisanne merely shook her head. She didn't trust herself to speak. Even if she could talk him into beginning the process of applying, having been fired would make it a lot harder for him to get a job.

"He told me it was because he left work early and one of his experiments melted down. I think there must have been more to it than that, don't you?"

Lisanne only trusted herself to shrug. A successful scientist not only would have been paid more by Querx, but they wouldn't have been *fired* either.

A failed scientist wouldn't suddenly have succeeded at achieving fusion when no one else could either.

Tiona shifted her head to look up at her mother and saw the tears running down her cheeks. "Mom! I'm sorry! I didn't know you didn't know! I'm so sorry…" she petered out, not sure whether she was sorry she'd told her mother or sorry her dad was crazy. She realized she'd entered the room hoping her mother would explain away her concerns about her dad. She'd only frightened her mother and hadn't made herself feel any better. "I'm sorry."

Lisanne sniffed, "It's OK kid. I needed to know." She hugged her daughter's shoulder and tried to smile. "We'll get through this... somehow."

Tiona said, "Don got a wrestling scholarship to ECU."

"Oh! That's great. Why hasn't he told me?"

"I think it's 'cause he's still hoping to get one at State."

"Oh, OK. I hope he gets it."

Tiona looked back up at her mom, "Are you gonna be OK?"

Lisanne nodded.

"I need to study, OK?"

"Sure Honey. I need to read up on fusion."

Tiona rolled over and gave Lisanne a momentary hug before she left.

Lisanne lay trying to remember when she'd last gotten a hug from her daughter. Too bad it took a crisis like this to bring it on. Sighing she looked up at the wall screen and started bringing up information on fusion.

After a while she cursed and brought up information on manic personality disorders.

Lisanne cried herself to sleep.

***

Phil Dennis knocked on Vangester's door but then entered without an invitation. "We have a request from Gettnor's attorney for a meeting about our failure to pay him his full share of royalties."

"Ah Christ! Do you know his attorney? Is he any good?"

"She, one Anbala Singh, and yeah, she's got a reputation, smart and aggressive."

"What do we do?"

"Negotiate a settlement."

Vangester's jaw worked and he turned a little red, but he didn't explode. "I told you to figure a way out of this!"

"There isn't a way 'out of this.' The law's on his side."

Vangester closed his eyes, then opened them again, "OK, we negotiate. We need to come to the table ready to play hardball though. What kind of leverage do we have?"

Dennis shrugged microscopically, "We can say that we're ready to take them to court on the basis that we think his failure to object constitutes acceptance of a modified contract. Remind them how expensive court can be."

"All right!" Vangester sounded cheered.

"She'll just laugh at us though. It's pretty clear cut and she should be able to hammer us flat and maybe charge us for court costs." He paused, "The other thing we've got on them is Gettnor stealing those discs. We could threaten criminal charges and claim knowledge that they are an important part of whatever new thing he's patenting, demand a share, or a reduction in what we owe in back royalties."

"Oh, yeah! Let's plan on that. Hire outside counsel too, have them look at everything. Maybe they'll see something we've missed."

Dennis shrugged, "OK. I think you're wasting your money, but it'll be a pittance compared to what we owe."

***

Lisanne eyed her husband during dinner. He'd cooked, which he'd been doing more nights than not lately. Occasionally what he cooked wasn't all that great, but tonight he'd cooked something vaguely Asian with chicken smothered in peanut butter that

175

tasted awesome. As usual, it wasn't out of a recipe book and it was hard for her to reconcile the notion that someone delusional could cook something that complex, off the cuff, and have it turn out so well. His behavior during dinner was… odd, saying little unless spoken to, seldom looking up from his plate.

But, it wasn't unusual behavior for Vaz Gettnor. She finally decided that if it weren't for her little talk with Tiona, she wouldn't even be considering that something might have changed about him.

After dinner, Lisanne cleaned up the kitchen, purposely delaying until Vaz had gone down to his basement. Once she thought he'd had time to settle in she tried the door. It was unlocked so she went down the stairs. She felt weird, as if she was invading his personal and private space, even though it was part of the house they both owned and she used to think of herself as welcome down there.

When she opened the door, like Tiona, Lisanne felt surprised by the markedly increased lighting. The old clutter had all been cleaned up and benches set up for the new equipment. Her eyes narrowed, it seemed like a *lot* more equipment than could possibly have been in the boxes that had been delivered the day they'd blown up. Had he been ordering even more stuff?

She took a deep breath and reminded herself that she'd checked yesterday and their shared accounts hadn't sustained any expenditures she didn't know about. If he'd spent more money it must have all come out of his personal account that she didn't have access to. Certainly, she didn't want to blow up on him if his psychological state teetered on edge. "Hey Vaz."

He regarded her warily, lifting a set of magnifiers off his head. After a moment, apparently remembering that she would expect a response he said, "Hey."

176

"Tiona tells me you're doing some pretty exciting stuff down here?"

Vaz nodded, but not as eagerly as she might have expected.

"What are you studying?"

Vaz blinked. "She didn't tell you?"

She tilted her head, "Hydrogen-boron fusion?"

He nodded.

Lisanne smiled brightly, "Wow! How are you doing it? Everything I read says it should be impossible."

He nodded again and his eyes dropped to the device he had been working on. After a moment he said, "It should be. Yes." A long pause ensued, then sounding frustrated he said, "I'm unable to work out any math that can explain it. The device results in a great number of hydrogen protons being tightly packed in around boron atoms that are immobilized in a boron-vanadium-palladium alloy matrix. I force new protons into the matrix with a surging electric current and simultaneously strike it with highly energetic ultrasonic waves transmitted through the highly compressed hydrogen. I believe… I believe that ultrasonically induced flexing in the matrix somehow forces protons into contact with boron nuclei. However," he shrugged, "by every calculation I've made, it should not… should not produce the numbers of fusion events that are occurring." His eyes rose to focus on her again, "So I must be missing something, because the fusion events are there."

"Can you show me?"

"The mechanisms are disassembled now. I could show you records from the last test if you like?"

"Why did you disassemble them?" she asked, stomach clinching. She'd learned while reading about claims for "cold fusion" that bad or fake science mysteriously could never be reproduced at the time that verification experts showed up to witness the

177

claimed scientific events personally. Equipment was always broken or not performing at such times.

"I'm building a third version."

"How come?"

"Trying to improve the efficiency, both by increasing the frequency of the fusion events and by more effectively harvesting the energy from the alpha particles."

Lisanne looked around the room. He sounded sane, for Vaz. Except that he thought he could do something that everything she read said was impossible. Why, after a completely unprepossessing period as a research drudge for Querx, doing who knows what, but certainly not exciting stuff, would he get fired and almost immediately discover something that no one, not even in the huge academic research foundations around the world, had been able to accomplish? Not wanting their pleasant conversation to languish she said, "What's the huge thing there?" she pointed at the enormous stainless steel tank.

"A boron lined water tank to stop free neutrons."

Lisanne looked back at Vaz. Magnifiers back over his eyes, he was back to working on his device. "I… I'm glad we're getting along better."

"So am I."

"Can we go out to dinner tomorrow night? It'd be nice to get out on a Friday night."

Vaz closed his eyes without lifting his head. He didn't want to go out, but reminded himself of his own concern that he was becoming less and less comfortable leaving the house. He resisted the temptation to point out that if she was worried about money she shouldn't be going out to dinner. "OK."

Lisanne smiled sadly at him. "It's a date then."

Back upstairs Lisanne stopped outside Dante and Tiona's rooms, knocked and got the doors to both rooms open. Looking from one to the other she said, "We're all going out to dinner tomorrow night." They both began to protest, obviously not wanting to be seen in public with their parents. Irritated to be standing in the hall trying to talk to her children through their open doors, Lisanne said, "Tiona, please come into Dante's room with me so we can talk."

Tiona made a face but acquiesced. They both picked their way through the mess on Dante's floor to sit on his bed. Lisanne turned to Tiona, "Have you talked to Dante about your concerns regarding your father?"

Tiona's eyes widened but she only shook her head minutely.

Dante said with a mildly disgusted tone, "You mean about him quitting at Querx and not even looking for another job?"

Tiona said quietly, as if imparting a horrible secret, "Don, he got *fired*!"

Dante turned wide eyed to his mother, doubt written large on his face.

Lisanne nodded, "He told Tiona last night that he'd actually been fired."

"Goddammit!"

Lisanne thought about asking Dante not to swear, but she reflected, he was nearly grown. She looked back and forth from one child to the other. "You may realize he's been spending almost all his time in the basement?"

They nodded, Dante suppressing the impulse to tell about his Dad's MMA adventure, still not wanting to admit he'd gone to the MMA fight himself.

"I was worried that he might become a recluse but then Tiona told me last night that she was worried too." She looked meaningfully from one to the other. "Tiona went down to talk to him and he claimed that he's achieved nuclear fusion and intended to finance your college educations with money from that invention."

Dante's head drew back, "Wouldn't that be a *good* thing?"

Lisanne smiled sadly, "Yes, if it weren't impossible. I went down a little while ago and asked him about it... He told me he'd "disassembled" the device to make a better one."

Dante said, "So?"

Lisanne shook her head sorrowfully, "You can't read much about fusion without reading about the large numbers of charlatans and simply deluded people who have previously claimed to have achieved fusion with 'tabletop fusion' setups. All those claims have in common that when others come to inspect the setup, it's never working. It's broken, or it's down for maintenance, or there's some other problem. It's called 'pathological science.' Many of the people involved aren't trying to fool anyone, they actually believe it themselves."

Dante said, "So you aren't going to give him a chance to prove himself?"

"Of course I am. And it *will* be amazing if he's truly successful... but we need to face the reality that getting fired may have driven him into holing up in his basement and simply fantasizing that he's doing important stuff there."

Dante and Tiona stared. Dante with dawning horror and Tiona with dismay over this confirmation of her worst fears.

After a pause without any questions from the kids Lisanne said, "I know your dad has always been a little weird." Dante whose head had drooped so that he stared at the floor between his knees snorted, "But in his own sweet way he cares about us deeply and I care about him too. I'm hoping you two will help me try to pull him out of this and save him and our family?"

They both nodded.

"I think that we've got to get him out of his basement and out of the house. He's got to get back into the world again. We need to be loving and supportive despite his being fired. We need to be enthusiastic about his science though not about fusion because we don't want to encourage any delusions he may be having. I want him to feel that we love him *even though* he's suffered a major failure. I want him not to be afraid to risk failure again, if and when he gets up the courage to apply for another job."

They nodded. Because Lisanne and Vaz had always been careful to hide any disagreements when the kids were smaller, this was the kids first experience with one of their parents suggesting that the other one wasn't perfect. And it came with the baggage that they might need to pitch in and help their dad work out a problem.

Tiona felt it hard. She'd personally been disrespecting her father's weird ways for so long now that she felt guilty contemplating that she might be partly responsible for his sudden loss of touch with reality.

"Do you guys have any suggestions for other things we might do to help?"

They both shook their heads and Lisanne said, "So, dinner tomorrow night, out. You guys have any suggestions for places where you won't have to be seen eating with your parents?"

Tiona leaned closer and put an arm around Lisanne, "It's OK Mom," she said throatily, "I don't *care* if my friends see us. Pizza?"

Lisanne stood, and Tiona stood with her. "OK pizza it is. Maybe next weekend it'll be 'dinner and a movie,' live large I say."

Dante quietly said, "Mom, can we afford to go out?"

181

"Eating out isn't all that much more expensive than eating in. Keeping your dad sane is immensely valuable by comparison. Besides, you guys shouldn't worry all that much about money. I've got enough in my retirement account to send you to state schools," she shrugged, "I just might have to retire a little later is all. And of course, any scholarships you get will be greatly appreciated." She waggled her eyebrows at them.

***

Vangester wanted to be present for the negotiation about Gettnor's royalties, but worried that having the CEO of the company present at a negotiation over a back pay issue would give Gettnor's lawyer the impression that the company was taking this more seriously than he wanted her to believe. Instead he settled for watching through a feed from Phil Dennis' AI.

Gettnor's attorney, Anbala Singh entered first and Vangester relaxed a little. She was short, slender, young woman of Indian descent with long dark hair. Because she was attractive, Vangester dismissed her as harmless. Next to enter was Gettnor himself walking with his peculiar gait that gave the impression he'd just gotten off a horse. Vangester was surprised to see someone else enter; it was that bastard Smint! "What is Smint doing here?" he hissed at Dennis over the link, "Did you call him as a witness?"

Dennis replied as they'd agreed, tapping his finger once as a "no."

Singh said, "Shall we begin?"

Dennis nodded.

She said, "You have failed to pay my client, Mr. Gettnor, the full amounts that were specified in his employment contract. I refer to his share of the royalties and profits on the inventions he made while working at Querx. This shortfall amounts to $27,891,752. We would like to arrange to receive that money as soon as possible."

Vangester's stomach roiled, that was almost exactly what the accounting drones at Querx had calculated. He'd hoped that Gettnor would be unaware of the total amount.

Dennis said, "Oh come now. Dr. Gettnor was informed that we were lowering the percentage Querx would pay on his inventions. He made no objection."

Singh laughed as if she'd been told a particularly funny joke. "Seriously? You're going to try to claim that having one of your minions just drop by to tell him that he was being paid a lower share constitutes a legal and binding modification of an employment contract? When he didn't even express agreement?" Singh leaned forward and put a finger on her cheek, grinning, "Perhaps Dr. Gettnor could just drop by and tell that same woman that he'd decided he wanted his cut of the royalties retroactively upped to 60%. As long as he left before she disagreed, I assume you'd be bound by the new agreement eh?"

A silence stretched. Vangester, unable to see the sour expression on Dennis' face finally hissed into the link, "Say something, dammit!"

Dennis tapped a finger deliberately a single time on the table. Then to Singh he said, "You are no doubt aware that Dr. Gettnor was far from an ideal employee while working here at Querx, coming in late, leaving early, often disregarding his assigned research to hare off into other areas that interested him."

Singh grinned again, "And coming in late at night for far more hours than he lost at the beginning and end of his workday. If you'd like to consider him an hourly employee we could talk about your paying him 'time and a half' for his overage hours which we could extract from his AI's records. Also I believe that it was while straying from his assigned research path that he made nine of the twelve discoveries that Querx patented." She lifted an eyebrow, "We'd be willing to pay back the company for those 'off track' hours if they'll stipulate then that the *entirety* of those inventions must then belong to Dr. Gettnor?"

Dennis didn't respond to this assault. Instead he said, "In fact, our security records document that Dr. Gettnor stole Querx property on the day he was fired."

Singh covered her mouth, saying, "Oh my goodness."

Vangester hopefully thought she'd been taken aback.

But then she said, "Are you referring to the alloy disks?"

Dennis nodded.

"Dr. Gettnor does regret the fact that some of those were still in his pocket when he left. Do you have use for them? If so, he could replace them. Or if you'd like, he'd be happy to reimburse you up to ten times their appraised value? Or," she grinned again, "you could press charges for the theft. That would nicely separate the disk issue from this present negotiation."

Dennis sighed and drew his last weapon, "We are aware that Dr. Gettnor has submitted another patent application."

Singh nodded, still grinning.

"We have reason to believe that the new invention relates to those disks and therefore is owned by Querx."

Unfazed she said, "Why, you're absolutely correct. The disks are of an alloy that Dr. Gettnor worked on as part of his assignment while working at Querx. He had been assigned to try to improve hydrogen storage and had calculated that this particular alloy, cast in that particular fashion, would absorb more hydrogen than pure palladium, which surprisingly is already capable of holding more hydrogen than is contained in the liquid state of hydrogen. You're welcome to patent the new alloy in his name per the original employment agreement he signed with you. He'll tell you how to cast the alloy, and he'll tell you which of the many alloys he cast at Querx is the most effective."

Dennis narrowed his eyes, "And in return you want what?"

"Why, nothing. Dr. Gettnor feels that this is only right. It follows from the employment agreement he signed when he came to work here.

Dennis felt shocked. It sounded valuable, and they weren't even going to fight for a bigger share? He put up a finger, "I'd like to take a small recess, can I get you refreshments?"

Singh smiled broadly, "Certainly. I'd like tea. Dr. Gettnor, Dr. Smint?"

Dennis hustled out of the room, told a secretary to get them the drinks they'd requested, and stepped down to Vangester's office. As he came through the door he said, "How valuable is that?"

Vangester smiled a predatory smile, "Tens of millions at least, probably substantially more than we're at risk for on Gettnor's contract dispute."

"So I should go for it?"

"No!" Vangester frowned as if Dennis were an idiot, "We have the disks, we'll just figure out which one absorbs the most, then assay it and cast them by the millions.

"Richard," Dennis sighed at Vangester, "They aren't asking for anything in return for the alloy."

Vangester cocked his head, considering. "I'll bet they want us to give up our right to prosecute him for theft of the disks."

"Maybe, but *we* wouldn't get anything out of prosecuting him for a crime you know?"

"OK but at the least, they'll want us to stop playing hardball on Gettnor's share of previous royalties."

Anbala Singh smiled up over her teacup at him when a disgruntled Phil Dennis reluctantly reentered the room. She'd stifled conversation amongst Gettnor and Smint while Dennis was gone, suspecting that someone would be listening. Gettnor hardly ever talked anyway, so it wasn't difficult. Once Dennis had seated himself, she said brightly, "Are you ready to pay Dr. Gettnor his share of the royalties?"

Dennis looked like he'd bitten something else sour. "Here is what we're willing to do. First, just in order to stay out of court, we're willing to grant Dr. Gettnor ten percent of the twenty seven million he claims he's owed but no more. We'd increase his share to two tenths of a percent of gross and six percent of royalties, i.e. double his current share. If he insists on more you'll find yourself in a protracted court battle."

Singh interjected, "Oh I don't think it will be all that protracted, these issues are pretty straightforward."

Dennis continued, "Second, we're glad that Dr. Gettnor is willing to fulfill the terms of his employment and tell us what he knows about the alloy that we're working to perfect. If he does, we're willing to grant him the same two tenths percent of gross that we'd now be paying him on his other inventions."

As if delightfully amused, Singh laughed until she had to get a tissue out of her purse and dab at her eyes. "Well!" she gasped finally, "We aren't going to agree to *that*. What we'll do is give you one week to sign the agreement I've forwarded to your AI. After that time point, we will then file suit and also ask the

186

court to have you recompense Dr. Gettnor for the $2,498,416 in interest that Dr. Gettnor would have earned on his money at prevailing interest rates had you paid it to him when it was owed. Also Dr. Gettnor will no longer agree to teach you how to manufacture the new alloy." Her eyebrows bounced up and down, "And, tell your handler," she pointed at her ear suggesting that she was fully aware that someone outside the room was telling Dennis what to do, "that I'd be *delighted* to take this to court." She giggled, "That would just be *so* much fun."

She rose and shepherded Gettnor and Smint toward the door. Vaz had no idea why she thought all this was so funny. However, Smint had assured him that, because in addition to her fee, Singh also stood to gain a two percent share of whatever she negotiated for them, she would have his best interests at heart. He felt bemused to realize that he would normally have expected to feel very angry about what Querx had been and was still trying to do to him. It didn't meet his expectations of what was fair or right. However, Anbala's laughing at them somehow kept it from being quite so infuriating.

Shortly after they'd left, Vangester stormed into the room, "Singh may look like a cute thing, but she's a real bitch!"

Dennis sighed, "I told you she was tough."

"Well, the lab guys are going to figure out how to make that alloy. And, *you're* going to figure out how to nail her hide to the wall." He stormed out, presumably to go light a fire under the lab people.

***

When Vaz came upstairs in response to Lisanne's call and found Dante and Tiona there too he wondered what was going on. They hadn't been

187

out to dinner as an entire family for years. He'd asked Lisanne once why not and she'd told him that teenagers didn't want to be seen in public with their parents. He looked back and forth from one to another, thinking that they were still teenagers and wishing that he was better at reading other people's emotions. He couldn't be sure whether Lisanne had told them that they had to go and they were angry about it or whether they had grown out of their reluctance to be seen with their parents. Since Lisanne had been complaining about their behavior only a few months ago it seemed unlikely that they'd grown out of it to him. He shrugged, "Are we ready to go?"

They took Lisanne's larger car to Sal's Pizzeria. Once they'd ordered and received their sodas, Lisanne lifted her cup and said, "A toast."

Vaz lifted his cup with the others and looked back and forth at the members of his family. This little celebration of whatever they were honoring made him feel warm and happy. Lisanne said, "To scholarships!"

Vaz tilted his head curiously, "Scholarships?"

"First you have to say 'Hear, hear.'"

"OK." Vaz said "Hear, hear," with the rest, then said again, "Scholarships?"

"Dante got offered a wrestling scholarship to ECU and is still hoping to get one from NCSU."

Vaz turned in surprise to look at Dante, "Congratulations!" A moment later, he belatedly put his hand out to shake and Dante took it.

Vaz looked back at Lisanne who said, "And, Tiona's counselor thinks she'll get an academic scholarship. He's putting her up for several. Though I know it isn't a sure thing, I'm very proud of her."

Dante stared at his mother a moment then said, "Mom, it *is* pretty much a sure thing you know."

Lisanne said, "Dante those types of scholarships are pretty competitive."

Dante stared a moment, then said, "You *do* know that 'T' has the highest GPA in the school?"

Lisanne, taken aback, looked at Tiona, "Really?"

Tiona blushed, "Yeah."

"Well, don't look embarrassed! Shout *that* from the rooftops!"

"Mom! Shhh, I don't want everyone to think I'm some kind of nerd!"

Lisanne laughed merrily. Vaz blinked, then leaned to Tiona and said "Congratulations." He held his hand out to shake.

Tiona, surprised that her father would offer to shake hands, nonetheless shook his hand and said, "Thanks Dad." Shouldn't he have given her a hug like her mother would have? Of course, as she thought back on it, even when he'd given her hugs as a little girl, they had been wooden and uncomfortable rather than the warm comforting embraces that her mother administered.

Dante said, "And, you know she got a perfect 800 score on the math part of her SAT?"

Lisanne let out a little whoop, "'T'! Why didn't you tell me?!"

Tiona shrugged, still blushing.

Lisanne said, "I am so, *so* proud of you! Can I give you a hug?"

Tiona glanced around and, seeing no one she knew, gave a little nod.

As Lisanne hugged her Vaz watched. This, he realized, made him very happy. He wondered if he was supposed to hug Tiona too. Hugs always made him uncomfortable. Except private ones with Lisanne of course. When Lisanne let Tiona go he settled for reaching out and patting her clumsily on the shoulder, "Congratulations," he said again and wondered how common 800s were. He himself had had an 800 on

189

the math section but had no idea whether a lot or a few were awarded, just that they were good scores.

As his family ate, they excitedly discussed scholarships, how much they might be worth and which ones Tiona might be up for. Though Vaz had little to contribute, he continued to feel highly contented with his family's new dynamic. He'd hated it when he and Lisanne weren't getting along and, though sometimes he hadn't personally recognized the 'surly' behavior of the kids himself, he had been able to tell when it upset Lisanne.

He hoped that this happy state would persist. He'd only had to work out to exhaustion once today and that had only been because he'd been frustrated once again by his failure to generate a successful mathematical model for the hydrogen-boron fusion events.

***

Stillman Davis examined himself in the bathroom mirror as he slid off his wedding ring, kissed it and put it in his pocket. He didn't feel guilty this time; after all, he was playing a single guy tonight in the best interests of his wife as well as himself. He ran his comb through his thick, dark hair, re-tucked his shirt and headed back out into the bar.

After a few minutes of apparently aimless wandering he fetched up next to his target at the bar. She was pretty, though since she was about five years older than he was, not someone he would normally have been interested in. "How's your Friday night going?" he asked as he flagged down the bartender.

An hour later he'd purchased a couple of "whisky starkies" for her. He'd drunk a couple with her, but as he'd specified to the bartender earlier, his had been weak and hers had been strong. "So where do you work?"

"At a paten' offish, you?"

"I'm a business consultant," he shot her one of the fake e-cards he'd made up for this evening and watched her glance up at her HUD to look at it. "I represent several manufacturing companies. Maybe I could hook up some of your inventors with manufacturers?"

She raised an eyebrow.

"Do you run the office? 'Cause if you do, maybe you could offer my services, you know, as kind of a 'value added' proposition?" He knew she was only an assistant but he knew the value of overestimating someone's importance.

She laughed, "I don' think so." She let her head fall to the side, obviously pretty drunk.

Stillman motioned to the bartender for another round. "Do you ever get to see any interesting inventions?" He raised his hands defensively, "Not that I'm asking for any secrets," he laughed.

She grinned knowingly, "Mosht of them are sooo boring, and even if I wanted to, I couldn't 'splain any secrets to you. The latest one is probably the bigges' thing we've *ever* tried to patent. An I couldn' give tha' secret away no matter how bad I wanted, hah, I'd have to be a nuclear fishi… fiz, physishist! They're patentin' a cheap way to make atomic energy… can you believe tha' shit?!"

Stillman tried not to let his eyes widen as shock flooded through him. Instead he tried to sound drunk himself, "You mean, like fusion, or some such crap?"

She pointed a finger at him, "Yeah! Fushion, fusion. Tha's it! *Just* tha' kinda crap, exac'ly."

"Oh, come on! No one can do that!"

"You don' wanna bet againsht 'dis guy. He'sh really weir' bu' he keepsh patentn' more and more shtuff an' it almos' alwaysh makesh a *lo'* o' money."

Stillman felt goosebumps, it had to be Gettnor! No one else was both weird *and* had a lot of successful patents. Fusion! This was *so* much better than he'd hoped for. He just needed to separate himself from this woman, without her suspecting his motivations. He found out that she was a Tar Heel fan so he talked to her about college basketball for a bit. Then he hunched a bit and said, "Shit! There's my girlfriend. She and I haven't been getting along, but I want to go over there and try to salvage our relationship." He got out of his chair and walked away, going over to talk to Esther, a girl he'd known all the way back in high school.

He hoped that his new friend was ready to drop him but that he could reconnect with her if he needed. If so, he could give her a story about he and his "girlfriend" breaking up for good.

    ***

Vangester stormed through the labs on Sunday. He'd demanded that all of Querx's scientists work as close to around the clock as they could until they had evaluated and recreated the hydrogen absorption alloy. He'd felt certain that a week would be plenty of time but decided to have them work over the weekend too in case making the alloy was harder than it sounded. Now he had this panicked feeling that a week wouldn't be nearly enough.

The lab had confirmed that the disks Gettnor had left behind did absorb huge quantities of hydrogen, in the range of 1200 to 1600 times their volume. By Gettnor's records they knew they were composed of boron-vanadium-palladium and the percentages of each element in the alloy. But, when they casted pellets of boron-vanadium-palladium in the correct percentages, the pellets absorbed pitiful quantities of hydrogen!

He'd asked why they made pellets instead of disks and they'd said that it was because pellets would be easier to use in a hydrogen storage tank. He'd demanded that they replicate Gettnor's work first by casting disks. They'd grumbled, but done it though it took hours to create molds for the discs. Like they'd predicted, it only increased the amount of hydrogen absorption to about 20% percent of the alloy's volume.

Then they'd assayed the Gettnor disks to confirm that the percentages in Gettnor's notes were correct.

They were.

That was when Vangester flew off the handle. He'd been yelling at people pretty much nonstop since then, but not getting the results he wanted.

One of the lab rat guys came down the hall, "Mr. Vangester, Dr. Ohcott would like to show you something?"

Vangester rolled his eyes, "I hope this is something good," he rumbled, mostly to himself, and followed the guy down to a lab at the end of the hall. Ohcott turned out to be a small, dark, birdlike fellow in a dark room. "What?"

Ohcott said, "Ah, Mr. Vangester, I think I've found the problem. Here, look at the surface of Dr. Gettnor's alloy."

Vangester snorted, "Come on Ohcott, I have no idea what I'm looking at here."

"Oh, sorry, I've put the specimen in our scanning electron microscope. This is one of Dr. Gettnor's disks on the left side of the screen and the disk we made here on the right."

"OK, I see they're different. What does it mean?"

"Well I'm not sure what it means, but the structure of Gettnor's alloy is much, much finer. In fact I can't really resolve *any* structure. It might be that the large crystals in our casting lock the hydrogen out of some areas. Or it might be that boron is clumping in some areas, vanadium in others and palladium in others. Personally I favor the latter. I think the palladium in Gettnor's alloy somehow dictates the arrangement of the boron atoms and perhaps serves as a catalyst to break H_2 into monomolecular hydrogen that enters the interstices like it does in pure palladium."

"So! Make our alloy with a fine structure!"

"Sir, we don't know how to do that. Gettnor's ability to create alloys with weird properties was astonishing. I don't think anyone in the world can hold a candle to him. Why don't you just hire him back?"

"Goddammit! He doesn't want to come back! Weren't you listening when I briefed you guys?"

"Well, just hire him as a consultant to teach us how to make the alloy then."

"We can't do that. You guys need to figure out how to make the alloy yourselves!"

"We can try," Ohcott said dubiously, "but I don't think we'll have any luck. We could probably spend years trying different methods of casting that alloy without getting the same results as Gettnor. Somehow he was able to predict the conditions necessary to produce different crystallizations. I think he'd worked out his own mathematical formulas that predicted crystal structures from casting conditions. It might be that he even had some other substance in the casting that evaporated during crystallization; he told me once that he used a lot of volatile elements to achieve the crystal structures that made some of his materials so amazing. You remember his patent for the J-Point battery? It depends on the cathode being made with an alloy that's casted using volatiles."

Vangester headed up to his office to get a couple of aspirin and a neat glass of Parker's Heritage bourbon. He leaned back in his chair, closed his eyes and contemplated the pain of accepting Anbala Singh's ultimatum.

***

Vaz accepted a call from Smint who excitedly said, "Vaz, you're not going to believe what I've managed to arrange." Smint paused to wait for Vaz to ask him "what," but the silence just stretched until he realized that Vaz probably wouldn't think to do so. "I've been talking to John Vernor at GE. You remember he was the one that ramrodded their licensing of your high temperature superconductor?"

Vaz said, "I remember him."

"Well, I told him that you had a new product he should look at because I thought it would be a good fit for GE."

"OK."

"I didn't tell him that it was fusion for fear that he'd blow us off as crazy, but believe it or not, I got him to come down and look at it without even knowing what we're going to show him."

Gettnor said curiously, "Is it OK to show it to him without having a patent?"

"I checked with Milton. He says it's OK to show it to them. We'll have him sign a non-disclosure agreement but we're confirmed as 'patent applied for,' so they can't very well steal it from us. If they want it, they may bear the patent costs and save us having to pay for patenting.

"OK."

Smint chuckled at himself for being disappointed that Vaz wasn't more excited, "He's flying down here tomorrow to look it over."

"It's not functional right now, can we show him recordings?"

Smint's sphincter's clenched. Was he about to hear that Vaz couldn't reproduce the effect? The same as so many other researchers who'd claimed fusion in the past? Heart in his throat he said, "Not functional?"

"No."

"Why?!"

"I've disassembled it to work on the new version."

"Can you put it back together?"

"No. That would be a waste. The new version will be *much* better."

"Vaz, this is important!"

"The old version really isn't very good."

"Come on, it produced enormous currents!"

"Yes, but there was a lot of leakage. Also, if my current theory is correct, the new model will reduce the number of side reactions."

"Reduce side reactions?"

"Produce fewer neutrons."

"Vaz that'd be great, but we can work on that later. If your new theory is wrong it might not even work! We might not get this chance to sell to GE again if we put him off now."

"Then we can sell it to someone else."

"Vaz... I know, and you know, that fusion will be an enormous boon to mankind. *We* know that companies would have to be crazy to pass up a chance at it. But, you've got to understand, it is *such* accepted dogma that low energy nuclear fusion is impossible, we won't even be able to get our foot in the door. We *can't* pass up this opportunity!"

"What time is he coming?"

"Tomorrow, he'd get here about 11AM."

After a long pause Vaz said, "I might have it ready by then."

"Might?"

"Might. I don't think so."

"Vaz, it'll be a disaster if we tell him we have fusion and then can't produce."

"Tell him to come Thursday then."

"I'll see what he says." After a pause he asked, "Would Vernor be able to bring his own meters and detectors."

"Why would he want to do that?"

"To be sure we aren't faking the results."

"Why would we do that?"

"Vaz, every previous claim of tabletop fusion has turned out to be a fake."

"I don't understand why anyone would fake it. The truth would come out sooner or later."

"Trust me on this? He's going to be worried if he can't check it for himself."

"OK."

"Please do your best to have it ready by Thursday?"

"OK."

***

Jerrod looked up to see Stillman Davis in his hallway again. A flash of irritation came over him, but he told his AI to release the lock on the door. "Hello Stilly," he sighed.

Davis pointed to Jerrod's AI with a questioning look.

Jerrod signaled that his was off.

"Jerrod, I've done a little recon on this new patent of Gettnor's. Get this, it's for *fusion*!"

Jerrod frowned, "You mean like the Ford?"

Stillman winced a little at the depths of Jerrod's ignorance. "No, atomic fusion. That's what the Ford was named after."

"Really?"

"Yes, it's a way to make energy, electricity. Solve the energy crisis." He saw Jerrod's interest waning, "It's worth *billions*."

Jerrod perked up, "And you think your Chinaman would pay how much for the plans?"

"Millions."

"And how are we going to get the plans out of Gettnor?"

"Um, that's your field. I was thinking you'd threaten him or something."

"How do we make sure he gives us the right plans?"

"If he doesn't," Davis lowered his voice and sounded threatening, "we'll be back."

Jerrod leaned back, staring at the ceiling and thinking. "Sooo, we show up at his place one night, scare the crap out of him, make him export his files to a drive, then tell him, if he talks, or if he stiffed us on functioning files, we'll be back to make him sorry he ever lived?"

Stillman nodded, "Something like that."

"What about what happened to Billy?"

"What do you mean?"

"I mean Billy's a big tough guy, how'd Gettnor manage to take him out?"

"There's got to be more to that story. A geek like Gettnor doesn't 'take *anyone* out.' I suspect Billy's too embarrassed to tell you what really happened. Maybe he fell down the stairs."

Jerrod grunted, Billy was out on bail awaiting trial on the home invasion charges but Jerrod hadn't talked to him directly, not wanting there to be any record that he had anything to do with Billy. Billy hadn't worn his AI to Gettnor's house and Gettnor's AV records wouldn't be available until the trial, so Jerrod hadn't seen an audio-video record of the events that day.

Davis said, "Besides, if you're worried that Gettnor's dangerous, just take some weapons."

"Guns will increase the charges if we get caught."

Davis shrugged, "Bats… or something else. And *don't* get caught for Chrissake."

***

Vaz looked up with some irritation as Lisanne opened the door to the basement. He would have a hard time finishing the new fusion setup if he kept getting interrupted.

"I was thinking that it might be nice for the family to go out to dinner and watch the new JumpGirl movie this coming Saturday night."

"OK." Vaz didn't want to go, but even more, he wanted Lisanne to be satisfied and go back upstairs, leaving him to work.

"Great! What're you working on?"

"Putting together the new fusion device. I need to get it done quickly, so please don't take up my time if you don't have to."

"Quickly?"

"By Thursday."

"Why?"

"Someone's coming to watch it work."

Excitement warred with alarm in Lisanne's mind. Did someone actually believe it could work, and therefore was coming to witness it? What would happen to Vaz's psychological balance when it didn't? After a pause she said, "Oh. Can I help?"

"No! Like when we cook together, *that* would be a disaster."

"OK. I'll leave you then." She said with some irritation and turned to go, hoping he'd call her back and apologize.

He didn't.

199

Upstairs she worried about what might happen Thursday to Vaz's stability.

***

Vangester stepped into Dennis' office and dropped into a chair, "We are well and truly screwed as regards that alloy! The weak links we've got working in the lab have absolutely no idea how to crystallize it correctly. Have you found a legal way to stymie Gettnor and his trained attack dog?"

Dennis stared at him a moment, then slowly shook his head back and forth. "You're 'well and truly screwed' there too. I've taken the liberty of seeking opinions from outside counsel, not once, but twice. They've both advised that you do your very best to negotiate favorable terms because the most recent court precedents regarding AV records and contracts are very much in Gettnor's favor."

"Shit, shit… *shit!*" Vangester reached up to put his palms on his forehead, rubbing his temples with his thumbs. "The board's gonna have my ass!"

Dennis said nothing. He agreed with Vangester's assessment.

Vangester peered up with bloodshot eyes, "Do you have any other ideas?"

Dennis shook his head, "You need to *take* Singh's offer. Save yourself the cost of the interest on Gettnor's money and get the formula for that alloy. If you can turn the alloy into a big success you might be able to convince the board that you actually made chicken salad out of chicken shit."

Vangester buried his face back in his hands and mumbled, "I doubt they'll give me time to turn it into a success."

"Get your sales and business people together and draw up ambitious plans for how you're going to turn it into a huge win for the company."

Vangester slowly raised his head, considering, then visibly brightened, "Good idea, thanks." He got up and left the office with purpose in his stride.

***

Smint called Vaz, "I'm going to the airport to pick up John Vernor. Is the device working?"

"I'm just finishing the assembly. I'll have it put together by the time you arrive."

"You haven't actually had a trial run yet?" Smint said in a panicked tone.

Oblivious to Smint's distress, "No, I just finished assembling it."

"Wait, which one are you setting up? The Mark 2 that we know works or the Mark 3 that you've been working on?"

"Mark 3, it'll be *much* better than the Mark 2."

"But Vaz! What if it doesn't work?"

"Then he'll have to come back another time." Vaz said this as if surprised that Smint could be so obtuse.

"Oh, Christ. We'd better hope it works, we'll never get him back if it doesn't."

"There's no reason it shouldn't work. I haven't changed any of the underlying principles."

"Shit happens, my friend, shit happens. Well, we should be there at your place just after noon, come what may."

***

Wondering what had his old friend Jack Smint so riled up, John Vernor picked up his bag off the luggage slide. He was only staying overnight and usually would have just carried on a small bag but Smint had suggested he bring a variety of radiation detectors, an ammeter, a voltage multimeter, and some thermocouples. He wondered why, surely they had such equipment available at Querx. Why he should bring his own was a complete mystery to him. Smint was practically dancing from one foot to the other and John couldn't tell if it was excitement or anxiety. As he got in Smint's car he said, "OK, I'm here. Can you tell me what I'm going to be looking at?"

"I'd rather not. It's a surprise you're not going to believe… I don't want to spoil it."

Vernor sighed, this all seemed a little childish to him. But GE had made some tremendous profits on Gettnor's high temperature superconductor, so if he had something new, it would be crazy not to come down and check it out. "Do you have patent protection?"

"Patent applied for."

The rest of the ride they talked about baseball.

To Vernor's surprise, the car parked itself on a residential street of ordinary two story houses. He turned to Smint in some surprise, "This isn't Querx."

Getting out of the car, Smint said, "Ah, no, I retired. Neither Vaz nor I work at Querx anymore. Vaz has set himself up with a pretty amazing research lab in his basement."

Vernor's heart sank. Had he come all the way down to North Carolina just to look at someone's home science project? Was this some shabby, poorly thought out garage experiment that he would be embarrassed to look at? He got out of the car and followed Smint up the walk, trying to remind himself that Gettnor had a truly amazing track record of fairly important innovations. However, his mind kept tracking back to just how weird he'd thought Gettnor was, the one time they'd met. "This is Gettnor's *house*?" he asked

"Yes," Smint said, introducing himself to the house AI which let them in. "Right this way, he's set up the lab in the basement."

Vernor practically cringed as he descended the stairs, *a basement lab! How could I not have checked this out a little more before I bought tickets and flew down here?* He started thinking about the work he could have been doing back home instead of wasting his time down here. He quietly asked his AI whether there was a flight he could still catch back to New York this afternoon or evening. Checking his HUD, he saw that it had found one in three hours, he whispered, "Find me a seat."

The door into the basement opened and Vernor stepped into a brightly lit, large space that, to his surprise, looked much the same as many industrial labs he had visited. *Maybe this won't be as embarrassing as I thought,* he mused. Then he noticed a cot and clothes in the corner with a punching bag and other exercise equipment. He sighed.

Gettnor sat at a bench wearing head mounted magnifiers and working down inside a long stainless steel pipe that was bivalved open on hinges. Smint said with a nervous laugh, "Isn't it finished?"

Gettnor looked up blandly, "Almost."

Vernor felt a muscle twitch in his cheek and tried not to grind his teeth.

Smint said, "Can I help?"

"No."

"How much longer?"

"I think about ten minutes."

Smint sighed and his shoulders drooped.

Trying not to fume Vernor said, "Why don't you tell me what it is while we're waiting?" He eyed the device which seemed to for the most part consist of a big coil. The part Gettnor was working on appeared to have a stainless steel frame around a

203

concave device, kind of like the mirror in a reflector telescope, except the concave device looked like it was a ceramic with a non-reflective metallic surface. At the focal point of the "mirror" was a thin disk then the beginning of the coil. The entire thing was hooked up to heavy duty tubing and wiring. It looked very professional, but Vernor had never seen anything like it and wouldn't have been able to hazard the first guess as to what it was for.

Smint cleared his throat. "Well, Vaz has found a way to achieve fusion."

Vernor waited a moment for Smint to finish the sentence by telling him what two objects, or processes Vaz might be fusing together. Then he realized that the sentence was complete. In an effort not to explode he slowly closed his eyes and tried not to squinch them. He opened them and looked at Smint, he forced a smile, "Fusion of?"

"Hydrogen and boron."

Vernor frowned, *maybe they weren't talking about nuclear fusion?* "Hydrogen and boron?"

"Yes, it should be much harder than deuterium fusion and, of course, even now no one has achieved positive energy yet with deuterium fusion. However, through a happy accident, hydrogen-boron is what he's accomplished. H B is much more desirable than deuterium fusion because it's aneutronic."

Vernor sighed, vaguely remembering some of this from his nuclear physics courses in college, "Come on. Surely you didn't bring me all the way down here..." He stopped as he realized that, of course, they had. And *they* must believe that it worked or they *wouldn't* have brought him down. But being called to look at a device that just happened not to be working at the time was such a classic story in scientific chicanery.

Smint said, "I know just what you're thinking, but it really does work. As soon as Vaz finishes..." he trailed off at the look in Vernor's eyes. "It really does work…" he trailed off.

"Sure it does. Sure it does," Vernor said and glanced up at his HUD. "Well, I'll give you 45 minutes. That's when my taxi back to the airport will arrive."

"But, I thought you were here until the morning!?"

"That was before I knew what you thought you were going to show me," Vernor said in an irritated tone.

Smint glanced at Vaz who was working on the device as if he hadn't heard a word that had been said. He pulled the soldering iron back, switched it off and laid it down. He picked up the leads of a multimeter and began touching them to points in the mechanism. Vaz spoke to his AI and the wall screens lit, showing the views from small cameras mounted here and there inside the stainless steel pipe. Then he spoke again and one of the screens popped up some graphs, all flat at present. He reached back in to the mechanism, touching a probe to points inside and looking up to see the graphs reacting.

Once all the graphs had responded to his probe, he set the probe down and started closing the bivalved cover on the tube. With a power socket wrench he screwed bolts along both sides to squeeze the pipe shut. Once he'd done that he turned to Smint, "Help me carry it to the tank." The two men lifted the pipe and carried it over to set it in front of a very large stainless steel box where they snapped ropes to it. This was the first part of the whole thing that struck Vernor as looking a little sloppy and unprofessional.

They pulled on the ropes, lifting the pipe up the front of the box and over the edge into it. Once it had disappeared their eyes turned to the screens. One screen showed a video of the pipe floating on a liquid. Despite his irritation Vernor couldn't stifle his curiosity, "What's the liquid?"

"Water," Gettnor said.

Smint clarified, "Even though the main reaction is aneutronic there are some side chain reactions that release a few neutrons. The water absorbs them."

"And the boron inside the tank," Gettnor said, motioning to Smint to pull on a different rope on his end. As they pulled, the pipe could be seen submerging into the tank. Once it was submerged they stopped and Gettnor studied the monitors for a moment. He said, "Leak. Let's lift it out."

Vernor hadn't seen any leak but they lifted the pipe back out with the rope and pulley set up. Gettnor tightened a couple of the bolts and they lifted it back in. This time Gettnor was satisfied and they pulled the pipe down into the water to rest on a cradle that appeared to be centered in the tank. The ropes were tied off and Gettnor said, "Check systems," to his AI. He looked up at his HUD a moment, then said, "Stop test." He turned to Smint, "We need to take it out," he said stepping over to the ropes holding the pipe submerged in the tank.

"What's wrong?" Smint asked, darting a nervous glance at Vernor. He began untying his rope and they started letting the pipe rise to the surface of the water.

Gettnor said, "The coil doesn't have a good connection."

As they carried the pipe back over to the cradle on Gettnor's bench Vernor looked up at his HUD. "Thirty more minutes," he said. He thought Gettnor might start moving a little more rapidly, but no, he continued moving deliberately, using his power wrench to open the pipe and bivalve it again. Once it was open he tightened a connection, spoke to his AI, looked at his HUD and then began closing the pipe back up.

Smint began fumbling bolts into place to help close the pipe. Gettnor looked up at him and said, "Calmly Jack."

Smint took a deep breath, "We don't have much time."

"We have plenty of time to run the test, what we don't have time for are mistakes." He began tightening the bolts with his power wrench.

Smint said, "But if Dr. Vernor has to leave before we get it working…"

Expressionlessly Gettnor said, "Then he will have made a serious mistake."

Vernor narrowed his eyes at Gettnor's arrogance but only said, "Twenty two more minutes."

The pipe went back into the tank, didn't leak, and was pulled down into its cradle. "Check systems," Gettnor said to his AI. After studying his HUD a moment he nodded, turned to the wall screens and said, "Begin test run."

Gettnor sat down and after a moment Smint pushed the other chair over to Vernor. For a moment he thought of politely refusing the chair since there wasn't one for Smint, but then, irritated, he sat down and turned his attention to the screens. He wondered what he was looking at. Smint must have thought the same thing because he bent, pointed to the different graphs and said, "If you look at the little graphs, the upper left graph is thermal, registering the temperature inside the device." Vernor saw that the graph had risen slightly. "The next one is the x-ray detector, then the neutron detector. The next lower ones graph the same things, but out in the tank. The bottom graphs measure the same things on the outside of the tank. The big graph at the far end is the current induced in the coil by the alpha particles."

As Vernor watched the graphs all began to rise. Well, except the neutron detectors. The neutron detector graph from inside the pipe occasionally had little blips on it. the other two stayed quiescent. As did the x-ray graph for the detector outside the tank.

Vernor blinked, the graph for current had just dropped suddenly and was rising again. It got near the top of the graph and dropped again. It happened one more time and he said, "What's happening to the 'current' graph?"

"It's going off scale, so the scale is being readjusted."

It readjusted again. Vernor whispered to his AI to bring him up a summary of the properties of hydrogen-boron fusion. He scanned a summary on his HUD. It should indeed produce heat, x-rays and some side chain reactions that would produce some neutrons. He looked back at the graphs. And *lots* of energetic alpha particles that would induce large currents in coils.

Current commercial energy production from nuclear reactions first produced heat, which then had to be used to heat water to create steam. The steam then turned turbines to produce electricity. He felt a frisson of excitement as he realized just how desirable H-B fusion would be.

Then he got to the part of the summary that reminded him just how impossible it was. He looked back at the screens where the graphs were leveling off. Gettnor sat immobile, watching the screens. Smint's eyes were focused on Vernor. With a sigh Vernor said, "You really expect me to believe you're achieving fusion… energy positive fusion?"

Smint looked a little panicked but Gettnor simply turned his chair to face Vernor and frowned, "Why not? You can see the readings for yourself."

Vernor's brow drew down, "That could be faked."

"I thought Dr. Smint told you to bring your own test equipment?"

Vernor's eyes widened as he realized that he did have his equipment out in the car. Smint had known he'd react like this. That was why he'd insisted he bring his own equipment.

Vernor glanced up at his HUD, "Sorry, but my time is up."

Smint said, "But…"

Expressionlessly, Gettnor said, "Dr. Vernon, this device *is* producing fusion. Someone *will* license it. We have no reason to care very much who. But if you leave without fully evaluating our claim; you, *and* your company, will certainly regret that decision."

Vernor stared at the bland Gettnor a moment then said, "Sorry." He turned to Smint, "Jack, I need to get my bag out of the trunk of your car. My taxi should be here by now."

Jack's shoulders slumped and he said, "I'll walk you out."

Gettnor turned back to his screens, then as if it was an afterthought said, "Goodbye."

The taxi was pulling up when they got out to Smint's car. Vernor lifted his bag out and turned to Smint, "Sorry." He put his hand out to shake.

Smint said, "Yeah," as he shook Vernor's hand. Then he firmed up and said, "You know, don't worry. Vaz is right. It *does* actually work. We *will* be able to sell it to someone else. This actually isn't a problem for us… Sorry you flew down for nothing."

"OK." Vernor turned and got in the taxi. Then he sat there.

Eventually the taxi said, "Destination?" A moment later it pulled away from the curb, evidently having been given the airport as a destination by his AI. He said, "Stop." Shaking his head, he got back out of the taxi and grabbed his suitcase. He dragged it up the walk to Gettnor's house and touched the doorbell.

The house AI said, "Yes."

"Please tell Dr. Gettnor that John Vernor is back."

Two hours later Vernor stretched a cramp in his back and said, "I'll be damned." By his measurements the device was consuming 1,250 watts and producing about fifteen thousand.

Gettnor said that by his calculations a small device the size they were testing should be able to produce up to eighty thousand watts, but he didn't have any way to dispose of that much energy. The local power company would let him dump fifteen kilowatts onto its grid according to a policy established so that people who had solar roofs could sell their excess energy on sunny days. Knowing that was as much energy as he could dispose of he hadn't built the coils or the power runs to handle more. "That would have to be the Mark 4 version," he said. He'd also pointed out that the device would produce that much direct electricity just from the alpha particles, the heat it produced could also produce steam which could be used to create even more power. With the correct set up the x-rays it emitted could also be turned into power. Gettnor calculated that an optimized device should be able to generate a megawatt on a consumption of about 10 kilowatts. The device would be almost the same size though the equipment to harvest the power would be significantly larger.

As Vernor prepared to leave he said, "I'm going to have to study up on fusion and look over these results. I might want to come over tomorrow and observe another run or ask questions, depending on what I learn. Probably I'll just head back to New York in the morning though. If so, GE will be in touch. That's assuming they don't just laugh at me when I tell them what you've got here."

Gettnor frowned, "Why would they do that?"

Vernor and Smint laughed because they thought he still didn't understand. When they realized that Gettnor actually had a sly grin on his face, they laughed even harder.

***

Vaz made chicken breast stuffed with sundried tomatoes, olives, and cheese for dinner Thursday night. It melted in their mouths and Dante asked for several extra pieces. Lisanne studied Vaz while they ate, desperately wanting to ask him about what happened during the day, as this was the day that someone had been supposed to come by to look at his fusion device. At the same time she *didn't* want to ask for fear that his apparent mental stability would come apart at the seams.

So Lisanne felt a mixture of anticipation and horror when Tiona looked up and said, "Dad, how's your hydrogen-boron fusion thing going?"

However, Vaz calmly said, "The third iteration is working well. It performs quite closely to what my calculations had predicted."

Tiona tilted her head, "How does it do it without generating billions of degrees of heat?"

Vaz shrugged, then frowned, "I wish I had a reasonable theory for that."

***

Friday morning, Vangester stared at Anbala Singh with a smile on his face and hatred in his veins. Phil Dennis had attempted to negotiate several points and she'd shot them all down.

However, neither Dennis, nor Vangester, objected to the language of the clause of the agreement which stated, "Querx will obtain a patent in

Dr. Gettnor's name for the use of Dr. Gettnor's boron-vanadium-palladium alloy for hydrogen storage. These rights to the use of the alloy for hydrogen storage follows from the fact that hydrogen storage had been Dr. Gettnor's assigned research task at the time of the termination of his employment and the alloy's capacity for hydrogen storage had become evident at that time. Royalties on this patent will be paid according to Dr. Gettnor's original employment contract."

Neither Dennis nor Vangester appeared to notice that this discharged Gettnor's responsibility regarding the alloy. That it specified that uses known at the time of his departure were covered but that other—non-hydrogen storage—uses of the alloy recognized after his departure would not be covered by the agreement. Anbala slightly regretted the time she had spent preparing arguments regarding Gettnor's retention of such rights, but was happy that it didn't become necessary to use them.

 ***

Lisanne came home early on Friday. Because of the current economic downturn, Radix, where she worked, had had a loss of demand for their prototyping services. Everyone had been running scared at Radix because there had been talk of layoffs, but today the CEO had called everyone in for a meeting and said he didn't want to lose anyone so he was going to try going to a four day work week for a while until things picked back up. They were to start by all going home at noon that day.

"I realize," he'd said, "that some of you won't feel like you can make ends meet on a reduced salary and may have to look elsewhere. But, I'm hoping we can turn this around, especially if the economy will just bounce back quickly. This way, perhaps it might be possible to keep every single one of you, people who I've come to respect and rely on as part of our team here."

Lisanne felt panicked. It wasn't as bad as if she'd been laid off of course, but with Vaz not working, she could hardly afford the reduction in salary. They not only wouldn't be putting any money away for the kids education, they'd have to start taking it out! She'd need to spend her Fridays applying for other jobs.

As she rode home she hoped that when Vaz encountered her at home, applying for jobs, that it might light a fire under him so that he would look for work himself. She didn't intend to announce what had happened. She just hoped that he would ask her why she was home on a Friday so she could then explain it to him in a nonthreatening way.

However, when she pulled in to the garage, his car was gone. At first she was disappointed, but then she counted it as a plus. When he came in, he'd encounter her immediately. She'd been worried that, as much time as he spent in the basement, it might be several Fridays before he realized she wasn't going to work. She set herself up on the couch in the family room to begin her job search process. There, Vaz would have to walk past her to get to the basement.

Lisanne had reformatted and updated her résumé and begun to search the net for possible jobs when the house AI said, "Ms. Anbala Singh is here to speak to Dr. Gettnor."

Lisanne frowned and had the AI throw Singh's image up on the screen in the family room. She was a slender, dark skinned woman of Indian descent wearing a business suit. Quite pretty too, in her early thirties, Lisanne estimated. *Why would an attractive young woman like that be visiting Vaz at home during the day?*

Lisanne's heart skipped a beat. *Did Vaz get himself in such excellent physical condition for* this *woman, who now has the gall to visit him at home during the day! How long has this been going on?* She got up and went to the door thinking how unlikely it seemed that Vaz Gettnor, of all men, would have an affair. She opened the door, "Hello," she said coolly.

Singh smiled, "Mrs. Gettnor?"

Singh certainly didn't look like someone who was nervous to be confronting her boyfriend's wife. "Yes?"

"Isn't Dr. Gettnor here?"

"No." Lisanne felt like she had controlled her voice well enough that her hostility hadn't shown. Well didn't show until she had cause anyway.

"Well," Singh said brightly, "maybe you can give him the good news that Querx accepted all of our requests this morning. I had hoped to give him the good news myself but I'm sure you'll enjoy telling him just as much as I would, eh? I also need to leave these papers for him to sign, assuming he agrees." She winked and pulled out a 9x12" envelope and handed it to Lisanne.

Trying to hide her dismay, Lisanne took the envelope, *is Vaz in legal trouble with Querx?* "I'll give it to him, thanks."

"Have a great celebration," Singh said airily as she turned and walked away.

Lisanne felt a little better that Singh felt they had reason to celebrate. Perhaps whatever problem he'd had there had been resolved by the agreement in the envelope? She retreated to the family room and set the envelope down in front of her. She desperately wanted to know what was inside but thought that, since she hadn't heard of Singh or of any issues with Querx, Vaz might consider it to be a secret. She fingered the envelope, then suddenly realized it wasn't sealed, just held shut with a tab. She could look inside and no one would be the wiser. She glanced toward the garage, no sign of Vaz.

She bit her lip and popped the tab, opening the envelope and pulling out the papers.

An hour later she was still intermittently re-reading it. She'd read it multiple times, then brewed a cup of tea and come back to it. She kept coming back to the section that said, "Querx agrees, within nine days of the signing of this agreement, to reimburse Dr. Gettnor for the $27,891,752.00 shortfall in royalty payments owed to him over the past nine years. Dr. Gettnor graciously rescinds any claim on interest owed on those monies."

That couldn't *possibly* mean what it sounded like, could it?

Lisanne sat trying to decide what it all meant. Her emotions ping-ponged all over the place. To start with she was excited, $27million! Then she fluctuated between being excited, angry that he'd let her worry about money, and then worry that he was keeping it from her for a reason? Did he want to leave her?

Finally she started to hope that his might mean that he wasn't delusional.

Tiona came in, "Hey Mom, how's Dad?" she asked quietly.

"Huh? Oh, OK I guess." Lisanne answered absently.

Tiona looked curiously at her somewhat dazed appearing mother. "Aren't you worried because he was still talking about fusion last night?"

"Uh, I'm… not sure. I'm just pretty happy that we've all been getting along better."

"But, Mom. *Fusion!* That's just crazy talk."

Lisanne frowned a moment, then focused her gaze intently on her daughter. "'T,' what if… what if your Dad actually did figure out how to achieve low energy nuclear fusion?"

"Mom!"

"Seriously, have you ever heard an old saying to the effect that 'a person is never famous in their own hometown'?"

Tiona frowned, "No, that seems… ridiculous."

"It just means that those who know the person well are the hardest to convince that he or she's extraordinary."

Tiona's eyebrows ascended. "You're saying that you think Dad's extraordinary?"

Lisanne stared off into the distance, "I *know* he's extraordinary." She shrugged sadly, "but, you're right I guess… not 'fusion' extraordinary."

Tiona said, "Meri and I are going to see Tonnisville tonight."

"Tonnisville?"

"It's a *movie* Mom," Tiona said, rolling her eyes.

"Oh, OK." Lisanne said, thinking, *that's the teenage girl with the lame mother that I've known for so long.*

Tiona went upstairs to study, then came back down to go out with Meri. Lisanne continued to sit on the couch, occasionally opening Vaz's envelope and rereading the contents, trying to make sense of it.

Dante came in, declared he was hungry and ate the last two of Vaz's stuffed chicken breasts from the night before. Lisanne asked him if he had any plans for the evening and he told her no, then went up to his room.

Lisanne started to feel hungry herself and worry about Vaz. It wasn't like him to be gone past dinnertime.

She'd just asked her AI to connect her to him when she heard the rumbling of the garage door. A minute later the door opened and Vaz stepped in. "Hey, Vaz," she said, so full of questions and so reluctant to ask them.

He gave her a little wave and a sheepish smile. "Sorry I'm late. I forgot to call."

"Did you eat dinner?"

"No." He seemed surprised to realize it.

"I'll make tacos. Tiona's out with Meri and Dante's already eaten, but I'll bet he'd eat more."

"OK."

"A lady named Anbala Singh came by this afternoon. She said to tell you the good news that 'Querx accepted all of your requests this morning.'" Lisanne got up and handed the envelope to him, "She left this for you."

Vaz looked upset, "Oh." He stood unmoving, holding the envelope.

"She said you needed to sign the documents inside if you agreed."

Vaz looked intently at Lisanne, then sat, popped the seal and drew out the papers. Not knowing what more to say, Lisanne went into the kitchen and started cooking hamburger for tacos.

As she cooked, Lisanne eyed Vaz, wondering what he was thinking. After a bit, he got a pen and signed the documents, then put them back in the envelope and took them as he headed down to the basement. She sighed. So much for her hope that he would explain to her what was going on.

Once the tacos were done she called down to the basement to tell Vaz to come eat. He arrived as she was setting out plates and she handed him one. "Was the news good then?"

Vaz nodded, seeming uncertain about something.

"What's the deal with Querx?"

"They've agreed to pay the back royalties on inventions that I made while I worked there."

"Back royalties?"

"Originally they didn't pay me what my contract specified."

"And they're paying that now?"

"Well, they *say* they're going to."

Lisanne felt like she was pulling teeth, getting this information out of him. "How many inventions did you have while working there?"

"Twelve. Well, thirteen, they haven't patented the last one yet."

"Wow! And they're all patented?"

He nodded.

"So do they owe you a lot of money?"

Vaz nodded again.

Lisanne grinned, "Enough to send the kids to college?"

He grinned sheepishly and said, "Yeah."

Lisanne threw her arms around him and squeezed him tight, "Oh Vaz!" she whispered in his ear. "That's so great!" She leaned back and looked him in the eye, "How much is it?"

Vaz turned his head to stare out the window and almost whispered, "Twenty seven million." With dread he waited to hear that she wanted to go on a trip or move to a bigger house or something.

Lisanne leaned back tight against him and said, "Holy mother of God! Vaz, I'm so proud of you! I'm so glad." She leaned back and looked him in the eye again, "I guess this means that you should be able to fool around in your basement lab as much as you want without your wife nagging at you to get a job, huh?"

Vaz turned to look at Lisanne and gave her one of his shy grins, "Uh huh."

From the stairs Dante said, "Something smells good. You guys going to invite me to dinner or what?"

218

Lisanne laughed, "I thought you already ate, hungry boy."

They all sat to eat and Lisanne teased Dante, "If you keep eating this way, you're going to jump a couple of weight classes in wrestling you know?"

Dante, surprised that his mother seemed so happy and upbeat for a change, winked, "Well, then I'll just have to beat even bigger guys, won't I?"

Lisanne was just about to say something about his not needing a wrestling scholarship when the house AI announced, "A fault has developed in the fiberoptic connection to the net. The door camera shows workmen at the site where the fiber enters the house so they may have inadvertently damaged it."

Vaz frowned and stood, walking to the front door. He looked out and saw a large man with a small power saw cutting a section out of the optical fiber conduit where it ran up from the ground to enter the house. Five other large men stood nearby, one on the porch. Vaz realized that they were wearing latex masks like the man who had entered the house demanding he "go back to work." He stared at the men for a minute, then turned. Walking back toward the table he said, "House AI, lock all doors. Personal AI, call 911, tell them we are victims of a home invasion." He stared out the back windows and saw a large man out there as well. To Lisanne and Dante who were looking up in startlement he said, "We need to get down to the basement!" When they stared at him rather than moving, he barked, "Now!" and grabbed Lisanne by the elbow. Dragging her out of her chair, he pulled her inexorably after him. He barked at Dante again, "NOW! A group of men are about to break into the house. We'll be safer downstairs."

Dante got up and followed, Vaz's AI said, "I cannot connect to 911 by wireless. Something is saturating the wavelengths that I use with digital noise."

Vaz headed down the stairs, Lisanne stumbling after. Once Dante entered the stairs, Vaz said, "Close the door." When Dante had closed it Vaz said "House AI, lock the upper door of the basement stairwell. Dante, check that it's locked, then come down to the basement."

When Dante entered the basement he found his dad manhandling a huge tank over next to the door. Dante tried to help him push it up against the door but Vaz said, "Stop, that's close enough for now." Vaz crossed the room and returned with a large bucket which he set next to the tank. He dropped a hose from the tank into the bucket and turned on a spigot. Fluid poured into the bucket giving off clouds of fog. Vaz handed the hose to Dante and said, "Here, fill the bucket."

"What is it Dad?" Dante asked.

"Liquid nitrogen." Vaz said crossing the room and opening a large drawer. He pulled out little tanks with shoulder straps and threw one over his own shoulder. He started toward Lisanne, dropping one over her shoulder as well, then pulling tubing from it and putting a lightweight facemask onto her head. He adjusted something on the tank, then brought the other one to Dante, putting it on him too.

"Vaz? What are these?" Lisanne asked tremulously.

"Oxygen," he said, then to the house AI, "Can you put a feed from the house cameras up on the screens here in the basement?"

Lisanne said, "Why wouldn't it?" Then she covered her mouth, "Oh, the wireless is out," she said in a faint voice.

Vaz nodded, "That's why I'm speaking loudly, the AI has to receive instructions through the house microphones since my AI can't transmit to it." There was a flicker and then the wall screens lit with pictures from the different cameras around the house. Some of the men were on the porch now.

The house AI said, "They are asking permission to enter. They say they are from Time Warner Network Services."

"Denied." Vaz barked.

Lisanne said, "What do they want?"

In an ugly tone Vaz said, "They've got to be working for that son of a bitch Davis."

At the same time the AI said, "They say they need to access the inside of the house to correctly repair the fiberoptic connection."

"Oh my God!" Lisanne breathed, sitting suddenly and looking pale.

Dante said, "What do we do Dad?"

Lisanne darted an unbelieving glance at her son, *why would he think Vaz would know what to do besides hide in the basement?* She turned back to Vaz, "Why are we wearing oxygen?"

"Because I'm releasing a lot of nitrogen."

"But nitrogen isn't toxic!"

"It is if it displaces *all* the oxygen."

"Why are you doing it then?"

"I haven't done it yet," he said enigmatically.

On the screens one of the men crashed into the front door with his shoulder. The door was solid and opened outward so he didn't budge it. They could be heard cursing, then the smallest of them—still a large man—put down the bag he had over his shoulder and pulled out a baseball bat. The others stood around him to block the view from the street as he punched out the window next to the door. He climbed through it and one of the other men knocked out the rest of the glass, evidently so that the broken window wouldn't be so easily recognized as broken.

Soon the one who'd climbed in the window had opened the front door and the rest of them filed in. The bag was opened again and all of them took baseball bats. One of them bellowed, "Gettnor! We need to talk to you." He smacked the bat into his palm, then twirled it.

Vaz said, "House AI, transmit my voice to the family room." He paused frowning a moment, then said, "What do you want?"

On the screen the men looked about, evidently wondering where the voice came from, then realized it was coming from the house AI's intercom system. "Where are you?" the spokesman growled.

Vaz said nothing and after waiting a few moments the leader pointed to three of the others with his bat. "Search the house." They started to go in different directions but he barked, "Stay together!" They left the family room through the kitchen toward the living room. There weren't any cameras in there so the Gettnors could no longer see them. However they could hear things breaking. A minute or so later the men came back into the family room and checked the coat closet and the bathroom.

They rattled the locked door to the basement. "Probably behind this door," one of them said.

The leader nodded, "Check upstairs first."

On the screens the three Gettnors in the basement watched the men casually striking things with their bats as they walked around and generally leaving a trail of destruction. Shortly they were coming back down the stairs. "No one up there," one said and turned toward the door to the basement.

Vaz had put on a pair of heavy work gloves. He opened the basement door, picked up the nearly full bucket of liquid nitrogen and tossed its contents up the stairs. He quickly shut the door as huge clouds of fog began blasting out of the stairwell. He told the AI to lock the door and leaned up to peer through a fish eye lens in the door.

Lisanne stared at the lens. She'd never noticed it before and wondered if it had always been there, or whether Vaz had recently installed it when he started living in the basement and locking people out.

Vaz started filling the bucket with nitrogen again.

Upstairs Ramos stared at the locked door. Fog poured out from under it—which creeped him out. He leaned down and sniffed. *Doesn't smell bad,* he thought. It reminded him of the fog in horror movies though. He said, "Jason, break that door down."

Jason was the largest of their group, six foot seven and muscular. He grinned and hefted his bat, then swung at the knob which flew off. He stepped to the side and took a few swings at the region of the door near the latch. When it splintered and cracked, fog began pouring out through that opening too. The next blow broke a large hole around the knob and, because the blow had separated the latch section from the main door, the door itself puffed open on the fog. He reached out and pushed the door further open with his bat.

The six men peered nervously at the clouds of fog emanating from the stairwell.

Ramos sniffed again, then shrugged. "Jason, Mike, Stivitz, head down there and bring Mr. Gettnor up to us. Remember, this guy is supposed to be able to hit, don't let him sucker punch one of you."

The three big men stepped a little apprehensively to the foggy stairwell and started down.

Ramos watched them troop down into the darkened stairwell wondering what the cold fog could be. He leaned closer. He was getting a headache!

He heard something thump. Then more thumping. The three guys dropped out of Ramos' view. He leaned closer to the door. They seemed to be crumpled on top of one another at the bottom of the stairs! Suddenly the door at the bottom of the stairs opened and Gettnor, wearing some kind of clear plastic mask, reached out and dragged a limp Stivitz into the brightly lit basement. Another dude dragged Mike in, then Gettnor was back and dragging Jason floppily into the basement too.

Eyes wide, Ramos watched the other dude toss a bucket of water into the stairwell. The water exploded into steam and fog and the door closed. Ramos' headache felt worse. Jerrod was gonna be *pissed*. Ramos stepped into the stairwell and took a couple of steps down, sniffing for anything weird and searching the walls for anything that might have knocked his guys out.

Suddenly the stairwell got very dark and he felt himself falling.

Dante had watched his father peering through the fisheye lens in the door. Then he heard thumping and thought the men were hitting the door with their fists. To his amazement Vaz jerked the door open, reached into the stairwell and pulled a large man off the top of two other, tossing the man into the room, "Get the next guy Dante." He turned to Lisanne and said, "Get the cable ties," he pointed, "in the box on the right end of the bench."

Dante found the large guy in the stairwell surprisingly hard to move. He grabbed a wrist with both hands and dragged him in next to the first guy. "Dad!" he frowned. "What happened to these guys?"

Vaz dragged the third guy in, saying, "Throw that bucket of nitrogen up the stairs and close the door." He paused but once he saw Dante doing it he turned to Lisanne, "Cable ties, quick." He held a hand out to her.

Nervously she fumbled some to him.

224

"Watch." Vaz said, taking a cable tie, wrapping it around the big guy's left wrist and threading the tip through the buckle on it. He dropped that wrist and picked up another. "Put cable ties on all their wrists."

Once Vaz had cable ties on both wrists he dragged the guy over to a vertical steel post that supported one of the joists in the floor above. He put the guy's wrists around the post and bound them together with a third cable tie. Then he helped Dante drag his guy over and they bound his wrists around the post just above the first guy's. When they returned for the third guy he was beginning to twitch around. There was another thump from the door.

Vaz quickly dragged the third guy to the post and said, "Tie him in," then he went to the basement door, opened it and dragged in a fourth unconscious man.

A little while later they had four men arranged radially around the post with their wrists bound around it. Vaz said, "Bind their feet together," and began cable tying the feet on the one he was closest too.

Dante asked again, "What happened to these guys?"

"The liquid nitrogen from the bucket expanded enormously when it splattered all over the stairs. It displaced almost all the air out of the stairwell leaving only nitrogen."

"But, if they weren't getting oxygen… why didn't they turn around when they felt short of breath?"

"You feel short of breath when you accumulate carbon dioxide, not because you're short of oxygen."

"Really?"

"Really."

"So… they didn't even know they weren't getting oxygen?"

"No."

But... you can go for *minutes* without breathing," Dante said with a puzzled tone.

"An oxygen free atmosphere is much worse than holding your breath. As you breathe the 'dead air' into your lungs, the blood passing through your lung releases the little oxygen it has remaining in it into the alveoli—since the air in the alveoli has no oxygen. So the blood that leaves your lungs has virtually no oxygen. Then that blood goes to your brain and starts absorbing oxygen from your neural tissue. You almost immediately lose consciousness."

"So that's why we're wearing oxygen, so we won't fall out before *we* realize there's a problem?"

Vaz nodded, then bent over the fourth man, pushed hard on his sternum, then lifted his shoulders. "Feel for a pulse!"

The man looked a little blue. Lisanne crouched over the man's wrist and said, "I feel a pulse, but it doesn't seem very strong."

Vaz pumped his chest a few more times then said, "Dante, do this."

Dante said, "I don't know how!"

Vaz said, "Neither do I, but it can't be any worse than doing nothing."

Vaz got another emergency oxygen bottle and put the mask on the man. Then he stood aside and watched Dante pumping the man's chest. Dante said, "Am I doing it right?"

Vaz shrugged. "I don't know, but he's getting pinker." He turned and went to the door. He pulled the nitrogen tank in front of it and began filling the bucket again. He turned to Lisanne and said, "Get me a Coke bottle out of the trash, please?"

The last guy they'd dragged out of the stairwell groaned and threw up. "Sheeit!" he moaned.

Vaz had filled the Coke bottle with liquid nitrogen while watching the four men. He loosely screwed the cap onto the bottle and turned to Lisanne. "Can you fill the bucket with nitrogen again?"

She nodded. He showed her how, then walked over to squat near the last man. He pulled the guy's latex mask off and stared at him.

"What did you do to us?" the guy asked somewhat fearfully.

Expressionlessly, Vaz ignored the question and said, "What did you guys want?"

The man pressed his lips together.

Vaz picked up the man's wrist and bent his small finger back until the knuckle popped, leaving the finger pointing crazily upward. The man screeched a little, staring wide eyed at Vaz.

Lisanne stared at her husband, somewhat horrified that he would hurt the man to get information, but also astonished that Vaz Gettnor would hurt someone at all.

"What did you want?" Vaz picked up his ring finger.

The guy wildly jerked his hand but hardly budged Vaz's grip on his wrist. Vaz popped that knuckle back too and reached for his long finger.

Cursing fervently the guy said, "Wait! Wait! They wanted plans…"

Vaz said, "What plans?"

"For the fusion… machine."

Lisanne and Dante's eyebrows rose and they looked at one another, *someone thinks his fusion device works?*

Vaz frowned "That won't do them any good. We've already applied for a patent."

"Not here in the U.S." the man groaned.

"Yes, here in the U.S." Vaz said.

"No, the guy who wants the plans isn't from here."

"We're filing for patents worldwide."

227

"Some people in other countries don't care."

Vaz stared at him a while, then grunted, "Humpf. What if I gave you fake plans?"

"Then the next time we'd take you and *your family* too."

Vaz turned to stare at the door to the stairs. He got up and went to peer through the peephole. "Looks like your friends aren't coming after you." He turned to look at the screens. The image of the family room showed two guys staring apprehensively at the door to the basement and talking to one another. The one of the backyard showed at least one man standing out there.

Vaz stood, said, "If they won't come here…" and walked to the door. He turned to Dante and Lisanne, "Toss another bucket of nitrogen into the stairwell every so often. If you get a headache, you aren't getting enough oxygen. There are more oxygen tanks in the safety equipment drawer where I got these." He opened the door and tossed the bucket of nitrogen out into the stairwell. He settled his mask over his face, put on some heavy work gloves and picked up the neck of the Coke bottle of liquid nitrogen between the fingers of his work gloves. He opened the door again and stepped out, closing the door behind him.

Lisanne called to him, "Vaz! Wait! Don't go up there! Surely help will arrive soon…" She petered out, he was gone.

Dante turned to Lisanne, "I should go with him."

She shook her head, glancing at the bound men, eyes wide. She put her hand on Dante's wrist, "Please. Stay with me."

One of the men jerked at his bonds, "If you know what's good for you, you'll cut us loose."

Lisanne stifled a hysterical giggle, "Right." She turned to watch the screens as Vaz exited the stairwell into the family room. The camera showed the two men there turn to look at him.

Over the microphone she heard one of them snarl, "Where are the other guys?"

Vaz said, "They fell asleep."

One of them aimed a pistol like device at Vaz, "Stop right there."

Vaz stopped.

"Put down the bottle and take off the mask."

Vaz screwed the lid tightly on the nitrogen and set it and the oxygen bottle with its mask on the floor. He stepped closer to the men.

"Don't move!"

He had covered two additional paces but Vaz stopped as ordered. "What do you want?" he asked.

"We need copies of all your files to do with the nuclear fusion thingy."

Vaz shrugged, "Oh, that's no problem. I can get you a download of the files from my house AI." He stepped toward the desk they kept in the family room. Lisanne noticed that moving toward the desk brought him still closer to the two men.

Suddenly the liquid nitrogen bottle exploded as the expanding gas in it ripped the bottle violently apart. The two men flinched, turning toward the explosion.

Lisanne could hardly believe her eyes. As the two men turned, Vaz swung and punched the closest one on the side of his head with his gloved fist. It laid the man out full length!

Vaz moved on the second man but he had recovered from the distraction and shot Vaz with the Taser. Vaz fell twitching at his feet. "Goddamn!" the man said, dancing away. Reaching in his baggy coverall pocket he pulled out a roll of duct tape and knelt to begin taping Vaz's wrists together.

Dante said, "Mom! I've got to get up there and help Dad!"

Lisanne choked back her objections and said, "Go!" She leapt to her feet to follow him up the stairs.

Dante stopped to pick up one of the bats the men had dropped in the stairwell so Lisanne did too. When they burst out into the family room the man was getting ready to tape Vaz's ankles together. Dante charged and tackled him, driving him off the top of Vaz. The two struggling men crashed in under the breakfast table scattering chairs.

Lisanne dropped to her knees and began picking at the tape on Vaz's wrists. Vaz moaned and said between gritted teeth, "Run, until your AI reaches the net, call 911!"

"As soon as I get you loose."

"No! Now! Before he Tasers you and *no one* can get away!"

Lisanne hesitated momentarily, then plunged out the back door and across the yard. Vas rolled his eyes to watch her go, thinking he should have specified which door since he *knew* there was another man out back.

Dante struggled mightily with the man he'd tackled. He hadn't hit him with the bat for fear of killing him. He had felt like he'd be better off wrestling him, wrestling was something Dante understood. But the guy was *big* and hard to control. Dante realized that the man would have no compunction about hurting Dante if he got free. Dante's arms were tiring. Dante slipped his arms under the man's armpits and up onto the back of his head for a full Nelson hold. "Hold still or I'll break your neck!" he grunted into the man's ear.

The man flattened himself to the floor. This had the effect of requiring Dante to force the man's head through the floor to be able to stress his neck. He reached back, grabbed Dante's wrists and started pulling on them to get them out from behind his neck. The guy was powerful and Dante's fingers began to slip apart.

At a sudden thump, the man let go of Dante's wrists, shrieking.

Dante unlocked his hands from the man's neck and sat up to see Vaz, wrists still taped, kneeling a little unsteadily beside him, holding one of the bats in his bound hands. The man's elbow was smashed and bloody where Vaz had hit it with the bat. Vaz said, "Get a knife and cut this tape."

Dante jumped up and ran across the kitchen. Returning with a paring knife, he cut his father's wrists loose. "Where's Mom?" Dante asked, glancing around for her.

"She's trying to get far enough from their jammer signal to call the police. Tape these two guys' wrists behind their backs, then tape their wrists to their ankles."

The back door slammed open and a man stepped inside. He had one arm around Lisanne's neck and the other holding a Taser to her head. "Don't move, unless you want to find out just how bad a Taser shot to the head'll scramble her brains."

Dante slowly raised his hands. After a moment Vaz did the same. Vaz raised his eyebrows at Lisanne, wondering if she'd reached 911.

Lisanne's shoulders sagged and she shook her head minutely.

The guy looked at them and said, "Jimmy, tape that bastard's wrists together."

"Jimmy" rolled over with a moan and said, "The 'bastard' broke my elbow Chuck. I can't do shit."

They all glanced at the guy Vaz had punched when the bottle exploded. He breathed and twitched but his lights were obviously still out. The guy who'd come in the door with Lisanne said, "Shit! What happened to the other four guys that were in here?"

Jimmy groaned, "They went down to the basement, and never came back."

"Chuck" cursed fervently, "What did you do to them?" He demanded, staring at Vaz and forcing the Taser's barrel into Lisanne's head. She winced and her eyes fearfully rolled toward it.

"Tied them up." Vaz said. "Call down there and ask them. They're fine."

Chuck bellowed, "Ramos? You OK?"

"Hell no! The son 'va bitch tied us up and broke my damn fingers! Get down here and cut us loose!"

Chuck darted his eyes around looking a little frustrated, "Jimmy, you're gonna have to get your ass up, broken arm or no, and go cut me loose some help!"

Jimmy raised his head and looked around a moment, then said, "Shit!" and struggled to his feet. He carefully used his right hand to put his left hand in his pants pocket. With this functioning as an improvised sling, he headed across the room and down the stairs, cursing in pain the entire time.

Vaz tried to sidle closer to Chuck, hoping he'd let his guard down a moment but Chuck pulled Lisanne away and barked at Vaz to stay where he was.

A couple of minutes passed then the first of the four men from downstairs came up and taped Vaz's wrists together. The others quickly followed up the stairs and taped Dante and Lisanne's wrists too. They removed the Gettnors' AIs, turned them off and put the AIs in a metal box. Ramos came up, staring sullen daggers at Vaz and then talked to Jimmy and Chuck in whispers for a few moments. He flipped a switch on the box evidently killing the jammer because he then spoke to his AI. A moment later he said, "Bossman?"

They couldn't hear what "Bossman" said, but a moment later Ramos said, "No, we ain't got no

Goddamned plans! Bossman, the son 'va bitch nearly took down the whole team!"

After another pause he said, "*I* don't know how he did it. He gassed the damn stairwell and knocked four of us out. *He broke my fingers!*" Ramos said this as if it was the most heinous crime imaginable. "Then he punched Arno's lights out and broke Jimmy's elbow. If Chuck hadn't caught the wife tryin' to escape and brought her back as a hostage the police would be here and we'd be toast!"

Another pause to listen, then "The daughter's not here and I don't think we should hang around much longer waitin' for her. The neighbors are probably starting to wonder what's going on."

Ramos listened a moment longer then turned to the other men. "Stivitz, go get the van. Pull it into the garage as soon as someone moves their car. Mike, throw some water on Arno, see if you can get him up. Chuck, drag the wife out to the garage and make her authorize starting their car and having it back out of the way. When the van pulls into the garage put her in it and cable tie her to a seat." He glared at Vaz, "Jason, cable tie this bastard's elbows back behind his back. He's too tricky."

Jason pulled out a bundle of cable ties and put one around each of Vaz's elbows, then connected them with cable tie loops passing behind his back. Combined with the tape holding his wrists bound in front, his arms were fairly well immobilized. Jason did the same to Dante.

Mike roused "Arno" and guided him as he staggered out to the garage. They heard the garage door rumble open and a minute or two later rumble shut. Stivitz came in through the door to the garage and took Dante out. Ramos waved a Taser at Vaz and said, "Let's go." He indicated the direction of the garage with a jerk of his head.

They'd just started to move when Vaz heard the front door open. At first his heart leapt with hope, *could it be the Police?* Then with horror he heard Tiona call out. "Hey, the window by the front door is broken." She came down the little hall from the entry, looking back over her shoulder at the broken window. When she turned her eyes widened as she saw the large, strange men with the latex masks and her father with his wrists bound, "What…?"

Vaz said, "Run," at the same time that Ramos spat, "Don't move."

Ramos turned to Jason, "Grab her." He jerked his head in Tiona's direction.

Wide eyed Tiona started to back away, then turned to run.

Ramos shot her with the Taser. As she fell twitching to the floor he muttered, "Bitch, I *told* you not to move!"

Vaz lifted a foot and stamped it into the side of Ramos' knee. The knee gave way with a sickening "cratch" sound.

Ramos screeched as he fell to the floor, grabbing for his knee with his hand. He bumped his dislocated fingers on it and shouted, "Goddammit! You *son* of a bitch! You're gonna regret that." He turned the Taser on Vaz and fired again.

The lightweight dart struck Vaz's sweatshirt where it hung loosely away from his abdomen. Vaz stepped forward and kicked Ramos in the face.

The Taser skittered away across the floor, passing near Jason who picked it up and turned it back on Vaz. Eyeing the unconscious Ramos, who had blood pouring out of his nose, he wondered how Gettnor had stood up to the Taser. Then he saw the dart hanging free on his sweatshirt. He shot Vaz in the chest and watched him drop quivering. He pulled out some more cable ties and used them to bind

Vaz's ankles. Then he stepped over to bind Tiona's ankles and wrists.

Eyes wide behind his mask, Stillman Davis stood to watch the men making their way into Jerrod's safehouse practically dragging the Gettnor family. The shambling Arno, still looking confused and unsteady was followed by Jimmy, carrying his broken arm and steadily cursing Gettnor. Chuck came in with Gettnor's wife and daughter, "Are we puttin' 'em in the basement?"

Jerrod nodded.

Davis turned to him, "The basement?"

Jerrod shrugged, "Doesn't have a window. Door's the only exit. We put in a reinforced door, pinless hinges and a security bar. Closest thing we've got to a cell."

Stivitz came in with Gettnor's son and followed them to the basement. Jason and Mike came in with Gettnor himself, arms bound front and back and shuffling with his ankles linked only about twelve inches apart. Gettnor stopped and looked right at Stillman. His eyes narrowed and he hissed, "Davis," with a sound of loathing. Jason shoved him and he shuffled off to the basement. Getting down the stairs with his ankles bound barely the height of a stair apart took a while.

Davis turned to Jerrod and whispered, "How'd he know it was me?" He tried to calm himself, but his heart was in his throat after hearing what Gettnor had done to the men.

Jerrod snickered, "Not likin' rough business as much as you thought Stilly? Ain't you 'Mr. Tough Guy' like you thought?"

Davis took a Rolaids.

A couple minutes later Stivitz came back out of the hallway and said, "What are we going to do with Ramos and Jimmy?"

235

Jerrod frowned, "For Ramos' broken fingers you mean?"

"Shit no! Gettnor busted up his knee and kicked in his face. He looks pretty bad. Breathin' funny."

Jerrod cursed, "How the Hell did that happen? I thought you had him tied up?"

"We did! Then Ramos Tasered Gettnor's daughter. When that happened, Gettnor kicked Ramos in the side of the knee. It was sick man! Ramos knee went 'cratch' and buckled sideways. Then Ramos tried to Taser Gettnor and Gettnor kicked him in the face. Ramos face is all messed up man! And he's out like a light." Stivitz face flashed with ugly rage, "Boss, when you've got what you need out of him, you got to let us have at him with a baseball bat."

Jerrod got up and they went out to the garage to look at Ramos. His face was indeed a pulpy swollen mass with blood dribbling out of his nose onto the flooring of the van. Several loose looking teeth were visible through a large split in his upper lip. His knee lay at a strange angle. Jerrod dispiritedly said, "Shit!" Ramos had been one of his more sensible men. After a beat he sighed, "Take him to the hospital… Jimmy too."

"How 'bout Arno?"

"We'll see if he gets better."

"What if he has a concussion?"

"Probably does. People been getting over concussions on their own for thousands of years now. We'll take him to the Doc in the morning if he ain't better."

Stivitz shrugged, "OK," he picked up a metal case, "Here's their AIs."

Jerrod said, "Give 'em to Davis here." He turned to Davis, "Time to earn your keep Stilly. See if you can find those plans you were so sure you could get out of Gettnor's AI."

Davis said, "We could just make Gettnor download them for us."

Jerrod grinned, "Why don't you just go in there and do that then?"

Internally Davis flinched at the thought of personally confronting Gettnor. The look he'd had in his eyes when he'd come in had been frightening. He said, "Let me see what I can do."

Shoved into the basement, Vaz stared at the heavy door that had been closed up the stairs above him. He glanced around in wonder. The stairwell shared a sheetrock wall with the hall next to it! He looked around the partly finished room they'd been locked into with more and more disbelief. He couldn't see a video camera—of course that didn't mean one wasn't present, they could be pretty small—but thought one *must* be present. Their captors didn't seem very sharp to him but he couldn't believe that they could be so dimwitted as to lock them in what appeared to be an ordinary basement as if it were a prison cell. A basement full of… things. The furnace/AC unit sat out in the middle of the basement with ducts radiating from the top of it to vents in the floors above. A washer and dryer stood over against one wall with an ironing board and to his astonishment, an iron! Big cabinets were over against the other wall.

Lisanne sobbed. Tiona, wide eyed, darted glances around. Vaz thought Dante looked angry, but as usual he was having trouble judging just what everyone was feeling. For a moment he considered his own feelings and found excitement bubbling through him like it did before a fight. He had been somewhat dismayed to realize just how much he'd enjoyed hurting the men back at his house. A frisson shot through him at the prospect of hurting more of them, *especially* Davis. He wondered, *am I some kind of psycho?*

Internally, he shrugged. Right now he'd just as well turn his inner demon loose if it might protect his family. Vaz shuffled over near Lisanne and whispered to the kids, "Hey! Let's talk."

Lisanne gasped, "What do they want?"

"The fusion device."

"My God! I heard them say that." Lisanne gasped, "Just tell them it doesn't work."

Vaz tilted his head curiously, "But it does."

"Oh Vaz!" Lisanne said disgustedly. "Even if *you* really think it works, *tell* them it doesn't."

He frowned, "But they'd find out eventually… Then they'd be back."

Lisanne moaned despairingly at the realization that her husband's delusion was about to destroy her family.

Vaz thought the kids looked distressed. He looked around at his family and continued to whisper, "Look, it was stupid of them to lock us in this basement. There are a lot of weapons in here, the iron for one."

Lisanne and Dante looked confused but Tiona's eyebrows rose and she darted glances around the room.

Vaz said, "Before we do anything, we need to figure out where their video cameras are. We don't want them watching us."

Everyone's eyes turned to look around the room, Dante said, "I think there's one in the wall there," he jerked his head at a spot near the far corner.

Vaz grunted. There was a small hole high in the wall. "If that's it, it'll be hard to cover."

Despite the cable ties on her ankles Tiona shuffled across the room saying, "It's a camera all right, but I've got that," she pulled a piece of gum out of her mouth and stuck it over the hole. Looking around she said, "There's another over your heads," and shuffled back, pulling out the rest of her gum.

They all surveyed the rest of the room without seeing another lens.

Vaz turned to Lisanne, thinking that if she had something to do it might calm her. "Can you untape my wrists?" As she, through blurry eyes, began picking at the end of the duct tape to start unwinding it, he wondered at the lack of thought the men upstairs had given this. He found it hard to believe that they were relying on duct taped wrists when they had put all of their prisoners in one room. *Could they be used to dealing with only one captive at a time? Or never have held people against their wills before? Even if I were alone, I'd be able to chew through the duct tape on my wrists.*

Tiona began working on Dante's tape.

When Vaz's wrists came free, he said, "Save the tape, we might be able to use it for something ourselves." He put his arms back and Lisanne managed to slide the cable ties down from his elbows and off his hands to free his arms. He then freed Lisanne's wrists from her duct tape. He surveyed their group. Tiona still had cable ties on her wrists and ankles and Vaz had them on his ankles but Dante and Lisanne were completely free.

Vaz got up, "Plug in the iron and set it on high. Let's check those cabinets and drawers. Maybe there's something we can use to cut these cable ties. If not, maybe the iron will melt them."

Tiona said, "Look for dangerous chemicals we can use too." She got up and shuffled along behind Dante, peering in as he opened things.

Lisanne got down a box of Tide and took it over to the bottom of the stairwell. She filled a measuring cup with detergent. Trying to sound brave she said, "I can throw this stuff in their eyes if they come down here."

Tiona said, "Holy crap! There are gallons of ammonia and bleach in here!"

Vaz frowned, turning to look into the big cabinet they had opened. There were boxes of trash bags and gallon bottles of many kinds of cleaners. "This probably isn't the first time they've done some dirty work. I'll bet they keep this stuff to clean up crime scenes."

In a panicked voice Lisanne asked, "Are they're planning to kill us?"

Vaz shrugged, not recognizing just how stressed Lisanne felt. "They probably don't want to leave witnesses behind."

Lisanne sobbed.

Vaz looked at her with a puzzled expression, "We're not dead yet."

Lisanne wiped her eyes on the back of her wrist but then stifled her sobs and glared up the stairs.

Tiona said, "We should be able to use the bleach and ammonia somehow!"

Vaz looked at her curiously, "Are you thinking we could throw bleach on them when they come down for us?"

Wide eyed she said, "No. But, if you mix bleach and ammonia you make chlorine gas. Well chlorine and something else noxious, I don't remember exactly what. But if we could make the gas and send it up there… we could make them miserable."

Dante said, "How would we get gas out there? Making gas seems like it would be worse for us than for them."

Vaz's eyes narrowed, "No, wait, good idea." He looked around the room. "Dante, pull the washing machine out from the wall and take a water hose off the back." Vaz shuffled over to the big air return duct that went down to enter the bottom of the furnace/AC unit. It seemed pretty solid, but there was a grate on the side of the big duct that led up to the ones that spread across the ceiling to the rooms above. It was probably intended to heat the basement though it was shuttered at present. He tugged and the grate came out leaving a hole in the duct down into the furnace. "Are there any clothes or things anywhere that we can stuff this hole with?"

Tiona shuffled over to where her Mom stood looking desperate with the cup of Tide in her hand. She said, "Until my wrists and ankles are free I'm not good for much but I can be the 'Tide tosser' Mom. If I take over that job, can you search for stuff to plug the duct for Dad?"

Lisanne got up and went to the dryer. Sure enough, there was a load of clothing in it. She passed a double handful to Vaz. She felt good to be doing something instead of just waiting, hoping that she would be able to do some good throwing detergent.

Dante had moved the washer and climbed behind it. After turning off the water he unscrewed a supply hose. He thought for a moment that both of them were too tight to undo. Just before he said it wouldn't come undone he remembered how strong his dad was and thought about how embarrassing it would be if the old man undid it after he said it couldn't be done. Besides, their lives could depend on this! He wrapped his sleeve around the fitting and taking a two handed grip lunged against it. That broke it loose, though he saw it had torn the skin in his thumb web a little.

After handing the hose to his dad, Dante watched as his dad fed the hose down into the air conditioning duct.

Vaz had Lisanne wet down some of the clothing from the dryer using the water tap to the washer that Dante had taken the hose off of. He

241

packed wads of wet clothing in around the hose in the duct opening to plug it against any back flow of air from the vent.

Because walking around with his bound ankles was irritating, Vaz had Dante open the door so he could see the contents of the cabinet. Bring me some of those gallon bottles of ammonia and bleach."

Dante brought the chemicals and set them beside Vaz on the floor.

Vaz pointed to a quart bottle of fabric softener and said. "Dump the contents of that one into the washer."

Lisanne said, "The iron's hot."

Vaz shuffled over and sat on the concrete floor by the ironing board, "Hand it down to me." When she did, he put a corner of the hot iron onto the cable tie between his ankles. It softened and after he thumped it a few times with the edge of the iron, the cable tie parted. Next he tried it on the bottle of fabric softener Dante had emptied and found that it melted quickly through the wall. This allowed him to remove the bottom of the bottle. He handed the iron to Tiona so she could work on her own cable ties.

Vaz walked back to the furnace and duct taped the top of the fabric softener bottle onto the end of the hose to act as a kind of funnel.

Holding the fabric softener bottle/funnel upright Vaz said, "Dante, pour the bleach down this."

Dante picked up the jug and unscrewed the top. "I thought we had to mix it with the ammonia?"

"We'll let it mix down in the furnace rather than out here in the room with us."

Dante pursed his lips and started pouring the bleach down the hose, careful not to let it overflow onto his dad's hands.

Once a gallon of the bleach had gone down, Vaz said, "Lisanne, can you hold the funnel while he pours in the ammonia?"

Lisanne came over and took the funnel while Dante unscrewed the cap from a jug of ammonia and started pouring it down too. A small puff of noxious fumes wafted out and Dante coughed, but then it stopped.

Dante cleared his throat, "That stuff is nasty! How come it stopped coming out?"

"The hose is full of ammonia. It's pushing the bleach down and blocking any back flow." Vaz looked around the room. He grabbed a couple of t-shirts from the pile of clothing, wet them and wedged them into the crack under the door at the top of the stairs. Then he climbed up on the dryer and pulled the vent hose off its fitting.

Tiona frowned, "Why are you doing that?

"Let a little clean air in for us from the outside." He peered into the duct. "Bring me a wire coat hanger."

Tiona brought him a hanger from the hanger bar near the ironing board. Vaz squished it nearly flat and pushed it out the vent to hold the flapper valve open. As he hopped down from the dryer his eyes narrowed as he saw a puff of vapor coming from a leak in one of the ducts. He picked up one of the strips of duct tape left over from undoing their wrists and, holding his breath, walked over to seal the leak. He sealed another with the last of the duct tape and covered a third with a soaking wet t-shirt from the pile of clothes Lisanne had found.

His family glanced intermittently and wonderingly at Vaz. Lisanne felt bewildered by the way her husband had stepped up to handle this situation. For years she, despite her love for Vaz, had kind of thought of him as a third kid that she had to mother. In her heart of hearts she would have expected him to completely decompensate in a situation like this. She would have expected to have to deal with their captors on behalf of the family

243

herself. She would have never dreamed that he might fight back.

Dante watched his dad with awe and pride, increased exponentially from what he'd felt the evening he had seen his dad win that MMA bout.

Tiona felt gratification over his quick uptake and use of her idea with the cleaning solutions. Putting the chemicals in the AC and letting the house's ducting take the gas to their captors would never have occurred to her.

Unfortunately, as usual, Vaz wasn't quite sure what their expressions meant when they glanced at him. Wrapping a t-shirt around each hand he walked over to the bottom of the stairs. He picked up the abandoned cup of Tide, "I'm not sure how noxious the gas will be to them up there. They might open the door and come down to stop us, in which case I'm pretty sure I can take some of them out. Maybe they'll flee the house, in which case we'll break out of the basement and run ourselves. Much as we'd like to stick together, we should all go different directions. Only one of us has to get free to call the police and the game will be up for these guys. We'll have a lot better chance of that if we go different directions."

Lisanne said incredulously, "How are you going to 'take them out'?"

Vaz blandly said, "Hit them," as if he thought it was obvious.

She raised her eyebrows in surprise that he could think that, "Come on, Vaz, those guys are huge... you're not a fighter!"

Vaz looked blankly at her, wondering how to explain.

Dante said, "Mom, you saw him punch that one guy out."

Lisanne, "He surprised that guy when the bottle blew up."

"Mom, that wasn't luck! Dad's *is* a fighter. He's been in some amateur MMA bouts and he's *good*!"

Three sets of eyes turned to stare at Dante in astonishment. Vaz horrified that Dante knew about it, Lisanne and Tiona unbelievingly in regard to Dante's outrageous claim, "What!!" they said together.

Vaz shrugged with embarrassment but said, "It's true," he said, "Better kink the hose," he pointed at the hose which—as the last of the ammonia drained away—puffed a cloud of noxious gas at Lisanne. She coughed and kinked the end of the hose. Vaz said, "I think you should pour another gallon of bleach in now." Dante picked one up and started unscrewing the cap.

The air in the basement had begun to become slightly irritating from small amounts of the gas leaking out of the duct system and the furnace itself. Vaz said, "If we can't get out and the air gets too bad, remember we can stand on the dryer and take turns breathing at the hole where the dryer vented to the outside."

Though she wanted to ask about Dante's MMA claim, Tiona focused on the issues at hand, "Dad, if they don't open the door how are we going to get out of here?"

He looked at her with some surprise, "I'll kick a hole through the sheetrock into the hall."

"Oh!" she said with some embarrassment, turning to look up the stairwell and realizing bemusedly that sheetrock walls like these couldn't actually hold them. She frowned, "Why would they think that they could lock us up in here?"

Vaz shook his head, "Damned if I know. Maybe they're just counting on guarding us? But I think it's simpler. Like most criminals they aren't all that bright. Let's be ready to run though." He focused his gaze on Tiona, "'T,' you're our best runner. So, once we're outside, you pick what you think is the best direction to get help. The rest of us will scatter other directions." Vaz, being a terrible runner, didn't plan to run at all but didn't want to tell his family that. He'd try to delay the men that might be going after his family. Besides, he was looking forward to hitting some more of them.

Stillman Davis got up from where he'd unsuccessfully been trying to break into Gettnor's AI. He'd realized that it was too well protected and he wasn't going to succeed. He'd just have to get Jerrod to threaten Gettnor's family until Gettnor opened it for them. He looked at the screens which had displayed the interior of the basement. They were dark. Stillman said, "Hey what happened to the view of the basement?" He looked at the four remaining men and saw to his astonishment that they were playing cards at a little table near the door to the basement.

Stivitz snorted, "The girl stuck her gum on it."

"Aren't you going to check on them and take it off?" Davis asked in surprise.

Stivitz shrugged, "They're locked in a windowless basement laundry room with a reinforced door. What're they gonna do, wash their clothes?" He sniggered at his own joke.

Davis looked around, "Where's Jerrod? We're gonna have to *make* Gettnor give us access to his AI."

"Takin' a nap. Said it would do 'em good to stew for a while down there."

"Where's he at? I'll talk to him about it."

"Wouldn't do *that*, were I you." Stivitz said without looking up.

Davis grunted, "Where's he at?"

Stivitz pointed down the hallway past the stairwell down to the basement. "Second room on the right… your funeral."

Davis got up and started that way, feeling a little nervous. He wondered if Jerrod might really be that irritable? He stopped to listen outside the basement. He heard a cough but it sounded like it came from down the hall. As he walked on down the hallway he heard someone begin coughing steadily in one of the rooms ahead. He raised his hand to knock on the second door but it slammed open and Jerrod, coughing violently, stepped out followed by a puff of acrid smelling smoke. "What the hell?" Davis said, giving way as Jerrod brushed past him, hacking like he could barely get his breath. After he got a breath of the smoke Davis coughed too. He followed Jerrod back down the hall. To his dismay he now heard coughing from the big room where the men were. "Is something burning?" he asked plaintively.

By the time Davis got back to the big room, the air there was bitter and acrid also. He coughed some more. Not realizing that the gas came from the AC ducts and that there weren't any ducts in the hallway, Davis wondered why the air in the hall was better than in the rooms at either end. Jerrod and the men were heading for the door to the back yard. Davis shouted after them, "We've got to get the Gettnors out of here!" But when he refilled his lungs from the shout he gasped at the burning sensation. He bolted across the big room to the door, feeling like he was coughing up chunks of his lungs.

Once outside Davis gasped a big breath of clean air, wiped his streaming eyes and turned to Jerrod, "What the hell is that smoke?"

Jerrod coughed a couple of times and blew his nose. He rubbed bloodshot eyes, "*I* don't know! *I* was taking a nap, what the hell were *you* guys doing?"

"Just watchin' 'em, boss man." Stivitz gasped out between hacking.

Davis wheezed "I haven't been able to break into Gettnor's AI. We need to drag him out of there and make him open it." He looked back into the house with concern, "Better get him out of there before the house burns down and kills our ticket." *Damn,* he thought, *I shouldn't have left them in there!*

Chuck said, "Doesn't smell like smoke to me. Smells like chemicals."

Jerrod and Davis turned to eye Chuck speculatively.

At the top of the stairs Tiona used the measuring cup from the box of Tide to listen at the door. She had the open end against the door and the other end against her ear. "For a while I heard a lot of coughing, then I heard a sliding glass door slam, now I don't hear anything. I think they've gone outside!"

Dante said, "Let's get out of here!"

"Dante, how do you think we're going to get out of here without getting gassed ourselves?" Lisanne asked.

Vaz opened the cabinet the bleach had been in. "We can hold our breath long enough to get out the door but we need to protect our eyes." He pulled out a box of clear plastic wastebasket bags, taking one himself. "Here, pull a bag over your head as you leave the room and hold your breath." Then he climbed the stairs, stepped up onto the top stair and kicked a hole in the sheetrock wall on the side toward the hall outside. He grasped the edge of the sheetrock and pulled big pieces out until they had a large opening through to the sheetrock on the other side of the wall. He looked at his family, "Ready?"

They all nodded.

"OK, remember, scatter. Get to someone's house and get them to call 911." Vaz pulled the bag over his head and kicked out the sheetrock on the other side of the wall. A faint white cloud came in as

248

he kicked out more sheet rock and forced himself through the opening he'd created into the hall. Stepping briefly out of the hall he saw the men outside in the back yard. Several of them were bending over, hands on their knees, coughing.

As Dante, Tiona and Lisanne came out he helped them up into the hall and directed them out the front door, using some of the lungful of air he'd been holding to admonish them to "run like the wind." As Lisanne went out the front door, Vaz turned back and headed for the glass door to the back yard. He saw the men there in the dim twilight. They looked up in surprise as he approached the door.

As Vaz pulled the door open and pulled the bag off his head Jerrod said, "Good, glad to see you made it out. Lie down there…" Jerrod was still pointing to the ground at his feet when Vaz lunged out, punching Davis in the head with a hand wrapped in a t-shirt. Jerrod backed up, pulling a pistol out of a holster under his shirt in back. Stivitz and the huge Jason advanced on Gettnor, arms out but Gettnor lunged again, punching Jason in the stomach and folding him in half. Stivitz grabbed him from behind but Gettnor's left elbow rocketed back and hit him in the temple. It didn't knock him out, but Stivitz let go and staggered back, dazed.

Mike and Chuck tackled Gettnor together, bear hugging his arms to his sides and dragging him to the ground with them. Jerrod watched in amazement as Gettnor, with two huge guys trying to hold him, flopped and flailed in their grip. His eyes widened as it began to look like Gettnor would wear the two men out and break loose. Chuck let go with one hand and pulled it back to hit Gettnor in the head, but then suddenly flailed back away from him. Jerrod could see that Gettnor's hand had gained some freedom when Chuck let go. It had immediately clamped onto Chuck's crotch. Chuck howled in agony and grasped at Gettnor's wrist as Gettnor's white-knuckled grip appeared to be crushing his genitals.

Jerrod fired a round into the ground by Gettnor's head. The three men suddenly stopped moving. Then Chuck moaned and rolled away, curling around and holding his crotch. Jerrod squatted and put the barrel of his Glock against Gettnor's head and said, "You *will* hold still, understand?"

Gettnor calmly said, "Yes," and laid unmoving.

Jerrod said, "Mike, get us some cable ties."

Mike looked nervously over his shoulder at the house. "But boss man, what about that gas… or smoke or whatever?"

"Open the door and let it air out." There was a pause and he said, "Go around front and have the AI open that door too, we'll get a little cross wind going through the house." He turned narrowed eyes on Gettnor, suddenly noticing that the man's eyes weren't red and he hadn't coughed. "Why didn't that gas or smoke or whatever hurt you? Did you make it somehow?" Gettnor just lay there unreadably eyeballing him which Jerrod found vastly annoying. "Answer me, dammit!" He swung the Glock back to pistol whip Gettnor but as the pistol left his head, Gettnor reached up and grabbed the gun. Wide eyed, Jerrod involuntarily squeezed another round off into the dirt as his left hand darted over to help his right turn the pistol back toward Gettnor. Unsuccessfully! Gettnor brought his other hand up to Jerrod's wrist and despite Jerrod's best efforts, Gettnor easily rotated the gun to point at the sky.

Wide eyed Jerrod glanced at Gettnor and saw a gleam of excitement in his eyes. Then Gettnor's right hand left the gun and drew back. Despite only Gettnor's left hand immobilizing the gun Jerrod couldn't turn it back on to Gettnor even using both of his hands.

Gettnor smiled and his right fist flew toward Jerrod's face. Jerrod's world disappeared.

Mike came back around the house, "Boss man, the front door was already open. I think those people might have gotten away…" He stopped as he saw Gettnor standing over a cowering Chuck, holding Jerrod's Glock. Davis and Jerrod lay sprawled bonelessly unmoving; both bleeding from their noses.

Gettnor pointed the weapon at Mike and said, "Don't move." He nudged Chuck with his foot, "Get up."

At gunpoint Gettnor forced Mike to go into the house and bring out a bundle of cable ties, then use them to bind Chuck's wrists and ankles. Gettnor took the bundle of ties and set the Glock down, saying, "Hold out your wrists."

Mike threw a punch at him instead, intending to connect one good one then run.

But Gettnor's forearm blocked it to one side and a punch Mike never saw landed in his gut doubling him over. Mike fell to the ground. As he frantically gasped for breath he felt Gettnor calmly pick up his hand and slip a cable tie around it. In the distance he heard sirens approaching.

Epilogue

Late Saturday afternoon Lisanne sat on the couch in their family room trying to come to grips with the events of the last 24 hours. The house they'd been captive in had proved to be somewhat rural. Tiona had had to run almost a mile to reach the nearest neighbor and get them to call the police.

When they first arrived, it had been hard to convince the police that Vaz was a victim rather than a perpetrator.

After all, when the police had arrived at the house they found Vaz with the Glock 9mm. Stivitz, Jason, Mike and Chuck were all bound hand and foot with cable ties. Jerrod and Davis lay unconscious. All but Mike had had to be taken to the hospital for evaluation.

They'd cuffed Vaz and held him until the family had been allowed to turn on their AI's and upload the AV records of their capture back at their own house. The house AI at Jerrod's safe house gave up records of the Gettnors being bundled into the basement. The record continued on up to the point where Tiona put her gum on the lenses. Not surprisingly, none of the men, nor the house AI, were making AV records of the rest of the goings on. In fact the house AI had instructions to delete all but the last thirty minutes of the video from the basement. Though it had been marked for deletion by the computer, it hadn't actually been recorded over so the police were able to retrieve it.

The whole family had spent time down at the police station giving statements separately, as the police still did when there wasn't a good AV record. Then this morning the police had been out to ask more questions.

A young policeman asked Lisanne, "Has your husband always been a fighter? We only find the record of his one fight with the guy who intruded into your house."

Lisanne shook her head wonderingly, "No. He's always been a geek. I would never have dreamed he would win a fight with anyone."

"Come on, he's incredibly muscular, surely you must have suspected."

Embarrassed to admit he'd gotten into the physical condition he was in without her really noticing she said, "Uh, that's a fairly new development."

"But he must spend *hours* at the gym!"

"I think he exercises in the basement."

"You think?!"

"Yeah, he's never exercised in front of me."

"And when he's been in fights before, he's won?"

"I don't think he's been in any fights before." She narrowed her eyes remembering Dante saying something about an MMA fight but didn't say anything to the policeman.

"Lady," the man said exasperatedly, "Your husband, by all accounts, last night knocked out three large men with single punches, two of whom have been admitted to the hospital. Two of the other men he fought with are spending time in the hospital getting surgical treatment for their injuries. And you expect us to believe that you didn't have *any* idea he was a fighter?"

She shrugged, "I had no idea," she whispered, stunned by this recitation of the facts.

"So they were after your husband's fusion technology?" another cop asked. He sounded a little excited.

"Well, yes, that's what they said, but…"

"But what Ma'am?" he asked frowning slightly.

"Well, I don't think it actually works," she almost whispered, even though Vaz wasn't there to hear her doubting him.

253

He tilted his head, "Why do you say that?"

Lisanne shrugged helplessly, "Well, everything I've read says that low temperature fusion is impossible," she said quietly.

His eyes narrowed, "We've called around... Dr. Smint, his old boss at Querx says it works."

Lisanne sat back a little, "Really?"

"And so does John Vernor, from General Electric. He says GE will desperately want to license the technology." He looked at her strangely, "You really should talk to your husband about this stuff."

Goose bumps skittered over Lisanne.

At lunchtime Lisanne had found Vaz in the kitchen making a pastrami sandwich. "Vaz..." She noticed his right hand was bruised and had a cut on the knuckle. "What happened to your hand?"

"I hit that Jerrod guy without any protection on my hand."

"Oh," she'd said, remembering the way Jerrod's cheekbone had been collapsed inward and that his lip had been split. Lisanne looked Vaz in the eye, "Where did you learn to fight like that?"

Vaz hung his head, "I'm sorry. I took some lessons at a mixed martial arts school. I uh... when I'm uh, angry... or frustrated or whatever... I like to hit things. It makes me less tense. And," he whispered, "it works even better if I'm in a *real* fight. I feel great today." He looked down and saw that he'd started twisting some hairs out of his arm. Dropping his arms exasperatedly to his side, he said, "I'm sorry. I'm kind of a monster."

Lisanne put her arms around him, snuggling in and pressing herself to his hard physique, thinking how safe he made her feel now that she had seen what he could do. "You are no monster Vaz Gettnor. You protected your family like... like a man should. I'm amazed, and gratified and happy."

254

"Oh," he said musingly, "That's good." He took his sandwich and went to sit at the table. Without looking up at her he said, "Querx deposited the first 10% of the back royalties into my account. I transferred 1.4 million into your account." Keeping his eyes on his plate he said quietly, "I don't want to go to the Caribbean."

Lisanne blinked. "Caribbean?"

Vaz hunched down, "Yeah, you know…"

"I… don't know. What about the Caribbean?"

"You wanted to go, but we didn't have the money."

"Oh."

"So you can go now… but I don't want to."

Lisanne sat down across from him thinking hard. He picked up and methodically began consuming his sandwich. Her eyes widened. Then narrowed, "Wait a minute. Where did the money for all that expensive lab equipment in the basement come from?"

Vaz paused in mid chew, looking like a boy caught with a hand in the cookie jar, but said nothing. His eyes flicked to her, back to his plate, back up to her, then down to stay on his plate.

"If Querx owes you for underpayment of royalties, they must have been paying you *some* royalties all along… and I've never seen that money, have I? Where's it been?"

Mouth full Vaz mumbled, "In a separate account."

"And that's why you kept saying we had the money to send the kids to school?"

Vaz nodded.

"And that's the money you spent on the basement?"

He nodded again.

Lisanne frowned at him, thinking back over her months of anxiety about Vaz and money. As

255

neutrally as possible she asked, "And... have you been hiding that money for fear I'd want us to go to the Caribbean?"

Vaz dropped his eyes to the table. He'd learned to look Lisanne in the eyes but it was really hard when she was mad. He nodded minutely, waiting for an explosion.

Suddenly Lisanne saw the funny side of the situation. He heard a snicker that grew slowly into a full blown explosion of laughter. Looking up he saw his beautiful wife, tears streaming out of her eyes, joyful laughter coming from her throat. "Oh Vaz!" she gasped, standing and stepping around the table to sit in his lap. She nuzzled her face into his neck. When she pulled her head back she saw Tiona and Dante uncertainly coming down the stairs.

Tiona hesitantly said, "What's so funny?"

Lisanne lifted an arm, reaching out to her children, still giggling. As they came into her embrace she hugged them to herself and Vaz. She pulled harder, "Turns out we're rich! We've actually been wealthy for a long time. And your dad has probably just solved the energy crisis, which will bring in a *lot* more money. You guys don't have to worry about money for college after all."

Lisanne shook her head and laughed again, "Just don't..." she giggled again, "try to get your dad to go to the Caribbean."

to go to the Caribbean."

The End

Hope you liked the book!
If so, please give it a positive review on Amazon.

Author's Afterword

This is a comment on the "science" in this science fiction novel. I have always been partial to science fiction that posed a "what if" question. Not everything in the story has to be scientifically possible, but you suspend your disbelief regarding one or two things that aren't thought to be possible. Then you ask, *what if* something (such as faster than light travel) were possible, how might that change our world?

This story poses several what ifs? First what if someone who is incredibly socially inept is also scientifically brilliant? This actually isn't all that implausible, the smart but geeky individual is a stereotype after all, but in this story it is at an extreme for both characteristics. Would such a person find love and have a family? Would the children be embarrassed by such a parent, yet perhaps still proud of his/her brilliant accomplishments (if they know about them)?

The second "what if" is of a more scientific nature. What if someone actually did achieve tabletop fusion, something almost every reputable expert believes is impossible? This truly *would* change our world. Fusion can produce about seven million times as much power per kilogram of fuel as the burning of gasoline. If you could do it you would *want* to use hydrogen-boron fusion because it would create *much* less radioactivity than deuterium fusion. What if some combination of previously falsely reported methods of achieving cold fusion (hydrogen in a palladium type matrix and ultrasonically induced cavitation, perhaps?) actually worked? Like the little boy who cried wolf, it would be hard to convince anyone of the validity of your experiment.

The third question is "what if" you needed to defend yourself from bad people with nothing but the dangerous materials that are commonly available in the average home?

As a final note, I'm a sucker for a story where no one really knows, or understands, or can even believe just how accomplished or dangerous a character actually is. I loved the movies *Target, True Lies* and *The Long Kiss Goodnight* all of which feature characters like that.

Acknowledgements

I would like to acknowledge the editing and advice of Gail Gilman, Elene Trull, Kerry McIntyre, Kat Lind and Nora Dahners, each of whom significantly improved this story.

38158556R00145

Made in the USA
Middletown, DE
15 December 2016